50 Ways to Hex Your Lover

Linda Wisdom

SOURCEBOOKS CASABLANCA™
AN IMPRINT OF SOURCEBOOKS, INC.®
NAPERVILLE, ILLINOIS

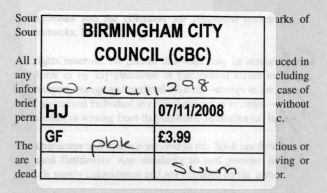

Published by Sourcebooks Casablanca, an imprint of Sourcebooks,
Inc.
P.O. Box 4410, Naperville, Illinois 60567-4410
(630) 961-3900
FAX: (630) 961-2168
www.sourcebooks.com

Library of Congress Cataloging-in-Publication Data

Wisdom, Linda Randall
  50 Ways to Hex Your Lover / Linda Wisdom.
    p. cm.
  ISBN-13: 978-1-4022-1085-3
  ISBN-10: 1-4022-1085-X
  I. Title. II. Title: Fifty ways to hex your lover.

PS3573.I774A613 2008
813'.54--dc22

                                    2007038727

Printed and bound in the United States of America
        OPM 10 9 8 7 6 5 4 3 2 1

In memory of my dad, Robert Randall, who left us in 1998. While he'd been there from the beginning of my career, I wish he could have still been here to see Jazz come to life. Something tells me he would have said that Jazz and I were too much alike. This one's for you, Dad.

Prologue

Alderley Edge, Cheshire, England
The Year 1313

"S omeone's thoughtless use of magick has put our school in great jeopardy."

Emerald velvet robes flew around the reed-thin body of the headmistress as if a storm brewed within her. Red and blue flames flashed from the foot of her staff as she tamped it to punctuate her words with the ring of cold stone. Not one of Eurydice's thirteen students moved a muscle as they stood in line awaiting her judgment.

On their first day at The Academy for Witches, the headmistress had laid down the rules and the consequences of breaking them. She pronounced that there would be no exceptions if any of those rules were broken. Yet today, her cardinal law had been broken—one of the students had gone so far as to cast a curse on a mortal. She walked down the line of girls, spearing each of them with her angry gaze.

"We are sor—" one of the girls sputtered.

"*Silence!*" Eurydice turned on her heel to face down the unlucky witchling. "Whoever cast the spell must step forward and be accountable for her actions."

Not one of the acolytes spoke up. All thirteen stared at the ancient stone floor.

"Your shared silence to protect the guilty one is laudable." Eurydice's dark eyes matched the flames flickering at the end of her staff. Still no one moved. "However this offense was committed against a member of royalty. A man with the power to close this school, do us harm, even destroy us. I am certain some would commend you for not betraying the classmate who cast this spell, but the culprit must step forward and accept her punishment."

The girls looked at each other, linked their fingers together and then, as one, all thirteen stepped forward.

"Very well. As you will have it," Eurydice said. The air around her swirled dark and purple as she pronounced judgment. "Henceforth, all of you are banished from this place and are cast out into the world for one hundred years with only the powers you presently control. If any of you dares to cast a spell not meant for the greater good, your banishment will be extended. At the end of your banishment you will be brought before the Witches' High Council to determine your final fate.

"And I hope—" she made eye contact with each girl who managed to meet her furious gaze "—you will learn just what a merciless mortal world you have been cast into."

Then she tamped her staff against the cold, unforgiving stone floor, and the thirteen acolytes vanished.

The headmistress turned to face the three elder witches standing quietly by the wall.

"Do you think they'll be all right, Eurydice, all alone in the world?" Allene, the softhearted, asked. "Do you think they'll be in danger?"

"Hardly, dear sister," the headmistress chuckled. "I fear more for the world."

One

Pasadena, California
The Year 2007

How long are we going to sit here?"

"As long as it takes." Jazz Tremaine shifted in the Thunderbird convertible's bench seat. She loved her 1956 aqua and white classic sports car, but there wasn't much legroom for her five-foot-eight-inch frame.

Nice neighborhood for a stakeout though, with its wide, posh swath of multi-million dollar homes set behind high iron fences and ornate gates. Still, Jazz hoped she wouldn't have to wait all night for Martin "The Sleaze Bag" Reynolds to come home. Her left foot was falling asleep, and that large Diet Coke she'd had with her dinner was warning her that bathroom time would be in her near future.

A scraping sound, a flare of sulfur, and a whiff of tobacco smoke from the passenger seat made Jazz's nose twitch. "Irma, put that damn thing out."

Irma clicked open the ashtray and heaved a put-upon sigh. "I'm bored."

"Then leave," Jazz snapped.

"Ha, ha," Irma snorted. "Very funny."

She sat in the passenger seat wearing her Sunday best, a navy floral-print dress with its delicate lace collar and navy buttons marching down the front. A dainty navy and white spring straw hat decorated with tiny flowers sat squarely on her tightly permed iron-gray hair. White gloves and a navy patent leather handbag completed her perfect 1950s ensemble. No surprise there because Irma had died in the passenger seat of the T-Bird on March 12, 1956.

Irma was the bane of the 700-year-young witch's existence and the sole drawback to the snazzy car she dearly loved. Her 100-percent success rate at eliminating curses had fallen to 99 percent when she'd failed, no matter what she tried, to remove the highly irritating Irma from the car. In the end, Jazz's client refused to pay her, and Jazz ended up with the classic sports car instead; with Irma as an accessory.

"I can make that lamppost disappear with a snap of my fingers." Jazz gestured toward a nearby post standing at the corner and did just that. Another snap of the fingers and the post reappeared. "But with you …" She snapped her fingers in front of Irma, but nothing happened. "With you, nothing. Nada. Zip. No matter how many times I try, you're still here!"

Jazz glared at Irma. Irma glared back at Jazz. The clash of witch temper and ghost tantrum lit the interior of the car with an unearthly silver light; then a gray Mercedes rolled slowly past the T-Bird, and Jazz swung her head away.

"Good," she said. "Martin is home."

The gates to The Sleaze Bag's Spanish-style mansion swung apart. The Mercedes drove past them and up the winding driveway. Jazz pushed her door open and slid out of the T-Bird. She glanced up at the night sky and felt the pull of the slowly waxing moon. She sighed and fingered the moonstone ring she wore on her right ring finger. The milky blue stone glowed faintly at her touch.

In two weeks she'd drive up to the small town of Moonstone Lake set high up in the Angelus Crest Mountains for the monthly ritual that kept her and her witch sisters centered. The lake and nearby town provided Jazz and two of her fellow banished classmates a much-needed sanctuary. While Stasia and Blair enjoyed living in the tiny mountain village, Jazz and several of the others preferred the darkness and grit of the city to breathing all that smog-free air.

"You could leave the radio on," Irma called after Jazz in the raspy voice of a long time smoker.

"Bite me," Jazz growled, moving silently across the street toward Martin's house.

She easily blended with the night in her black leather pants, black silk t-shirt, and black, waist-length leather jacket. Her coppery hair hung in a tight single braid down her back. Tonight she was Scary Witch, the better to teach Martin a lesson.

She paused long enough to flick her wrist at the gates, which opened just enough to allow her to slip through before they swung shut again.

Her nose wrinkled against the overpowering scent of heirloom roses lining the driveway. Malibu lights bathed a lawn that had been trimmed with mathematical precision.

"You pay a landscaping service a small fortune to keep the grounds looking perfect, and yet you dare cheat me," Jazz muttered, stopping a short distance from the house. She drew a breath, lifted her hands and murmured, "Resume."

A faint flicker traveled from her fingertips to the house. When the witch light slid through the windows, a woman's shrill, shrieking voice erupted within, so loud Jazz could hear it standing a hundred feet away.

"What have you done to this house?" Martin's harpy ten-years-dead mother-in-law screamed. "There is no way you can tell me my daughter had any hand in the decorating in here! What did you do? Hire one of your bimbos to design this interior like a brothel? Or did the slut do *you* instead? I told my baby not to marry you! You're a pig, Martin Reynolds! A pig!"

Jazz smiled and sauntered up the driveway to the front door. Figuring Doreen Hatcher's screaming inside would be too loud for Martin to hear the doorbell, she leaned on it long enough to be downright annoying.

"You just can't live without the booze, can you, Martin?" the voice shrieked. "Your liver ought to be pickled by now! *Pickled,* do you hear me? If not pickled, you should at least be dead from all that alcohol, you drunken slob! If I didn't know I had died from a heart attack I'd think you arranged my death."

Martin Reynolds flung the door open, wide-eyed and grim-lipped, a highball glass in one hand, a cordless phone tucked under his chin.

"Hello, Martin," Jazz purred.

"Jazz! I was just—uh—calling you," he said, stepping quickly backward, unease flashing across his face, though she noticed his forehead didn't move, even if his lips did. She guessed his Botox job had been fairly recent. "Your spell didn't work. You said she would be gone, but she isn't, and she's back with a vengeance. She showed up all of a sudden, just now. I walked in the house and bam, she's here, ten times worse than she was before." He waved his hand toward the other room. "You've got to take care of her."

"Come back here and face me, you coward!" Doreen screamed from the confines of the cookie jar she'd been cursed into before her death.

Martin flinched. Jazz did not flick an eyelash, but she wondered how a man reputed to be a driving force in the television industry could fail to connect her unexpected appearance at his front door with the return of his curse. A curse she'd effectively eliminated—until the sleaze tried to cheat her.

"Maybe she came back," Jazz said, "because you were a bad boy."

Martin looked wary. "I don't know what you mean."

"You know exactly what I mean. You stopped payment on the check you gave me." Jazz stepped into the foyer, plucked from her pocket the check with its giant red *Stop Payment* stamped across the surface and waved it under Martin's nose. "Not a smart way to do business. Especially with a witch."

"I wouldn't do that!" Martin cried, aghast. "It must have been my wife who ordered the stop payment!"

"Oh, that's right! Blame it on my sweet, precious Lenore!" Doreen's voice cried out. "You are such a worm, Martin Reynolds! You won't even take responsibility for your own mistakes."

"Don't be shy, Doreen," Jazz said. "Please join us."

She waved a hand at the closest wall and Doreen's features—high forehead, hawklike nose, and sharp chin—bulged out of the stucco. Her sightless eyes zeroed in on Martin and he shrieked.

"Did you think you could get rid of me so easily, you slime?"

"You miserable bitch!" Martin threw his highball glass at the wall.

Before it could explode in a shower of glass splinters, Jazz flicked her fingers again. The glass floated down to stand neatly on a nearby table, and Doreen's face instantly shifted to the boldly splashed oil painting over the fireplace. Jazz thought it might be a Picasso; a real one.

"What a cheap painting," Doreen sneered. "Bought this at one of those starving artist sales, didn't you?"

"What the fuck are you doing?" Martin screamed at Jazz and flung a pointing finger at the fireplace. "That's a Picasso!"

"I told you what would happen if you stiffed me, Martin." Jazz shrugged. "I told you the curse would come back ten-fold."

"All right, you win." Martin pulled out a handkerchief and mopped his perspiring brow. "I'll write you another check. Anything to get rid of that miserable old bitch."

"Ah, ah, ah, no B words, and no more checks. Now it's cash." Jazz held out her hand. "Five thousand dollars, please."

"Five grand?" Martin howled. "Our deal was for five hundred."

Jazz smiled. "That was before you cheated me out of my fee, Martin."

"I don't keep that kind of cash here at home."

"Yes, you do. There's twenty-five large in the safe in your office," Jazz said. "The safe your wife knows nothing about. Would you like me to open it for you? I can from here, you know."

"No," Martin snarled, spinning on his heel toward the back of the house. "You wait right here."

"The first number is four!" Jazz called after him, always ready to help.

Then she grinned and headed for the kitchen. A handful of chocolate chip cookies lay scattered on the countertop where Doreen's angry face distorted one side of the cookie jar sitting in the center of the counter.

"Good grief, Doreen. You blew your top." Jazz picked up the lid and helped herself to a cookie from the jar. One bite urged her to take a second one. She could never resist chocolate chip.

"I told her he was no good, but did she listen to me? No," Doreen seethed. "She should've divorced him before the network started canceling his shows. And I'm sure he's hiding money in offshore banks."

"Too late now." Jazz gave Doreen's Gingerbread Girl decorated lid a sympathetic pat. "Lenore will have to figure that out on her own."

Martin stalked into the kitchen and thrust a packet of bills at Jazz. "Here. Now get rid of the old bitch."

"No name calling, Martin." Jazz moved her fingertips over the money, counting it by touch to make sure the bills totaled five-thousand. Fool witch once, shame on you. Fool witch twice, oozing sores and an eternal rash in private areas.

It was all there. She tucked the cash into the inside pocket of her jacket, glanced at the scowling cookie jar and said, "Be gone."

Doreen's face vanished as Jazz's final word lingered in the air. Martin blinked and his mouth fell open.

"That's it?" He glared at Jazz. "You say two fucking words and she's gone? No fancy fireworks or arcane rhymes? No waving a wand around?"

"You've been in television too long, Martin." Jazz opened a drawer, pulled out a meat hammer and smashed the cookie jar to smithereens.

"*What have you done?*" Martin screamed, clutching at his hair. "My wife treasured that damn thing!"

"Blame it on the maid," Jazz said. "Or find one just like it on eBay."

Martin moaned and wiped a hand over his face. His stress etched on his face was warring with his Botox job. "Lenore is going to kill me when she gets home."

"Had to be done, Martin. The cookie jar carried the curse. Now you need to bury the pieces. And you have to bury each piece separately, at least three feet apart. Be sure you say, 'Be gone,' over each one as you cover it with dirt."

Martin gaped at her. "There's a million pieces here!"

"Hm, not that many. Maybe only a thousand, but you'd better get started right away, hadn't you?" Jazz turned to leave, paused in the kitchen doorway and looked back at Martin, staring at the shattered cookie jar. "One more thing, Martin."

"What?" he asked, not bothering to look at her.

"It's never good to cheat people. It only messes up your karma."

When Jazz climbed into the T-Bird, Irma quickly extinguished her forbidden cigarette. "Lands sake, I could hear screaming all the way out here. What did you make this one do?"

"I broke the cookie jar and told him he had to bury each piece at least three feet apart. Good thing he has a lot of property because he's going to need it." Jazz started the engine, sneezed from the cigarette smoke lingering in the car, and pulled the money Martin had given her out of her jacket. "And I charged him five thousand dollars."

"Don't tell me." Irma held up one white-gloved hand. "You're going to give every penny of it to the Save the Witches Fund."

"These are weird times for witches, Irma. I wish the Fund had been around years ago when my sisters and I needed a hand." Jazz pulled away from the curb. "It's not like I need the money. I make enough driving for Dweezil."

"Oh, yes. All Creatures Limo Service." Irma made a face. "I'm sure your mother would be so proud that you grew up to be a taxi driver."

"Stuff it, Irma," Jazz snapped and headed for the freeway.

"I swear, curse elimination always puts you in a bad mood, so let me guess." Irma sniffed, staring up at the freeway signs that whipped past. "We're going to see that alcoholic."

"Nooo," Jazz said. "*I* am going to see my friend Murphy. *You* are going to sit in the car, which you've been doing for the last …," Jazz did the math in her head, "fifty-odd years."

"Then let me go in with you sometimes when you do your work," Irma said. "I could help, you know."

"I eliminate curses, Irma, not add to them," Jazz said with a laugh, "You haven't been able to leave the car in fifty years as it is. Plus what would you do in there? Find a bed sheet and wander around flapping your arms?"

"If you gave me a chance, you could find out just what I could do."

Irma stuck her nose in the air and turned her head to look out the side window. A cigarette smoldered between her white-gloved fingers. Jazz had never been able to figure out how a fifty-year-old ghost managed to obtain Lucky Strikes on a regular basis.

Twenty minutes later, Jazz whipped the T-Bird into a parking spot in front of Murphy's Pub. The one-story weathered building near the waterfront had a faded, gilt-lettered sign over the door. No ambiance here. She could hear tinny music coming from the nearby pier, where the amusement park's Ferris wheel glittered with multi-colored lights.

"This is a No Parking zone," Irma announced, a fresh Lucky Strike appearing between her fingers. She sighed and made it disappear when Jazz shot her a warning look.

"Relax, Irma." Jazz pushed her door open. "I'm not lucky enough to have you towed away to a nasty, dirty impound lot." Instead of using a car alarm, she set an illusion spell that allowed anyone without magickal sight to see the car only as a rusting Pontiac instead of the snazzy T-Bird. And anyone who happened to stumble past the spell and still try to steal the car would be in for a nasty surprise. When it last happened in 1980, the hysterical car thief babbled on about the car being filled with snakes. No wonder the police thought he was flying high on drugs.

Fiddles playing *Morrison's Jig* engulfed Jazz as she stepped inside the pub. The music swept her back in time to the little Irish village where she was born. Memories were so strong, she swore she could almost smell peat burning on the hearth. Seven hundred years ago there had been no pubs, but there were meeting places for the men to gather, drink ale and brag. She was the little girl sent to fetch Da home, cuffed for her efforts as often as not. She shook off the memory as Murphy caught her eye and raised his hand in greeting. She returned the gesture and wove her way between the maze of tables and chairs. The patrons of Murphy's Pub cheerfully ignored the statewide restaurant smoking ban. The two local cops sitting at the end of the bar weren't about to enforce the law when they each had a cigarette in their hands.

"Don't you look like a hot and sexy lady of the night?" Murphy said as she slid into her usual place near the beer taps. He pushed a basket of pretzels toward her and rested his elbows on the bar's surface.

"Thank you, kind sir," Jazz said, letting a hint of Old Ireland creep into her voice.

"So tell me, darlin', you have any whips and chains hiding under that scrap of a jacket?" He leaned across the space between them as if to get a better look.

She picked up the mug and sipped the warm, yeasty ale with a grateful sigh. "You're such a flatterer, Murphy. Is that why the boys in blue are showing up here instead of heading over to one of their usual hangouts?"

His gaze momentarily shifted toward the cops, then came back to Jazz. "Some vamps have come up missing lately, so they're checking all the bars in the area. I told them vamps don't tend to come in here. We don't serve the right kind of refreshment." He chuckled.

"I bet they chose this place because they knew no vamp would come in here. They just wanted a place where they could kick back and drink," she replied, picking up a handful of pretzels and munching away. In seconds the basket was empty. Murphy replaced it with a filled one.

"They've sure been doing that." He winked at Jazz. "And what brings you to my establishment wearing a hot outfit like that?"

"Getting even with a client who tried to cheat me out of my fee."

"One of Dweezil's clients or a cursed client?"

"Cursed," she replied

"The world was saner before creatures came out of the woodwork," Murphy muttered, nodding acknowledgement at someone's shout for another Guinness. "And according to the boys in blue at the end of the bar, a lot safer."

"But not as exciting." Jazz winked back. "Live and let live, Murphy." She started to say more when she felt a faint stroke of cold trail across the back of her neck. She lifted the mug to her lips and tilted her head back just enough to look in the gilt edged mirror behind the bar. That's when she saw him, sitting at the rear corner table, ready to intercept her gaze in the mirror. Proof positive that a vampire without a reflection is nothing more than an old Bela Lugosi tale.

Nikolai Gregorivich. Tall, dark, and arrogant. Eyes the color of the Irish Sea. Features cold as ice. And a vampire.

Jazz had not seen him in over thirty years. What was he doing here?

White-hot anger settled deep inside and flowed through her veins like lava.

Focus, Jazz, focus.

What in Fate's sake was he doing here? Why wasn't he hanging out at The Crypt down in the warehouse district? There the undead found everything from O Positive to A Negative on tap.

He sure as hell wasn't here to see her. Maybe he was here for the same reason as the two mortal cops were. Nikolai worked as an investigator and enforcer for a vampire security agency. From experience, Jazz knew that vampire cops and mortal cops in the same place didn't always play well together, even if Nikolai seemed to get along better with mortal law enforcement than most of his kind did. A quick glance at the end of the bar assured her the two cops had no idea a vampire was even in the bar.

"Uh, Jazz."

She tore her eyes away from the mirror and saw the mug of ale bubbling in her hand—bubbling like, well, like a witch's cauldron.

"Is there something wrong?" Murphy asked, raising an eyebrow.

Jazz snuffed her temper and smiled, watching the bubbles recede. "Not a thing."

He frowned as he wiped up the liquid and then glanced up at a rumbling sound overhead. "What was that?"

"Probably a low-flying jet," she lied, dialing her temper back a few more notches. At this rate, she'd be sent to witchy anger management. She pushed the mug away. She knew any ale that reached her stomach now would only turn sour. "It's been a long night. I think I'll head on home, Murphy."

"It's not that late," he said with a hint of invitation in his voice.

She smiled and shook her head as she pulled out a twenty and left it on the bar, ignoring Murphy's attempt to push it back toward her. She turned away and headed for the door.

Another boom of thunder rattled the windows as she reached the exit.

"Damn it," Jazz muttered, hurrying outside before her witchy tantrum drew the two cops' attention. "And damn him for invading *my* territory."

∾

"Jazz."

She had barely stepped onto the sidewalk to walk toward her car, which meant there'd been no time for her temper to abate. She spun on her heel. Her watcher blended with the shadows on the edge of the alley next to the pub. She didn't bother wondering how he'd gotten outside before her. She only reacted.

"Nikolai Gregorivich, you bloody son of a whore!" She pushed enough power through her hands to send him flying deeper into the alley's gloom. She stalked after him, her fingertips glowing a bright orange-red. Strands of hair flew around her head, crackling with energy. A furious witch could generate enough power to light up an entire city. Jazz was rapidly moving past furious. "You are so dead!"

He landed on his ass, but bounded back onto his feet in a flash. His elongated canines flashed white in the darkness. "Yes, I am."

His wry comment momentarily threw her off balance and stopped her in her tracks. He had an uncanny knack for being able to do that to her: infuriate her and tease her at the same time, so she could not decide whether she was coming or going. For sure she wanted to kill him, but whether quickly or slowly was always at issue.

Gathering her sidetracked senses, she shot a fireball straight at him. He leapt out of the way just in time. The fireball struck the side of the building, leaving a large scorch mark on the faded bricks.

"I see you've added something new to your skill set." He looked up at the sky where clouds appeared overhead streaked with lightning. Thunder rumbled, and the air snapped from the energy of her rising temper. "I don't think Mother Nature will be too happy to find you stepping onto her turf."

She gnashed her teeth so hard it was amazing they didn't grind down to nubs. Their eyes remained locked as she struggled to bring her temper under control. Clouds floated away, and thunder and lightning disappeared, but the sparks emanating from her body were still bright enough for a Fourth of July fireworks display.

"You had me locked up," she snarled, advancing on him with fury tight in every muscle. She did not worry about him flashing his fangs at her. No way he'd come near her neck or any other part of her body. Witches' blood tended to give vampires heartburn—or worse. "I was imprisoned in that small town jail for more than a month before the sheriff realized you had lied to him. For Fate's sake, anything could have happened to me there! Didn't you ever watch any of those old prison movies?"

"I'm sure if you wanted out of there you could have cast a spell to get you out of there. Besides, it was for your own good." He wrinkled his nose. "Do you mind if we step out of this alley? The smell of a drunken man's piss never appealed to me."

She stood firm. Even if he could easily move her, his ingrained manners would prevent him. So why not make him suffer for another minute even if it was nothing more than screwing with his sense of smell.

He hadn't changed since she last saw him in 1972. Six-foot-two, slightly shaggy hair the color of her morning coffee, and eyes a blend of green, blue, and gray that always brought a shiver to her spine. So many vampires' eyes turned black or a glowing cobalt blue when they were turned. *The better to mesmerize their victims with, my dear.* But Nikolai's eyes had remained that uncommon blend of green, gray, and blue that she always compared to the Irish Sea at twilight. The same color eyes that had belonged to another man centuries ago. The memory of that man haunted Jazz still.

The stink of the alley mixed with the subtle earthy scent that clung to his skin. She knew it to be a special blend from an exclusive chemist's shop tucked away in London's most elite shopping district. Nikolai might not care about amassing wealth the way so many of his kind had, but he didn't purchase his toiletries at the neighborhood drugstore either. The scent brought back memories she swore were better off tucked away and forgotten.

The strong attraction she felt for him didn't stop her fingers from twitching for some witchflame. A very old soul resided in the sexy bod that didn't look a day over thirty-five. But that didn't mean she could stifle the instinct to drag out every piece of silver she had in her jewelry box and remind him it was a metal that didn't like him.

A dark intensity surrounded him that had nothing to do with his existence as a vampire for the past eight centuries. She always suspected that he had been a predator long before he became a never-ending night person. Although his black leather duster hung loose in perfect vampire fashion, his faded jeans and brick red t-shirt did not. They clung lovingly to him like a second skin.

She pretended not to notice how good he looked. Damn him.

"I need to talk to you," Nikolai said, his voice barely above a whisper. His husky voice still sent trembles to her limbs and memories of nights when he had whispered words of desire in her ear as he made love to her.

"We have nothing to say." She turned and walked away, only to stop short when he flashed past and appeared in front of her.

"It is important," he persisted, but he made sure to keep his distance. Jazz packed quite a wallop when her temper was up. Right now her temper could send the Richter scale off the charts. He would survive, but a mortal would need a full body cast after being thrown against the building.

She held up her hand. A glowing ball of orange-red fire danced in her palm. Her smile was not the least bit pleasant.

"Get out of my way, Nikolai, or end up looking like a Roman candle."

But he was as stubborn as she was, and he refused to move. He silently dared her to throw the fireball at him. Her fingers twitched. Was it more effort not to throw it or to make sure it hit its mark? Jazz paused to consider.

"Have you picked up any new tricks other than calling on thunder and conjuring up fireballs?"

The witchflame disappeared as she moved closer in a blur of speed to jam one arm against his throat.

"Like this?" She snapped her fingers and a sharpened stake appeared in her other hand. A breath later it was pointed at his heart. She gently tapped the area. "X marks the spot, darling," she purred. Her green eyes flared with a witchy fire that echoed the witchflame she still held in her hand.

He didn't flinch from the imminent threat of ending up a pile of ash at her feet.

"You can't do it, can you? After all, you didn't stake me in London," he murmured in the voice that always warmed her blood and gave her hormones a healthy jumpstart. "Nor in Florence, New Orleans, or Boston. And then there was San Francisco." A wealth of meaning stoked that last sentence. One she chose to ignore. She had felt the earth move in more ways than one during the predawn hours of that fateful April morning in 1906.

"There's always a first time." The stake disappeared as quickly as it appeared, and she stepped back before she gave in to temptation and ran her tongue up the side of his neck, grazing the area where the carotid artery had not pulsed in centuries. She wanted to bury her nose in the curve of his shoulder, run her fingers down his spine to that slight curve at the base that brought a growl to his lips. She knew his heightened senses wouldn't miss her quick indrawn breath or rapid heartbeat. She feared he could smell the pheromone rush in her blood and feel the increased heat along the surface of her skin. She knew that was the one thing Nikolai missed the most. His skin never felt any kind of warmth, even on hot summer nights. Many a night she had wrapped her body around his to give him the illusion of body heat, but he could never retain it for long.

"Not this time." That whiskey and velvet murmur followed her, trapped her within its selective intimacy—tumbled her desperately resisting psyche onto its back, legs spread, arms open wide in invitation. "No splinter, no toothpick, no stake, Jazz."

"Fire it is then," Jazz agreed, keeping the raggedness out of her voice through superwoman effort. Forcing herself to focus, she rekindled the simple witchflame in her palm and thrust it into Nikolai's face. He blanched instantly, rearing back.

"Jazz…"

"No." She was harsh, determined. "Don't even …" Deliberately she turned her back on him and— without extinguishing the witchflame—headed out of the alley. Toward what remained of her sanity—her car and …

That damned ghost.

"Jazz." The vampire's footsteps sounded behind her, an intentional effect by a being whose normal approach was more silent than fog. "Wait. I—we— need your help."

"Of course you do." Jazz didn't stop, didn't turn, until she was within two feet of the T-Bird. She merely allowed the orange-red ball of flame in her palm to grow visibly. "There could be no other reason to come find me after thirty years, could there?"

"That was a generation ago, Jazz," the vampire told her without emotion. "Needs must—then and now."

"Go f—" Jazz began, but a delighted, ghostly squeal interrupted her, putting an instant kibosh on the building tension between witch and vampire.

"Is that Nikolai?" Irma chirped, leaning out of the car as far as she could go. "It is! Nicky, sweetie, it's been so long since we've seen you. Come give your Auntie Irma a kiss!" She puckered up, her Tangeed lips almost glowing eerily under the dim streetlight.

"Not now, Irma." He concentrated on the glowing ball of fire dancing in Jazz's palm. "Jazz, members of my kind have gone missing."

"And this is a bad thing?"

"Don't be petty. It's not your style." The shadowy anger in his eyes matched her temper perfectly. It had made them ideal as lovers. "If you wish to hold a grudge against me personally, so be it, but I need you to listen for ten minutes. Surely, you can give me that."

"Get staked," Jazz advised, feeling behind her for the car door handle before her natural curiosity, Nikolai's obvious attractions, and her traitorous libido got the better of her.

"Tell *me*, pookie," Irma invited. "When she's not as cranky as she is now, I'll make her understand why you need her help."

He darted a glance at the ghost, then gauged the diminished witchflame Jazz still controlled.

"Back off," Jazz snapped, climbing into her car and slamming the door behind her. With a quick twist of the key, she gunned the engine, taking off with a squeal and smell of burning rubber.

"Merciful heavens, one day you're going to get us both killed!" Irma's protest echoed in the night.

⁓

Nikolai shook his head in frustration as he watched his ex-lover race off. He knew it wasn't retreat on her part. Jazz never retreated. She only regrouped. The world might change, but Jazz never did. And he thanked the Fates for that.

He wasn't surprised that she had displayed her temper the moment she saw him. That was the first thing he had noticed about her, the heated passion that seemed to fuel her soul. If he were a vampire who fed on emotions, he would have been well sated by her alone. Instead, Jazz had sustained him in other ways through the centuries.

He knew it wouldn't be easy to chip away at the hard exterior she had erected over the years, but he was a stubborn man.

And Jazz Tremaine was worth it.

Two

Jazz ignored Irma's mutterings about the late hour and her rude behavior toward Nikolai. The warm buzz from the ale she'd drunk had dissipated the minute she spied the vampire cop. Now all she was left with was a bad mood hangover. In the words of Dr. Phil, she had a lot of issues with her ex-lover.

Unfortunately she could not still the insistent niggle of his voice inside her head when he'd said, *"Members of my kind have gone missing"* and *"Ten minutes, Jazz. Surely you can give me that."*

She did not want to give him anything, damn it. Not again. Not ever. And yet ...

No. Firmly she shook off all thought of Nikolai—at least for the time being. There would be ample time to dwell on him later, in her dreams, whether she cared to admit the vulnerability to herself or not. Right now, she had other vermin to boil in oil and—if she was very lucky—blow up in lieu of her ex.

"It was bad enough you wouldn't take me inside that bar. And I know you have the power to do so if you would bother to try," Irma complained. "It wouldn't hurt you to do something nice once in awhile. Instead you leave me at the mercy of any drunken bum that might stagger by."

Jazz so did not want to deal with the cranky ghost occupying the passenger seat of her car. Why did Nikolai always have to show up when she was downright happy and felt she had her life together? And why did she have a sinking feeling this wouldn't be the last time he'd do this? Probably because he had done it in the past, and each time she gave in and helped him and along the way fell once more back into his bed. So either she gave in and allowed him to pull her into whatever mess he was dealing with right now or she avoided him at all costs until he got the message she didn't want to talk to him ever again. She knew him well enough to know that if he felt he needed her help, he was going to harass her until he got what he wanted. The problem with the stubborn vampire was that he could make her life miserable indefinitely. The pit of her stomach turned into a trampoline. After all these decades, he still affected her strongly. She just didn't know if she wanted to stake him or make love to him.

"The least you can do is speak to me!"

She pulled back from her musings about Nikolai and affected concern. "Irma! I'm shocked to hear you wished to enter an establishment serving alcohol! I would never dream of offending your sensibilities that way. You being such a fine upstanding member of the community and all. Where was it? Raspberry, Iowa?"

Irma lifted her chin. "Jasper, Nebraska. My grandfather was one of the founding fathers of our town and opened the first bank. And if it hadn't been for my father's generous nature and contributions to the community, the farmers would never have done as well as they did during the Depression." She glared at Jazz. "Many of them didn't lose their farms because he was willing to work with them instead of going in and repossessing their property right and left. Oh, that's right," her glare turned to a smile that wasn't the least bit friendly, "you were flitting around back then, weren't you?"

Jazz winced. Irma in a snit was worse than Irma any other time. She steeled herself to listen to the woman ramble on about the town of her birth and death. Luckily, their destination was not far from Murphy's. She was still ignoring Irma's babbling ten minutes later when she turned down a street that looked as if the dwellings on either side had been frozen in the 1880s. Old-fashioned street lamps stood like silent sentries of a long forgotten past and highlighted three- and four-story Victorian mansions. Wisps of fog wrapped their ghostly fingers around the iron bases of the lampposts, giving the night an eerie feel that fit right in with the houses and Jazz's own mood. Luckily, the closer she got to her home the more her dark disposition lifted. From the moment she had first driven down the street and saw the houses she felt as if this was the place she wanted to stay forever.

If she had her way no land developer would ever build twenty-story apartment buildings or housing developments in this particular area. Many of the homes in a five-block area were registered historical landmarks, but she always feared the city council's greed might find a way to override a home's olden past. This section of the city portrayed a part of its history she wanted to see kept intact. From the beginning she had been tempted to set up special wards around this block, but the Witches' High Council had all these pesky rules about not using magick for anything but the greater good. Protecting her home didn't seem to fall under that category. But if someone grew too proactive about developing here she'd have to rethink her "be careful where I interfere" policy.

"Would it hurt you to buy a nice little space heater for me?" Irma sniffed as Jazz pulled into the carriage house and parked her car next to a sleek fire engine red Porsche. "It's like a meat locker in here."

"The car doesn't need central heat and neither do you."

"Then what about a pet?" The ghost twisted in her seat to look at Jazz. "What would be wrong with my having some company?"

Jazz sighed. "Irma, while a pet might sense your presence, it wouldn't be able to interact with you because it wouldn't hear you talking to it. It wouldn't be fair to a pet to keep it out here just so you can have something to keep you company. Besides, you have the TV/DVD combo out here to give you something to do." Jazz had fixed it so that Irma could change channels verbally and merely say the name of a DVD in her collection for it to insert itself into the machine. She knew the ghost also enjoyed staying up late watching infomercials.

"A house isn't a home without a pet," Irma said primly.

"I've managed just fine without one all these years, thank you very much."

"What do you call those furry monsters you keep in the house?"

"Footwear." Jazz headed for the open door.

"Then what about a canary?" Irma wasn't about to give up. "I'd need a heater in here though. They're very delicate creatures."

But Jazz wasn't listening. She activated the sensor that automatically closed the carriage house door when she exited the building.

As she approached the back door she looked up and noted lights highlighting the elaborate stained glass windows that decorated the second floor. Krebs was back. Hurray and damn, all in one package.

All she wanted to do was go up to her third floor suite of rooms and sulk. Maybe throw a good witchy tantrum that involved pictures falling off the wall, vases dancing *The Hustle,* and sparklers flying around the room. Nothing too involved and something easily rectified. Instead, she'd have to stop by Krebs' floor and make nice because he'd wonder what was wrong if she bypassed him.

She liked that her roomie worried about her and was willing to talk when she needed a willing ear. Especially since men weren't known to want to listen to a woman's angst.

She now wished she had stayed at Murphy's for a couple of hours, drank more ale, and just plain kicked back. Instead, her evening had been ruined when Nikolai showed up and all sorts of memories were dredged up that were better left tucked away in a corner of her mind with the door firmly closed and locked with multiple deadbolts.

Her sitting in a filthy cell in Prague because he decided she was part of a gang of thieves.

Nikolai making love to her in a mountaintop villa in Italy where the moon glowed over them like molten silver.

Running from the *gendarmes* in Paris.

There were many exquisite reminiscences courtesy of the somber-faced vampire who made her heart race just by touching her face, but there were also too many recollections over the past five centuries or so that involved manacles, jail cells, and the threat of hanging or beheading.

That was when she had decided it was best she stay out of Nikolai's sphere. If they remained together too long she'd only come up with new ways to make the vampire suffer. And she'd suffer in the process. It wasn't worth it.

Ah, hell. She liked Krebs. He was cute and funny and he made her laugh. Nikolai and his demons had screwed with her mind long enough; she'd take the cheering up for now and work on the sulking later.

Always best to do it later, an inconvenient gargoyle in her mind suggested.

She felt like punching herself in the jaw to shut it up. Too bad she couldn't punch it in the jaw.

A stop at the refrigerator netted her two glasses of Chardonnay before she ascended to the third floor that housed her living quarters. Jazz quickly changed into a pale blue tank top and boxer shorts decorated with clouds. She slid her feet into her favorite slippers and loosened her hair from its braid. She dug her fingers into her scalp, massaging away the tightness as she headed for the door. She noticed a faint glow covering the bedroom wall she deliberately kept blank. She paused, thinking it would be "wallmail" from one of her sister witches. The elaborate dark gold script scrolling across the wall warned her otherwise.

Be advised that Griet of the village of Ardglass has sixty days added to her banishment due to the wrongful use of her power this night.

Eurydice,

Mistress, Witches' High Council

The ornate lettering slowly faded from the wall, but the memory of the words was embedded in her brain.

"Could be worse. I wonder what they would have given me if I had actually thrown that last fireball," she muttered, making her way down to the second floor. "And my name is Jazz and has been since 1921!" she informed the empty wall. Not that it would do any good. The Witches' High Council didn't hold with modern names. Using her birth name was their heavy-handed way of thinking they kept their outcast witches in line. As if!

Soulful jazz music drifted from the second floor. Jazz reached the front of the house where the walls had been knocked out to create an open floor plan with the perfect working environment for its resident. While the house's exterior portrayed the richness of the past, the second floor's interior was pure new millennium. Long tables were covered with state-of-the art computer equipment that would make any techno geek drool. A dark haired man faced a thirty-inch flat panel monitor that displayed scrolling lines of computer code.

"Whom are we mourning tonight?" she asked, setting one of the wine glasses on the table close enough for him to reach but far enough away to not endanger the equipment if it fell over.

"Who says I'm mourning anyone?" he said in a monotone of concentration as he continued to stare at the monitor. He nodded his thanks for the wine before picking up the glass, taking a sip, and setting it back down again.

"You only play Miles Davis when you're having a pity party." She hitched herself up on the table then moved down to the end when he frowned at her. "I wasn't sitting on anything," she protested, looking around to make sure she was telling the truth. "Come on, Krebs. Dish the dirt." She cradled her wine glass in her hands.

Krebs, aka Jonathon Shaw the Third, kept his focus on the monitor, his fingers flying over the keyboard. After watching a Dobie Gillis marathon on TVLand together, Jazz had affectionately dubbed him Krebs, for Maynard G. Krebs, when Jonathon said he identified with the laid-back beatnik.

"Heather wants to see other people."

Jazz winced. She knew he had hoped Heather was "The One." Jazz knew better. It didn't take a witch's power to know that the clichéd blue-eyed blonde saw Krebs as her very own golden ticket into old California society. What she didn't know was that he had blown off his family, and their fortune, fifteen years ago. In typical Krebs fashion, he had rejected the family tradition of attending Harvard and joining the family business and pursued his own path. After some rocky years spent roaming the sex, drugs, and rock 'n' roll beat, he managed to get himself back on track. Thanks to a flair for the unusual in web design and a knack for real estate investment, he had no money worries. When he rented the third floor to Jazz four years ago, she'd found a good friend. For one brief wine-soaked evening they had even toyed with the idea of becoming lovers, but sanity won out and their friendship had flourished until they were closer than they ever would have been as lovers. She was grateful that he understood her witchy side.

The sound of low mutters in an incomprehensible language finally penetrated Krebs' concentration. He looked down at Jazz's feet and groaned.

"Did you have to bring them in here?" he asked. "It's bad enough they manage to find their way in on their own to make a mess when I'm not around. I swear they'll think there's an open-door policy, and this is the one place they don't belong. I'm still positive they were behind the disappearance of two important CDs."

Jazz looked down at her off-white fuzzy slippers topped with bunny faces that would have looked downright adorable if it hadn't been for their large and very sharp teeth and the fact that the sweet-faced bunnies snarled instead of squeaked. Their ears twitched back and forth as their heads moved from side to side while they chattered away to each other. An intricate gold chain with a tiny gold broom charm circled Jazz's bare ankle. A small but perfect amethyst winked from the broom handle.

"Come on, Krebs. You have no proof they ate those CDs. Besides, they were lonely. And they really like you."

"Sure they do. As dinner, perhaps. Can you really understand what they're saying?" he asked, resting his hands on the keyboard. Jazz knew that past experience had taught him not to touch the bunny faces if he wanted to keep his fingers intact. They loved to nibble on anything that got too close to their mouths or anything they could catch. They also had the digestive system of a garbage disposal.

She nodded as she continued sipping her wine.

"What are they saying now?"

"You don't want to know." She looked around the table. "Do you have anything to eat up here? I didn't get any dinner." She'd planned on hitting the drive-through at In-N-Out on her way home, but her run-in with Nikolai had ruined her appetite for their Double-Double with onions and a large order of fries topped off with a large chocolate shake. The best thing about being a witch was that she didn't have to worry about calories and fat grams. And because she was still mad when she came home, she hadn't thought to check the fridge contents when she got the wine. She was too lazy to trek back down in search of food if there was a chance there was something up here. Still, the thought of that hamburger sent her mouth watering. Damn him for ruining her dinner plans!

A faint rumble overhead shook the house.

Krebs cocked his head to one side. "Man, I sure hope that doesn't mean we're in for an unexpected thunderstorm. I can't believe you didn't stop off somewhere for food. The day you don't have time to eat is the day the world ends." He slanted a look at Jazz whose gaze slid to the left. "Lucee, what 'ave you done?" he asked in an incredibly bad Ricky Ricardo accent.

She showed great interest in a pile of papers lying nearby even though she couldn't read one symbol of the computer code. "Nothing." But, coupled with Nikolai's unexpected appearance at Murphy's, her own—literally—fiery response to him and his plea for help, and Eurydice's wallmail, the question bothered her.

He shook his head, mumbled what sounded like "which means you did one hell of a something," and returned to his work.

"No, really, don't you have anything up here to eat?" She was prepared to beg as long as he didn't ask her about the thunder. One mega temper tantrum in 1965 and all of a sudden the Great Blackout made national news. It cost her an additional 400 years.

"If you want food go down to the kitchen where it's normally kept." He cocked his head to one side to better listen to the slippers' babble. Jazz knew it sounded more like gibberish to him. "Seriously, what are they saying?"

One rabbit looked up at him and gnashed its teeth. Jazz grinned.

"Fluff and Puff are debating if it's true that humans taste like chicken." She lifted one leg straight out in front of her. The slipper swiveled his head to look down and uttered a shrieking cry. It exhaled a sigh of relief when Jazz obediently lowered her leg. "They're not fond of heights."

Krebs shook his head. "You are a very sick woman." He looked down at the chattering slippers. "One thing I could never figure out. Are they male or female?"

She shrugged. "I've never been able to tell and they've never said. I think it depends on their mood and if there's any chocolate nearby."

Krebs winced when Fluff, or maybe it was Puff, looked up at him. Its ears stood straight up and drool slid down over its teeth, dripping onto the hardwood floor. "If they leave any bunny slipper turds around you have to clean them up." He turned back to the computer monitor.

Jazz leaned over for a better look. "Whose website are you working on?"

"I'm doing some maintenance for *Dates After Midnight.* Leticia wanted an edgier look to the site." His fingers flew over the keyboard. Within seconds the code disappeared and a digitally enhanced black lace curtain dropped over the screen. A small silver box set in the lower right hand corner of the monitor winked to life.

"Welcome to Dates after Midnight," a feminine digitized voice sounded over the speakers. "Please input your password to enter the portal."

"It sounds more like an online brothel special-izing in dominatrices than a dating service," she commented.

"Not just any online dating service, but one for vampires," Krebs pointed out, typing in the pass-word and checking out each page. "Leticia is a smart businesswoman. There're other dating services out there, but hers has more class and she makes it so exclusive that there's vampires everywhere begging to be accepted. A lot of it due to my website design, of course."

"Gee, Krebsie, vain much?" she grinned, and then burst out laughing. "Vain. Vein. Get it? I crack myself up."

"Oh yeah, a laugh a minute." He rolled his eyes.

Jazz hopped off the table and leaned over Krebs' shoulder to read the members' profiles.

"'After dark accountant seeks numbers-minded match. Former NFL star looking for athletic type O+.'" She shook her head. "Are you sure not just anyone can get into this site? Ads for blood bars and vamp self-help groups tend to put off most of the living. It even creeps me out a little."

He grinned. "Not the way I have it set up with enough firewalls to rival the U.S. Government. Leticia's site hasn't been hacked into once."

"Who knew creatures of the night and the magick-minded would enjoy surfing the net so much. And li'l ole warm-blooded you designs most of their business sites," she teased, dropping a kiss on top of his head. She peered closer. "Missing Vampire announcements?" She pointed at a series of drawings that were remarkably lifelike for creatures whose DOAD—date of actual death—meant the subjects had been long dead in the mortal sense. Nikolai's words about members of his kind disappearing teased the back of her mind. She ruthlessly pushed the thought into a mental compartment that held any memory to do with the sleaze fang, slammed the door, and locked it. The last thing she wanted was a reminder of the man who could make mind-blowing love to her one moment and betray her the next.

A faint rumbling sounded overhead.

Krebs swore under his breath. "That better not mean we're getting a thunderstorm. This has to be finished tonight."

"It sounded more like a low-flying jet to me," Jazz said with a nervous twitch. The last thing she needed was a few hours listening to Mother Nature lecture about not venturing into her territory. She quickly changed the subject. "There's sure a lot of missing vampire ads posted. Vampires move around all the time. They can't stay in one place too long or people start to notice they're not aging. So why are vamps thinking others are missing?"

"This is different. Some say they've been snatched. There're even rumors that there's some kind of cure to vampirism and that those who were treated successfully have taken up a mortal life again. So far, no one's come forward to say what's true and what's not. There are even articles about the disappearances posted on some of the vamp news feeds."

She studied the drawings. "Hmm, I guess it

wouldn't be the same to have the pictures of the missing vampires plastered across blood bags, would it?"

He looked up and grinned at her reference to a vampire version of pictures of missing children once posted on milk cartons. "Hey! How did it go with your deadbeat client? Did he pay up?"

"Of course he did. With a little help from *moi*." She held up her wiggling fingers. "A cookie jar, not to mention pretty much the entire house, cursed by your dead, but totally insane, mother-in-law is nothing to ignore." She grinned as she performed an impromptu soft shoe on the polished hardwood floor. "Martin 'The Sleaze Bag' Reynolds learned his lesson to the tune of five extremely big ones."

Krebs let loose a low whistle. "That's some markup from your original fee."

"Expanded curse, expanded fee. Plus he totally pissed me off." Her bunny slippers starting singing an off-key ditty as she continued her dance. "I warn my clients up front there are consequences if they cheat me out of my fee. Martin learned just what those consequences could be. He's lucky I didn't make it worse." She walked over to the small refrigerator set in a corner of the room and rummaged inside. She cast aspersions on a man who couldn't bother offering fat and cholesterol-filled snacks to his visitors. She finally settled on a butterscotch pudding cup. "I don't know what I enjoyed more— seeing his mother-in-law's face pop out of the Picasso hanging over his mantel or the way he panicked when he realized how long it would take him to bury all the pieces from the cursed antique cookie jar I broke."

"And you know your antiques well," he murmured.

"No age jokes, thank you very much." Further exploration among napkins and single-size non-dairy creamers earned her a plastic spoon that looked reasonably clean.

"Exactly how old are you?"

Although Jazz had related bits and pieces of her history to Krebs, she hadn't told him everything. A woman had to have a few secrets, after all.

She merely smiled, "Old enough."

She walked over to one of the front-facing windows and looked out. The brightly lit amusement park rides at the nearby boardwalk were easily seen from where she stood. The immense multi-colored disk doubling as a Ferris wheel overlooking the ocean lent magick to the night. One of the reasons she loved the house was that it was only a ten-minute walk to the beach and boardwalk when she needed a cotton candy and carnival ride fix.

Krebs glanced up from his work and noticed her pensive expression. "You're not exactly dressed for the boardwalk, love. Plus I thought your man-eating slippers were considered bunny *non grata* after their last visit."

Jazz laughed as one of her slippers snarled a response. "They're convinced they were framed. Fluff said there was no way he could eat an entire man on his own. And Puff had a sore throat that day."

•

Krebs gave a mock shudder. "Jazzy, love, I'm glad you're on my side."

She hitched herself back up onto the table and polished off her pudding.

"In the wastebasket, please." Krebs glared at the cup she set on the table. She wrinkled her nose at him and executed a perfect toss into the basket by his chair.

Jazz sat quietly, content to watch Krebs work his own brand of magick. She doubted he'd appreciate knowing she thought of him as her very own calming influence, something she sorely needed after her emotional confrontation with Nikolai. The sexy vampire never failed to stir up her hormones, whether she wanted them stirred or not. She was determined to do what she could to make sure not to run into him again. It should be fairly easy to manage. It wasn't like she had a lot to do with the undead community. Vampires weren't her favorite companions, and they didn't like witches much either. She tended to steer clear of them, except for the times she had to drive those who were automobile-challenged. With her blood poisonous to a vamp's digestive system, she was safe from becoming a late night snack. They weren't her favorite jobs—vampires were also incredibly bad tippers.

Despite the large room with its high ceilings she felt a slight pressure building up around her. Without saying anything, she slid off the table and wandered back to the front window overlooking the street.

The first thing she noticed was a neighbor's calico cat skidding to a stop in the middle of the sidewalk across the street. It stared into the darkness and arched its back. She imagined she heard the hiss that escaped the feline's mouth as it gazed intently at something the normal human eye couldn't detect. When the cat ran away, Jazz noticed a faint blur of movement near the neighbor's front gate. Then all grew still. She did not need her powers to know what the nearly invisible figure was.

"You just couldn't stop, could you?" she whispered. "You had to remind me that you're back and intend to find a way back into my life again by claiming you need my help. Go find yourself another witch, Nikolai. I'm not going to play with you anymore."

She didn't stop to wonder how he had discovered where she lived. If there was one thing Jazz understood, it was that in the preternatural world there were few secrets. And ex-lovers had even fewer.

⟡

Nick ignored the cold fog that swept around him and partially obscured the house across the street. With his enhanced vision, the fog was not a deterrent. He easily saw Jazz standing at the second-floor window, just as he heard the soul-stealing jazz music. He imagined he could smell the spicy scent of her perfume mingling nicely with her natural scent. He noticed she'd smothered the Gael in her voice, but what she didn't realize was that her heritage showed anytime she was emotional. No matter how many centuries had gone by, she still couldn't hide some things.

He unashamedly eavesdropped on the conversation between her and the roommate who did not appear to be her lover. Thinking back to the bar scene, he recalled that the only sentiment exchanged between her and Murphy's bartender had been teasing flirtation. That was unexpected since he knew only too intimately that Jazz had a strong sexual appetite. It was difficult to believe neither man was her lover, but it was a relief to know she was free.

Considering what he'd just heard her whisper, he knew that knowledge wouldn't do him any good. She hadn't exactly welcomed him with open arms when he approached her. He winced when a movement to one side reminded him of his bruised hip; it seemed to be healing more slowly than usual. Jazz's power had increased quite a bit since he'd seen her last. From the size of the fireball she conjured in the alley he was lucky he hadn't ended up a charcoal briquette.

A brief smile touched his lips. Some things never changed.

He slowly moved down the street toward the boardwalk. He knew he'd been right to find her, that Jazz was the only one who could help him and his kind—the only witch with enough power and enough guts to defy the Witches' High Council in order to use it—to help him figure out how and why vampires in the process of seeking an elusive cure to vampirism didn't return to a mortal life but disappeared for good.

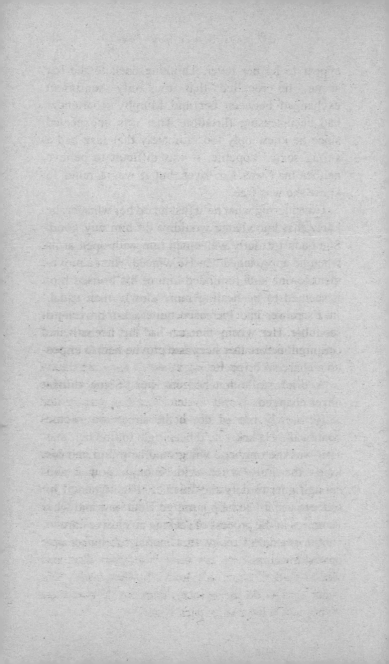

Three

"Krebsie, there is no jam." A seriously sleep-deprived Jazz stared at the refrigerator's interior as wisps of cold air tickled her toes. Five minutes of study and the refrigerator shelves were still as empty as they had been when she first opened it. Examination of the shelves in the door proved just as futile. Her witchy tantrum had left her so wired the night before that sleep had proven next to impossible. She woke up feeling so out of sorts she hadn't even bothered with a glamour spell to look suitable for the outside world. Instead, her hair was matted against one side of her head and pillow creases tracked her cheek.

"No butter either." She glanced over her shoulder at Krebs who sat at the table. He spooned up oatmeal from the bowl in front of him. "Krebs, my love? We have no food." She made sure to sound as plaintive as it was possible without shifting to outright pathetic.

He concentrated on his breakfast, making sure nothing dripped on his navy blue polo shirt and khaki slacks. "Jazz, my love," he shot back. "It's your turn to do the grocery shopping. If you want food, you'll have to go pick it up."

Her shoulders hunched over and her head hung down at the prospect of her least favorite chore. "I grocery shopped the last time."

"*I* did the shopping the last three times," he reminded her. "Sorry, babe. You have to step up to the plate and do the job. Pull up those thong panties and deal with the situation. Or wiggle your nose and conjure up breakfast."

She flopped down into a chair at the table. "That is so not allowed. And thanks to Fluff and Puff no one will deliver here anymore. Besides, I have stuff to do today." She used her favorite excuse. "I have to go by Dweezil's to pick up my pay and I have a curse elimination appointment at a sorority house." The more she thought about the latter, the more she wished she hadn't answered the phone a half hour ago. She took the job in hopes that using some magick would dispel, pardon the pun, the last of her irritation from the night before. Plus she wouldn't get dinged again since, in a sense, she was using her powers for good. She hoped the girls hadn't used some sort of crazy spell to improve their grades or get dates for the next dance or she would be delivering them the lecture from hell. Literally.

Krebs' interest perked up. "Sorority house? Are we talking nubile sweet young things running around in crop tops and tiny shorts and maybe even less? The kind who'd just love to learn the finer art of sex from an experienced older man? Maybe I should go with you."

Jazz smirked. "You wish. Besides, at that age they'd see you as decrepit."

"Shall we compare birth certificates?"

She flicked her fingers at him. A light shower of sparkles fluttered about his head like a swarm of multi-colored bees. "I think I can handle it. Considering the hysterical twit I talked to a few minutes ago, I'd say these girls' shoe sizes are way higher than their IQs. She refused to give me specifics. Said I'd have to see it for myself, which worries me. She said this is an extreme emergency and begged me to come out today. I'd gather whatever is out there isn't pleasant."

"Interesting. It's an emergency, but you're not going over there until after you see Dweezil."

"Her idea of an emergency and mine probably don't mesh. And since she didn't use the term life-threatening, I'm not going to worry."

She stared longingly at the coffee maker. She really should have gotten a cup before she sat down. A tired Jazz was a snarky Jazz. "Now do you understand why I can't go grocery shopping today? And maybe you could stop at the store after your meeting?" She stared at him hopefully.

Krebs got up and walked over to the coffee maker. He refilled his cup and filled another mug. He looked over his shoulder, cocking an eyebrow. "Try another one."

"But I don't wanna go to the grocery store!" Her forehead connected with the table's surface. "It's a mean nasty place with soccer moms blocking the aisles as they talk to their friends or on their cell phones, kids running and screaming all over the place. And Fred, the produce guy, fondles his melons while looking at mine. And I'm not allowed to zap any of them!" she moaned. "It's so not fair!"

"Stop the whining, Jazz. It doesn't become you and you're not going to make me feel sorry for you." He pushed the second mug in her direction. "Drink this. You'll feel more human once you've got some caffeine in you."

She raised her head and offered him a snarl worthy of her beloved Fluff and Puff. "I want toast and eggs." A glimmer of hope brightened her eyes. "Do we have any toaster pastries or frozen French toast sticks? Maybe I should check the freezer." She started to get up.

Krebs shook his head. "You ate the last of those three days ago. If you're so hungry, fix yourself some oatmeal. It's healthier for you anyway." He grinned, knowing full well she wouldn't eat anything that smacked of natural grains or good cholesterol. Spooning up the last of his oatmeal, he slurped his orange juice before standing up. "I've got to go. To make it easy on you I wrote out a shopping list and left it by the phone." He dropped a kiss on the top of her head and headed for the back door. "Considering we need, well, everything, I am afraid it will take you awhile. So good-bye, sweetheart, and have a wonderful day."

"Have a good day yourself, Krebsie, darling. I hate you for making me go to the grocery store," Jazz sang out in her best June Cleaver voice. "May you come home and find fleas in your bed."

"Nah, you don't hate me." Krebs grinned and winked at her. "You just want me as a sex toy."

"You wish, darling!" she crooned.

A few moments later she heard the muted growl of his Porsche roll down the driveway.

Jazz picked up her green and purple over-sized mug with *Wicked* written in bold script on one side and sipped the hearty brew. In her mind's eye she easily read the shopping list lying on the counter across the room.

"Healthy food, out." Black lines ran across half the items neatly printed on the paper. "Fun food, in." Graceful calligraphy covered the rest of the lined paper. Health-conscious Krebs would consider the new items listed as nothing more than empty calories. Jazz considered Hostess cream-filled cupcakes essential to a well-balanced diet and the basis for an excellent midnight snack.

She finished her coffee and poured a good measure in a travel mug. On her way out she snatched up the grocery list along with a leather jacket to battle the morning chill. As she headed out to the carriage house, reflex had her staring down to the end of the driveway. She searched for someone she knew wouldn't be there. It wasn't just fiction that vampires had to stay out of the sun. It was a cold hard fact. Yet it didn't stop the sense that a well-known voice whispered her name on the wind.

"You couldn't bring me coffee too?" Irma's flat Midwestern twang assaulted her ears the moment she slid the large door open. "You never think of others, do you?"

"Yeah, like you can actually drink it." Jazz slid into the sports car and nestled the travel mug between her thighs. "You try drinking coffee and it will only end up on the seat, which will royally piss me off." The car started up with a muted roar.

"Everything pisses you off lately," Irma muttered. "Maybe you should have talked to Nicky. Maybe done even more than just talked to him. He could have put you in a better mood."

Jazz knew exactly how Nikolai would have put her in a good mood too. And it didn't involve either talking or listening; just a lack of clothing. Actually, a little rearrangement would work too. She ruthlessly ignored the heat skimming along her nerve endings. How many times had she vowed no more where the sexy vampire was concerned? How many times had she sworn she would have nothing to do with him again? More times than she could count on her fingers and toes many times over, yet, damn him, he always managed to seduce her all over again. This time she was determined to avoid being pulled into his sphere. Of course, every slip-up in her past where he was concerned told her that was easier said than done.

Besides, didn't she have enough problems in her life without once again adding a "he makes me crazy" vampire to the mix?

She wrinkled her nose at the sharp tang of cigarette smoke. "Get rid of that fucking cigarette, Irma! How many times do you have to be told this car is a no smoking vehicle?"

"As if you haven't conjured up some smoke of your own. I will have you know that Preacher Morris wouldn't appreciate the language you use in front of a lady," Irma sniffed as her cigarette disappeared from view.

"Then Preacher Morris never knew the real you, did he?" Jazz pulled out onto the street without looking either way.

"You drive like a maniac," the older woman muttered. "Am I allowed to know where we're going today or do I have to guess?"

"Errands. It's turning into a gorgeous day, so why not sit back, be quiet, and enjoy the ride." Jazz sped up as they passed the palm tree-lined road that led to the beach and the boardwalk. In the bright daylight, the tall Ferris wheel looked drab—almost shabby—without its bright lights and tinny music adding to the mystique.

Tourist shops were likewise quieter with many of the store owners and employees standing outside to enjoy the last of the morning calm. Jazz honked and waved to those she knew. With one hand on the wheel, she was able to sip her coffee to keep her caffeine buzz intact. Irma's obeying Jazz's suggestion of silence lasted until Jazz made a quick stop at a local fast food restaurant for a breakfast burrito.

"You should think of eating something healthier than that thing you're eating. I cooked my Harold a hearty breakfast every morning," Irma said. "Three eggs over easy, bacon or sausage, country fried potatoes, and my buttermilk biscuits with preserves I put up myself. He wouldn't have dreamed of going to one of those places for a meal that doesn't look fit for a dog."

Not for the world would Jazz admit that her mouth was watering at the idea of a full country-style breakfast. For that alone she was tempted to try, one more time, to charm Irma out of the car—as long as she could manage to get her into the kitchen.

"I'm amazed good ole Harold didn't die of a heart attack from all the cholesterol he shoveled into his mouth every day. I bet you fried everything in lard and real butter, too." She finished the last of her breakfast burrito and daintily licked her fingers clean.

"What I should have done after finding out he was doing the dirty deed with Lorraine Bigelow was put rat poison in his biscuits instead of killing *myself* in his precious car." Irma uttered an unladylike growl.

For a moment, brief as it was, Jazz thought of offering the woman a bit of comfort. Sure, Irma drove her crazy, but if she hadn't killed herself in Harold's car and remained a curse inside the vehicle, Jazz wouldn't have been the lucky recipient of the T-Bird. Driving it fast was almost as good as great sex. Almost.

"Although, my doing that meant he didn't want to drive that tart around in the car," Irma finished with a self-satisfied smile. "And even if you drive like a maniac, I have been able to see a lot of the country."

So much for thinking the woman was mourning her old life. But she couldn't miss that hint of sadness crossing Irma's face.

"And now I suppose we're going to see that ugly man who has all those nasty dwarves working for him," Irma sniffed.

Jazz swallowed a sigh. The moment was gone.

Jazz drove past various auto body and repair shops in the commercial district until she reached one small business complex and pulled into the driveway. A long low-lying building was tucked into the back with several garage doors pulled up and various limousines and town cars being washed and detailed for the day's work. The sign over the office declared it to be All Creatures Limo Service. Jazz parked the T-Bird in one of several slots marked Visitor and climbed out.

"No honking the horn or flashing the lights because you get bored," she warned Irma. "Dweezil's threatened to blow up the car if you throw a tantrum out here. He said you freak out the customers when you do that."

"The man who looks like an olive claims *I* freak people out?" She gestured to a troll that exited the office. "Oh yes, *I'm* the odd one here."

Jazz swallowed her laughter. The last thing she needed to do was encourage the irascible ghost.

"And why would I want to draw attention to myself? That hideous man would only send over those creatures to commit disgusting acts on my body," Irma sniffed, nodding her head toward the tiny men swarming over the cars being readied for the day's work. "Lord knows what perversions they would think of. At least if we have to come here at night I know that Nicky would come and protect me."

Jazz ignored the skittering sensation in her stomach at the name said out loud. "If they try anything I promise to protect you as well as he would. Plus, vampires and dwarves don't get along very well, so I don't think Nikolai would care to come by here." She knew that to be fact, not rumor. "Maybe it's my imagination, but I don't think they want to deal with you any more than you want to deal with them." She watched the cleaning crew scurry around like busy three-foot-tall imps. Every once in awhile, one of them would pause and stare at the T-Bird and then turn to a co-worker and say something, prompting more stares. Jazz didn't experience any warm and fuzzy feelings coming from any of them. She reached for her door. "Oh yeah, you're safe."

Jazz winced when she walked into the office and was immediately assaulted by the pounding beat and explicit lyrics of Lucky Cock's *Linger Ficken' Good.*

"Fates preserve me," she muttered, wishing for a soundproof bubble. She was tempted to silence the stereo system, but Dweezil in a snit at the loss of his precious music wasn't a pleasant sight.

"Hi, Jazz!" said the Barbie doll come-to-life seated behind the counter. Shiny golden blonde hair was swept up into a slightly messy ponytail that looked cute rather than unkempt. It made a perfect frame for the delicate heart shaped face and big Dresden blue eyes. In keeping with the image was the baby pink tank top tucked neatly into a pair of immaculate white linen pants that didn't show one wrinkle. Gold stud earrings decorated the Barbie's equally delicate, but faintly pointed, ears. If it wasn't for that barely-seen point on the tip of her ears and the shift of otherworldly colors in her blue eyes, Jazz would have thought the young woman was pure human. Except what human would knowingly work here?

"Hi, Mindy. Is Dweezil back there?" Jazz nodded toward the rear office.

The woman nodded, "But he's on the phone right now. Do you want to wait?"

Jazz wished she could just ask Mindy to mail the money to her—except that Dweezil tended to "forget" to pay his people unless they came by in person to collect. Jazz's resume might be lengthy, but it didn't list the usual 9-to-5 jobs that many employers liked to see. Plus Dweezil paid well and he also, quite desirably to someone who liked to stay off the income tax radar, paid in cash. So Jazz avoided headaches by showing up for her pay. And while Dweezil made her crazy, his antics also entertained her. Even after all these centuries wandering the world, Dweezil was in a category all by himself. At least, she hoped so—she hated to think there were more Dweezils running around somewhere.

"Nah, too easy for him to try to sneak out the back door. I'll just go in and wait." She headed for the closed door.

"What do you mean that car wasn't clean? My fuckin' cars are cleaner than your arse!" The growl that greeted Jazz was as pleasing to the ear as fingernails on a chalkboard. The faint burnt almond scent that always clung to Dweezil's leathery olive-green skin stung her nostrils. That was another reason why she tried not to piss him off. The angrier he grew, the more burnt-almond stench came off his skin.

"You're sayin' my people don't clean the cars so you can get out of paying the bill. You don't pay the bill, you never use one of my fuckin' cars again. You got it?" The sound of cracking plastic indicated the call was finished.

Jazz dropped into the leather chair placed in front of the L-shaped mahogany desk meant to impress and intimidate anyone who ventured into the inner sanctum. A wide variety of vintage sex toys graced a floor-to-ceiling cabinet and erotic artwork lined the walls. Jazz hadn't been daunted the first time she'd seen the collection, although she wondered about the bedlike antique vibrator a woman had to lie on in order to use. She wasn't curious enough to try it though. Dweezil had offered to loan her the device as long as he could watch. She wasted no time turning down his oh-so-generous suggestion.

She returned his glare with a sunny smile.

"What the fuck is your problem?" Dweezil's voice was a combination of growl, rusty cough, and ground glass. He dropped the broken phone into the wastebasket and pulled out a replacement from the bottom drawer. Several phones lay there in wait for his next tantrum.

"You really need to work on your interpersonal skills, D."

"Why should I change what works for me?" he growled.

"Yeah, why bring in more business when you can so easily drive it away with your charming personality?"

The skeletal creature known as Dweezil—whose last name was unutterable by any human tongue—was a good seven feet tall and immaculately attired in a charcoal Armani suit. When she called him olive-skinned, she did not mean someone of Mediterranean heritage, but a preternatural creature with skin the color of a ripe green olive. While it was a good look for the fruit, it wasn't all that good for anything remotely humanoid. An unruly thatch of mud brown hair flew every which way on top of his football-shaped head. As if he wasn't ugly enough with the thin skin stretching over his bones—at least she thought they were bones—the overbite of yellowish-green teeth didn't add a thing to his lack of looks. His black eyes snapped at her, showing his usual ill humor.

Even though Jazz had worked for Dweezil for almost five years, she still hadn't been able to figure out his lineage. He was too short to be a giant, not ugly enough to be a troll, and most definitely not a goblin. She settled for seeing him as a combination of all three. She had heard rumors he paid his tailor extra to make sure his third arm was well hidden from the world. Gossip also hinted there was a second dick hiding somewhere in there too. Confirming the rumors wasn't anywhere close to the top of her to-do list.

"Damn vampires. First they complain my cars aren't clean, and then they demand some kind of protection 'cause so many of 'em have gone missing. Like that's my problem?" he grumbled. "Everyone knows they're not missing. They took some kind of weird cure and became mortal again. They're all probably at the beach working on their tans. Plus, they want any kind of protection, they're gonna have to pay for it, and it won't come cheap either." He looked up with his usual glare. "So what're you here for?" The burnt-almond scent became stronger. He smelled like he wasn't happy with the way the day was going and she was about to make it worse. Dweezil could make Ebenezer Scrooge look like a philanthropist.

"It's the end of the month." She lifted her eyebrows. When he didn't move, she abandoned the cute smile. "Pay day."

The staring contest lasted all of fifty seconds. Dweezil dropped his gaze first. He mumbled a few choice curses as he reached inside a desk drawer and retrieved a long white envelope. He held it between the two fingers that topped his left hand and tossed it across the desk.

Jazz picked it up and quietly made sure it was the amount he owed her. She tucked the envelope into her jacket's hidden inner pocket.

"Got a job for you for tomorrow night."

Her first thought was of a man with dark brown hair and eyes the color of the sea. Except she knew for a fact he already knew how to drive and was smart enough to not request her services as a driver. "I'm off tomorrow night."

"He asked for you specifically. And he'll pay extra just to have you." He wiggled his caterpillar eyebrows at her. For all she knew the hairy appendages over his eyes were fashioned from real insect fuzz. Something else she never cared to investigate.

"Just to have me? Eeuuww factor, Dweezil!" Jazz mimicked gagging.

"I'll pay you double your fee," he tempted.

"Hot date, hot man, ocean view, candlelight, fine dining," she fibbed. She couldn't remember the last time she'd been out on an actual date. As for sex … well, that was another subject better left in the land of Not In This Lifetime.

Dweezil attempted to display a smile on his bony face. His expression was guaranteed to scare the dead. Jazz swore she felt worms crawl up her flesh when he smiled.

He threw his arms in the air. Something shifted under his jacket. "All right, I'll pay you triple."

Jazz's mind raced at the idea of a triple fee. It could only mean this client was very special. Which meant it was someone who Dweezil didn't want to piss off and who was willing to pay him a lot of money. This sent all her senses on full alert.

"Who's the client, D?"

"He's a very well-connected member of our community," he said so quickly Jazz was sure he had rehearsed the speech in anticipation of her refusal. "He also likes that you can conjure up a strong protection spell if he requires one while he's out."

"*Who,* D?" Her voice hardened just a fraction. "And, for the record, those protection spells are extra and I get 100 percent of that extra."

"The job is for all evening, so we're talking a lot of money. It's not like he's demanding you go topless or something. But it wouldn't hurt, ya know. Get you bigger tips." He chortled at his twisted sense of humor. Jazz didn't join in.

"*D.*" A scattering of purple, black, and gold sparks sprinkled down around her. A sign she was *so* not happy!

Dweezil muttered a few words that Jazz guessed were curses in his language. He had already learned the hard way not to direct any at her. The one time he had it had taken him three weeks to pick all the maggots out of his flesh. An equal amount of time was added to her banishment. It had been worth it.

Just like the time the Witches Council added on for what you did to Nikolai, muttered that pesky gargoyle, sometimes doubling as her conscience, residing inside her head. *He wants your help. So give it already!* She wasted no time mentally stuffing a wad of cotton in its vile mouth.

"All you have to do is drive him to his favorite club and back to his house," he muttered. "No biggie."

"No."

He slammed his hands on the desk surface, causing a jade dildo to roll around on the polished wood. "You agreed to drive him for a triple fee!"

Now she knew she didn't need to hear the name to know exactly who the special client was, and as far as she was concerned, even a triple fee wasn't enough.

"I didn't agree to anything. Besides, he's disgusting! Find someone else." She instantly dismissed his demand.

"Tyge Foulshadow pays in gold bars!" There was nothing Dweezil loved more than money, but a client who paid in gold bars earned a special status in his avaricious little mind. He made *Star Trek*'s greedy *Ferengi* look like spendthrifts. "Do you know how hard it is to get clients who pay in gold? Just about fuckin' impossible!"

"His farts are noxious! Literally!"

"Which is why it's good that you're one of the few who can survive them," Dweezil happily pointed out, his hands lifted upward as if to say *See what a good deal this is for both of us?*

"I can never get that disgusting stench out of my clothes! I have to throw them away because I couldn't dare give them to a charity. And I can't burn them because the smoke is revolting. Only the Fates know what the clothes are doing to the landfills!"

"His tip alone will cover a replacement wardrobe." He paused. "I can't tell him you're turning him down, Jazz. He only wants you to drive him. Master Foulshadow doesn't take rejection lightly."

Jazz narrowed her eyes at the hint of vulnerability edged with fear written on Dweezil's face. She did not think anything could deflate her employer's mega-confidence, but the thought of losing Tyge Foulshadow's business seemed to. It was interesting to watch avarice compete with fear on his repulsive face. She wondered just why fear, though. What did Tyge have on him? She knew Dweezil was greedy, but was he so greedy he'd push her into taking a job he knew she didn't want?

"Then you have to foot the bill for my clothes," she stated.

"I'm already paying you a triple fee and he always tips well."

She stood up. "Try Vasal. He'll do anything for money. Put a red wig and high heels on him and maybe Foulshadow will think he's me."

Dweezil jumped to his feet. "All right, I'll pay for your fuckin' clothes! But you're cutting into my profit." He adopted the stance of a man teetering on the threshold of poverty. "It's no thanks to bi—," he quickly backpedaled as more sparks flared up around Jazz, "drivers like you who take advantage of my generosity."

Jazz knew better. She was positive that if her employer offered to pay her a triple fee the client would be charged much more than Dweezil's usual percentage.

"I am so out of here." She didn't need any more time added to her banishment, which would happen if she stuck around much longer. The idea of maggots once again covering Dweezil was growing more appealing by the minute. But that extra sixty days because of Nikolai still left a bitter taste in her mouth.

"Pick Master Foulshadow up at ten tomorrow night," Dweezil called after her. "And wear something sexy. Show off the assets. If you're going to be paid triple, you might as well earn it."

Jazz walked out, waving her extended middle finger over her head.

"You *must* show me respect! I still pay your salary!" he shouted after her. The sound of his agitation shattered a glass sculpture sitting on the reception desk. Mindy didn't flinch as she calmly picked up a brush and dustpan to sweep up the shards. If Dweezil didn't throw a tantrum at least once a day, those around him figured he was at death's door.

Jazz muttered a few of her own curses as she headed for her car.

"Those disgusting little men were staring at me," Irma sniffed as Jazz started up the T-Bird. "I just know they were imagining me with my clothes off."

"One, they're too busy to stop and stare at you. Two, there is no way in hell they'd think you were Snow White, with or without clothes." If she was lucky, her appointment at the sorority house would be long and involved and she would have an excellent reason why she didn't make it to the grocery store and why she was serving pizza for dinner.

Four

"What are those strange-looking letters on the house?" Irma asked. She squinted up at the two-story house they were parked in front of. Jazz wondered if there was a pair of glasses tucked away in that handbag that usually rested in Irma's lap.

"The letters are Greek because that's a sorority house," she replied, looking at the dwelling. She was positive she'd been here in the early 1930s. All the homes were that vintage, and if she recalled correctly, several minor film stars owned homes out this way. In fact, if she wasn't mistaken, she had met Clive Reeves at a party here. She could not stop the involuntary shudder that ran down her spine at the thought of the man who'd almost destroyed her soul and her life. She'd done her best to forget one fateful night, but some memories weren't easily erased.

Damn that man, he's moldering in his grave where he belongs, so why can't he leave me alone?

"Ah," Irma nodded. "I know about those groups. They're nothing more than girls just looking for a good time. They never bothered to learn anything when they attended college. They only went there to look for a husband to take care of them. Then once they got caught up with the campus activities, they joined sororities and acted like tarts, thinking they were better than the girls who didn't join one. All because they lived in a special house and wore one of those fancy little pins on their sweaters. Well, they were no different then, and I can tell you now, they're still no different than the rest of us."

"Bitter, party of one," Jazz muttered.

Irma's glare could have stripped paint. "Just because I hold myself to a higher standard doesn't mean you can make fun of me." She sat back in the seat with her arms crossed under her generous breasts.

"Tell you what. One evening I'll come out to the carriage house and we'll watch my DVD of *Animal House*," Jazz offered, to placate the grumpy ghost. "You can see a sorority tart get what she deserves."

"Don't let those hussies try to give you something funny to smoke," Irma advised as Jazz started up the driveway. "I've heard it can make you do all sorts of crazy things."

"Yeah, yeah, yeah." She adjusted her cropped aqua leather jacket that topped snug-fitting white jeans and a white silk t-shirt. An ornate moonstone pendant set in gold rested comfortably in the middle of her shirt. She thought too much black would scare the girls off, so she decided she would go with her version of witchy college girl chic.

Earsplitting squeals emanating from inside the house warned Jazz that what she found inside wouldn't be pleasant. She rang the doorbell, waited, and when no one appeared right away, she rang it again. Each time she rang the bell the squealing inside grew louder and more frantic. The sound was eerily familiar.

"Fates preserve me," she muttered. "Don't tell me they did what I think they did."

"Just do something about them! The smell is getting so gross I'm ready to hurl!" A high-pitched exasperated feminine voice hit Jazz just as the front door swung open. A petite brunette wearing grubby denim shorts and a lilac tank top stared at her. "Can I help you?"

"I'm Jazz Tremaine. You called for my services."

"Thank God, you're here." She reached out and grabbed Jazz's hand, pulling her inside. "We don't know what to do." She lifted her hands in a helpless gesture. "You have to save us!"

Jazz's first warning of the approaching tornado was a flash of pink and a series of squeals that hurt her ears. She jumped to one side as a pig raced past her with two girls on its heels. When they saw her they skidded to a stop while the frightened pig kept on running, its cloven hooves sliding on the hardwood floor. She wrinkled her nose against the barnyard aroma that permeated the entryway.

"Bloody hell," she whispered, looking around at the chaos with horrified fascination.

"You have to watch where you step," the girl who let her in warned with an apologetic air. "They, uh, aren't housebroken and we can't get them to go into the backyard to do their business, so… ." Her voice drifted off as she looked around at the disaster area.

Jazz ignored her and the other girls who now crowded around her as if she was their last hope.

From what she sensed in the air, they weren't far off the mark. She could feel the tangled threads of magick clouding the air like a crazy quilt, emphasis on the crazy.

There was no doubt that whatever they did here had gone very wrong, and she didn't need to look at the small herd of pigs to know that the girls had messed up big time.

"When the Wizard was passing out brains did any of you ever think about standing in line to get one?" she asked, not expecting an answer and not receiving one.

Jazz gently pushed away a curious pig chewing on her jeans. If she'd been warned about the pigs she definitely wouldn't have worn white.

"What did you do?" Her voice was low with the same dangerous edge she had displayed earlier to Dweezil.

The girls fell back. At that moment, their fear of Jazz was as thick as the magick filling the air.

"It was a joke," the first girl whispered. Her wide eyes were wary, but she still had the courage to face Jazz. Jazz gave her points for bravery even if her common sense appeared to be on hold.

Jazz took a deep breath and reminded herself that the girls didn't realize they had fooled with something dangerous.

"What kind of joke would involve all this?" She stalked toward the living room and found four more pigs running around. The sharp stench of offal was everywhere. For a moment, she was taken back to her childhood. Then her memories became more recent as she realized just what kind of mess the girls had conjured up. A wave of her hand brought the girls tumbling one after another into the room, whether they wanted to be there or not. With another swish, she froze time.

The wallpaper and furniture were different, but she knew this was the same house Josh Levine had owned back in 1931. For a moment, old memories swamped her and she saw the house as it had been. The debonair Clive Reeves had been out back naked in the swimming pool with five giggling starlets and not one of them was doing the backstroke. That should have been her first clue that the charismatic film star wasn't exactly the happily married man profiled in *Photoplay* magazine. But she always had a weak spot for tall, dark, handsome men, which was why she'd been so excited at the prospect of attending a party at the film star Clive Reeves' mansion. She only wished she could go back and redo that night. *But Nikolai* … . She clamped her lips shut to stop the curse that threatened to erupt. The way she felt at the moment, she would probably turn the girls into sheep and this area of the city wasn't zoned for livestock. She brought her mind back to the problem at hand, namely, pigs running all over the place. She waved the room to life again and cocked her head at the leader of the group. As she waited for an explanation, she wondered if she had ever been that young.

"It was 'Get Even Night,'" the petite brunette murmured, her gaze flitting everywhere but at Jazz. "We all know guys who have been mean to us or acted like total shits." She started to gain some confidence and stood a bit straighter and then met Jazz's gaze more openly. "They thought they were coming over for a party."

Jazz had no doubt what the boys expected to happen at said party. "And … ?"

A girl with a wide stripe of pink running through her white blonde hair piped up, "A girl in my Psych class is a witch and she goes to these awesome parties at some mansion up in the Hollywood hills." She faltered under Jazz's withering stare. "She gave me a spell she got there. She said it would make the guys act like pigs. We thought it would be funny if they ran around thinking they were pigs, when they actually are, so to speak," her words drifted off.

For a minute Jazz thought the top of her head would explode. She took a few deep breaths. "And you called me because?"

"Something went wrong with the spell," the brunette explained. "They were only supposed to act like pigs. You know, run around on all fours and squeal. They weren't supposed to," she cringed as a pig nudged her bare leg, "like, turn into pigs!"

Jazz held out her hand and snapped her fingers. "Give me the spell."

The girl with the pink-striped hair dug into her shorts pocket and pulled out a folded piece of paper. She gingerly stepped forward and handed it to her.

Jazz unfolded the paper and scanned the words. She mentally vowed to find the idiot who gave the girls this spell and give her a taste of her own medicine.

"This wasn't supposed to happen!" one of the girls wailed, kicking out at a pig who was trying to climb up her leg.

Jazz looked down at a once lovely rug that even a major shampoo job wouldn't rescue and furniture that had been shredded by tiny hooves. Nearby, one pig was happily munching on a bouquet of silk flowers that lay scattered on the floor.

"Eight hundred dollars. Cash only." The look of horror on their faces told her they didn't have that amount between them. No surprise there.

"We pooled our money together, but we only have four-hundred and eighty dollars." The brunette walked over to a table and opened a small drawer, pulling out the bills. "Unless you take Visa or MasterCard." Her smile grew faint at the expression on Jazz's face. "I guess not."

"Good guess." Jazz hesitated just long enough to make them worry. "All right, but ...," she tucked the bills into her jacket pocket and then she paused as their smiles quickly dimmed as she finished her sentence, "you have to do something for me."

"You can really turn them back?"

"What? You want references now?"

"No, no!" One other girl punched the disbeliever. "What do we have to do?"

"First you better make sure to clean this house from top to bottom yourselves. No finding a way to bring in a cleaning service to handle a mess that all of you are at fault for. If you want my spell to work, you have to clean this place yourselves."

A bunch of noses wrinkled with disgust. "Clean it? With what?"

"It's easy. Try buckets of hot soapy water, scrub brushes, and mops," she said firmly. "And last, you allow me to put a binding spell on all of you to prevent this ever happening again." She made eye contact with each girl to make sure they understood her conditions. If she knew her manner and stance mirrored Eurydice, Headmistress of the Witches Academy, she probably would have screamed in horror.

"How long will this binding spell last?" one girl asked.

"Forever."

A horrified silence followed her words.

"But midterms are coming up," one girl whispered.

Jazz's eyes sliced through her. "Be original. Study." Her anger at the girls was as palpable as the barnyard aroma in the room. "What you girls did was dangerous. Magick is not something you play with like a board game. You have no idea what you could have wrought last night with this badly written spell." She stalked past them, unconsciously echoing the headmistress's lofty arrogance. "If I told you what could have happened, you would suffer from nightmares for the rest of your thoughtless lives."

"We didn't know." The brunette's lower lip trembled as a tear trickled down her cheek.

"And now you do." She crumpled up the paper and with a flick of her fingers, let it burst into a bright orange flame. The girls gasped and stepped back. "From hence on ye shall do no harm. Ye shall speak no charm. From now on, ye shall retreat from all that hovers on the edge of your lives. Because I say so, damn it!" She waved her hand over each girl's head and a shower of multi-colored sparks fell over them. The air suddenly felt cleansed. She turned on her heel and walked to the center of the room. As if understanding it was now their turn, the pigs wandered into the room and milled about her. "Little boys go to a party. Little boys don't leave. Little boys turn into piggies. Little girls don't grieve. Now piggies must return to former selves and little girls will...." She paused for effect. "Behave. Because I say so, damn it!"

"That doesn't rhyme," one of the girls whispered. "Ouch!" She rubbed her arm, where she had been pinched hard.

A thick vapor drifted along the floor snaking itself around the pigs that squealed and tried to escape, but the fog was not to be denied its victims. As the mist floated upward, the girls screamed and the squealing grew loud enough to shake the ground underneath them. Then the sound transformed gradually into something deeper and more human. As suddenly as the fog appeared, it slid away leaving a dozen naked young men lying sprawled on the carpet.

"Shit!" One boy with a jock's beefy build leaped to his feet. He quickly grabbed a pillow off the couch and held it in front of his lower body. "What kind of drugs did you bitches give us?" He shouted at the girls, moving forward with retribution burning in his eyes. There was no doubt he was furious and intended to inflict some serious damage on the first girl he could grab.

"Okay, no reason for that." Keeping her gaze determinedly set above his waist, Jazz walked over and tapped his forehead with her fingertips. "Forget," she whispered. A look of consternation formed on his angular face. She moved among the boys, repeating her instructions. She looked over her shoulder at the girls. "If their clothes are destroyed, I suggest you find something for them to wear fast and get them out of here. You have a lot of cleaning up to do." She walked toward the front door.

"Uh, Jazz?" The brunette almost ran after her. "Does this mean they won't remember they were pigs?"

"It means they won't accuse you of drugging them," Jazz said. "You were idiots to mess with a spell you had no business using, but it's still no reason for him to call you bitches." She opened the door and looked at the girl. "That binding spell I cast will make sure you never try or go near magick again no matter how tempting it is," she warned. "Trust me, you don't want to even try reversing my spell. The consequences would be nasty."

Her head bobbed up and down. "Thank you."

Again Jazz wondered if she had ever been that young. "Just don't do anything so stupid again. And clean up those rooms until they can pass the white glove test!" She walked out.

"How was it?" Irma called out. A flicker of light flew out of the car.

Jazz sighed. She knew Irma wouldn't have been able to go too long without a cigarette.

"A bunch of Twinkies with no brains thought they could use a spell to make idiot boys act like idiot pigs." She secured the money in the glove compartment.

"Nothing unusual about that. When boys drink too much they always act like pigs."

"Only this drink actually turned the boys into real swine."

"Oh, my!" Irma patted her breast in ladylike shock. "That is not very sanitary either."

Jazz thought of the smell that had seeped right into the walls. She was positive the girls would never get it out of the house.

"No kidding." As she started up the car, she realized her next destination wouldn't be as easy. She swallowed the groan that threatened to rise up her throat. "And now I have to shop for groceries."

"You're a witch. Why can't you just wave your hands and let the food appear in the kitchen?"

"Because I'd be punished for it." Jazz thought of the produce manager who always leered at her while he fondled the melons. She couldn't imagine the council would tack on an additional sixty days for an exploding grapefruit ... or five. Not when the man deserved it. "Today, he just might find out what it feels like to be sprayed by a grapefruit," she whispered to herself.

Sometimes, the punishment was worth the crime.

⁀

The coming of dawn pulled at Nick's power, reminding him it was time to rest. He caught a last glimpse of the full moon, which the weres revered and gave them strength, and wondered why the same full moon would also have a centering effect on Jazz. Admittedly, with her energy level that said a lot.

Damn that witch!

After a frustrating night of tracking down a deadbeat vampire—even the undead were required to pay their bills—Nick was ready to spend the daylight hours resting. He had been a vampire long enough that he didn't have to sleep the day away and could even go out on sunless days without fear of bursting into flames. But he spent bright days like today in the shadowed darkness of his office, where he either caught up on paperwork or took a nap. After the night he had, today was definitely a day for recharging his batteries.

The two-story building near the boardwalk was as antique as the nearby carousel. He took the cagelike elevator to the second floor and headed for the office at the end of the hallway marked Gregory Investigations. The moment he stepped into the reception area his senses detected he wasn't alone. Just as quickly he knew that his uninvited visitor was a welcome one. He did not bother turning on a light. Neither of them would require one.

"You're very trusting, my friend. Even a mortal child could pick that sorry excuse for a lock." A blond-haired man uncoiled his lean length from the chair in front of Nick's desk and approached him. His broad smile pronounced him friend rather than foe. "By the sign on your door I see you have also modernized your name. I must say that Nick

Gregory suits the vampire facing me more than Nikolai Gregorivich did."

"Flavius!" Nick threw his arms around the man in greeting. "When did you arrive in L.A.?"

"Last evening. I had some meetings to attend out this way and thought I would stop by to see you." He glanced around the office filled with 1940s era furniture that fit with Nick's casual clothing and contrasted greatly with Flavius's sleek Italian cut suit, Egyptian cotton pale blue shirt that mirrored the color of his eyes and tasteful black diamond cufflinks. "I see you still think you're Sam Spade."

"And I see you still view yourself as James Bond." Nick's grin revealed a hint of fang. "Where are you based now? New York City? Paris? Rome?"

"I've been based in Madrid for the past few years."

"Making use of the Protectorate's private jet again, are you?" Nick teased.

"As befits a company executive. As I recall you once had free use of any jet in the fleet."

Nick silently admitted that giving up some of the perks of the Protectorate did hurt. Every jet in the fleet was set up to handle a vampire's every need from protection from daylight to blood on tap whether bottled or fresh from a willing vein.

"True, even flying first class doesn't provide the amenities Vamp Air did." He grinned when Flavius winced at his flippant tone. "You're still too serious, my friend."

"And you still fight authority when it suits you." The elder vampire settled back in a chair. "So tell me what you have been doing. I understand Jazz is living in the area. Have you seen her? It's been awhile for you two, hasn't it?"

Nick was not surprised that in only a few hours, and with very little effort, Flavius had ascertained Jazz's location. Even if he didn't admit it, Flavius knew to the day just how long it had been since Jazz and Nick had seen each other. The elder vampire had endured his share of run-ins with the snarky witch over the centuries.

"It's been a little over thirty years," he admitted. "Jazz never changes."

Flavius cocked an eyebrow, silently asking for details of the first meeting he sensed was more than a casual run-in. "You sound as if the two of you did nothing more innocuous than go out for coffee. That I can't believe."

"Not even close. I tracked her down the other night and she brought up witchflame and threw a fireball at me. She next threatened to stake me."

"And that's a new thing?" The elder vampire chuckled.

"This time she actually held the stake to my chest and made sure it was right over my heart."

Flavius winced. "Jazz has always been gifted in holding a grudge."

Nick looked at the being that knew him better than anyone. Flavius was more than his friend; he was his sire. He was the vampire that had turned him and then taught him the skills necessary to survive in a world that denied its residents sunlight and knew only violence. Flavius had spent his mortal adult life serving as a Consul, one of the highest-ranking officers in the Roman Army at the time when Ancient Rome ruled the world. He understood just what it took to exist among predators. Their friendship strengthened with each passing century. Nick wouldn't know what to do if anything ever happened to his friend.

Nick studied the bland expression on Flavius' face. "You're not here just to talk over old times. You mentioned meetings. They had to do with the missing vampires, didn't they?"

The elder vampire inclined his head. "It has come to the Protectorate's attention that the numbers have greatly increased in the past year. They are now quite anxious since the problem has become more public among our community due to rumors going around of a supposed cure for vampirism."

"They're worried *now?* A little late, aren't they?" Nick pushed his hands through his hair, dislodging the thick strands. He paced the length of the dark office. "Why weren't they worried five years ago? Ten? Even seventy years ago when the rumors first began? When I first brought this to their attention? You are one of their senior members, Flavius. Hell, you're probably their most senior member. Yet they did nothing to protect their own when the disappearances first started and continued to ignore the situation as they increased over the years," he ground out.

"At the time they thought of them as isolated incidents. You know as well as anyone that similar happenings have occurred over the centuries. Members of our kind disappear for many reasons. We also didn't have the resources we have these days."

"Isolated?" Nick barked a laugh. "I have been away from this city for some time, but even I know these aren't *isolated incidents*. In the beginning, one or two a month went missing. Now it is that number each week and possibly more." His grim expression spoke volumes. "Come on, Flavius, we both know who is behind this and he needs to be stopped."

Flavius shook his head. "You have no proof that Clive Reeves is behind the disappearances."

"Do you honestly doubt I am wrong?"

"Ever the hard-headed policeman. You should have stayed with the Protectorate instead of striking out on your own, my friend. You would have been running a division by now."

"No thanks. Too many rules." Nick looked around at his cramped, funky office. If he had remained with the Protectorate, he would have had a suite in a high-rise building downtown, elegant antique furniture and rare paintings decorating his office, an unlimited expense account, secretaries, assistants at his beck and call, and any information he needed in the blink of an eye. Not to mention a healthy bank account.

Instead, his office took up one corner of a crumbling building where smells of cotton candy and popcorn drifted through the window, his furniture had been found at a flea market, voice mail handled his calls because he couldn't afford a secretary yet and his bank account straddled the fence between red and black, leaning more to the former than the latter. Still, he was content because he had no one to answer to but himself.

Flavius rested his fingers together steeple fashion. "The Protectorate wishes to hire you to look into this matter."

"Been there, done that, never again."

Flavius shook his head. "We wish to hire you as an outside contractor." He named a figure that had Nick's bank account whistling *We're in the Money*. "And we are willing to pay off the mortgage on this building, so you would have it free and clear."

Nick wasn't surprised they knew he struggled to make the mortgage payments every month. Just because he was no longer an agent with the Protectorate didn't mean they stopped keeping tabs on him. He knew leaving the organization didn't mean the organization left him—something he'd never share with Jazz even if he ever managed to talk to her without her bringing up witchflame. "I don't think so. They would probably want to keep the deed. What is really going on, Flavius?"

Flavius shook his head. "I promise you the deed would be handed over to you. As to what's going on, we acknowledge there have been problems in the past...."

Nick threw up his hands. "Problems? Flavius, you are like a father to me. And once upon a time the Protectorate was my family. But I have not talked to any Protectorate agent besides you for the last eight years. Why would they come to me now? You have plenty of agents more qualified than I to take Reeves down."

"What happened then could not be helped."

Nick took a moment to gather his thoughts. He did

not want to argue with Flavius. It had been too long since they had seen each other and he would rather spend the time reminiscing about better times than dredge up old hurts.

"If they want to hire me, they will sign *my* contract and pay my daily rate and expenses." He automatically quadrupled his usual fee. The Protectorate had access to unlimited funds; Nick didn't.

He carried a decent caseload at the moment working for a couple of vampires who wanted him to find their missing mates, but they didn't have much money and he took the cases because it gave him a legitimate reason to investigate the disappearances. Contrary to popular myth, not all vampires were wealthy. Many of the ones he worked for could barely afford to pay his expenses, but he refused to turn down anyone in need. Now, he figured if he was going to investigate the increase in disappearing vampires, he may as well let the Protectorate pick up the whole tab.

Flavius burst out laughing. "You have not changed at all. Dare I say you are as hard-headed as your witch?"

"She's not *my* witch and, trust me, she wouldn't appreciate you calling her that." The fireball had been a close call and the stake even closer. "If I'm to do this I want full access to all the Protectorate's records on the disappearances."

"We will provide you with whatever you require."

Nick shook his head. "No, I want *everything* the Protectorate has. I know how you work, Flavius. You would give me what *you* feel is crucial and not necessarily what I need. This has been going on for decades and I'm sure you have records covering all those years."

Flavius waved a languid hand. "Agreed. I will give you the proper passwords to access all our records."

Nick nodded. "Thank you. A contract will be delivered to your office within a few hours. You can sign it and return it along with my retainer."

Flavius smiled. "That will be acceptable." He stood up. "Have you talked to Jazz about Clive Reeves?"

Nick fought hard to conceal the direction of his thoughts in regards to that question. "Jazz's memories of Clive Reeves aren't exactly Hallmark material," he muttered, grimacing at the colossal understatement. He regretted every day since that fateful night that he hadn't destroyed the creature that looked human but had no human qualities. And they called Nick's kind monsters. Those who did had never met Clive Reeves.

"Neither are yours," Flavius reminded him. "Don't allow that prejudice to get in the way of your investigation, Nico. We can't interfere in a mortal's life just because you have a hunch—and perhaps a grudge."

Nick whipped around to face his sire.

"Then tell me this. Why have so many vampires attended parties at the Reeves mansion, and yet not all leave the property? And even with that knowledge, why has no one done anything about it?"

Flavius' smile showed the weariness of a man who also had more questions than answers.

"Since the Protectorate has engaged your services, I would say that it is now up to you to find out."

❧

"I'm sorry, Callie, but I don't do that type of work. I don't follow alleged cheating mates," Nick sighed, keeping the phone to his ear as he wandered the office. He glanced at the old-fashioned clock on the wall. He was late meeting Flavius at Club Insolence, an exclusive club for wealthy vampires who were willing to pay the outrageous membership fees for their privacy. The club wasn't Nick's style, but Flavius enjoyed the elitist ambiance there. Nick planned to take Flavius to The Crypt, a more down-and-dirty club, the next time they got together. Knowing Flavius, he would enjoy what both clubs offered.

"But I was told you're the best, that you can do what others can't! Please?" the woman begged. "I need to know the truth about Thomas. I want to know that he still loves me as much as I love him."

Nick stifled a groan. He wanted to tell her that ten-to-one her mate was cheating on her. The couple had been converted together only twenty years ago because they wanted to be together always. The trouble was, male vamps tended to be extremely promiscuous for the first couple hundred years just because they could and the sex was so mind-blowing that it turned into an addiction. If it hadn't been for Flavius teaching him that quality definitely outweighed quantity, Nick would have been screwing a new woman, or four, every night, too.

"Do you truly love him?" he asked her, already knowing what her answer would be. Fates save him from lovesick baby vampires.

"Yes." Her heart might no longer beat, but her sobs were without a doubt the heartbroken kind. "We vowed we would love each other always. That's why we got converted together. But now he goes out almost every night and he doesn't want me going with him. He said he's expected to hunt with other males. I don't believe him. Oh, he brings food back for me, but we don't spend time together the way I thought we would."

Nick pressed his fingertips against the bridge of his nose and closed his eyes. Spare him from fickle young love. It never lasted as long as they thought it would. "I'm sorry, Callie, but I truly don't take on this type of case. I'll tell you what I can do. I want you to talk to a friend of mine. Her name's Rowena."

"Rowena," she repeated the name. "So she can find out if Thomas is cheating on me?"

"No, but she can help you find your own way in the vampire world." He winced at the muffled sob on the other end as realization hit hard that one night Thomas might not come back. Nick never did well with emotional females. At least Jazz never teared up when she was in an emotional state. She was more into throwing things at his head. "You admitted you personally have had few contacts with other vampires after the two of you converted. What about your sire?"

"Who?"

Nick swallowed a groan. "The vampire who made you. He or she should be instructing the two of you in how to survive in your new world."

"No, we just paid this guy to do it." She sounded totally clueless about the undead existence ahead of her.

He mentally spat out more than his share of curses and wished for a few of Jazz's fireballs. "He shouldn't have done that. It was his job to teach the two of you how to exist in our world."

"Thomas has vampire friends who do that," Callie said.

"You've relied too much on Thomas to take care of you and handle things for you. If, Fates forbid, something happens to him, you would be fair game for others. You need to know how to take care of yourself, Callie. In our world, it is essential that you be able to do for yourself or you'll be fair prey for any vampire stronger than you, and right now you're still as weak as a newborn kitten." He had this vision of the constantly disappearing Thomas coming home at the stroke of dawn with a supersized to-go cup of blood for Callie. What better way to keep her under his self-imposed power than to ensure she only fed if he brought the food to her? It was tempting to hunt down the bastard and show him what could happen to young arrogant vampires who did not follow the rules set down by the Vampire Council ages ago. But then the younger vamps saw the Council as nothing more than a bunch of old fogies who didn't believe in living in the new millennium. He feared the time would come when a war would be waged between the old traditions and the new, far more progressive but often self-destructive ways.

When he hung up, he got the feeling that the young female vampire wouldn't call Rowena and take that first step to independence, but he hoped he was wrong. He didn't want to think that the emotionally frail Callie might grow so depressed she would greet the dawn, which was the vampire way of committing suicide. All because she was in love and wanted to be with her boyfriend forever.

No thanks to the internet, too many people, most of them troubled and lost, had the ability to seek out vampires, who, for a fee, would convert them with the promise of an eternal existence of wealth and decadence. What these hapless fools didn't understand was that the fee only covered the conversion. Then they were left to fend for themselves, and without any training on how to understand their enhanced senses and thirst for blood, some turned feral, while others couldn't handle it, and insanity turned to death. When Nick had been a member of the Protectorate, his main job was hunting down many of the vampires who performed the conversions and destroying them before their wasteful practices destroyed the balance with humanity. And since he managed to blend easily enough with the human community, he was able to work under the guise of a mortal law enforcement agent when it was needed. His hand behind the death of so many vampires, even if they deserved it, had been the main reason he had left the organization that had nurtured him from the beginning of his time as a vampire. He hated the destruction of any being if there was a way it could be prevented. Rowena, an old friend, had come up with a solution by running a sort of half-way house for fledgling vampires who had no clue what they had gotten themselves into.

Nick made a mental note to call Rowena when he got back and tell her about Callie. Thanks to Caller ID he had the young vampire's phone number. Perhaps Rowena would be successful where Nick himself hadn't been in helping the young vampire understand what she needed to do besides simply awaiting the return of the constantly wandering Thomas.

Lost in contemplation of miserable—though often self-imposed—vampire fortunes, it was pure chance that he glanced out his office window and saw Jazz walking along the boardwalk. Although he always thought Fate had a twisted sense of humor where he and Jazz were concerned, this bit of synchronous interference certainly beat all.

He took the quickest way out of his office by climbing from the window onto the narrow iron fire escape and going up instead of down. The buildings' flat-topped roofs made it easy for him to follow her as she headed for the boardwalk's arcade and pier.

He wasn't surprised to discover she lived near the boardwalk. The child in Jazz had always loved the energy and bright colors of carnivals and fairs. Once upon a time they had spent many a summer evening at Coney Island riding the large wooden roller coaster, visiting the exhibits, and dancing under the stars. Those magickal nights had more to do with Jazz, the woman, than Jazz, the witch. He smiled. She had been known as Jessica Tremaine back then. She had favored voluminous skirts that swirled gracefully from her tiny waist and she'd worn her hair up in an elegant twist. Nothing like the faded jeans and baggy sweatshirt she wore tonight with her coppery hair tied back in a loose ponytail.

But the magick between them never lasted long. His work would intrude on their lives and she would lose her temper because he would be forced to take her into custody for some infraction or another since she had a habit of interfering or getting in the way. So they would part amid colorful shouts and curses. There'd been so many partings, both past and present. Yet, they always managed to find their way back to each other. He liked to think the Fates had a hand in that.

Tonight Nick was content to follow Jazz's leisurely progress past the usual Midway games that were guaranteed to take your money as easily as any Las Vegas craps table. As she walked by he noticed the workers cease their usual patter in hopes of luring passersby to stop at their booths to try their luck with one of the games. In fact, they managed to avoid looking at her altogether. She could have been a ghost freely strolling the weathered boards. Or someone who didn't need luck in pitching dimes or trying the ring toss to win a prize.

"You've won their games too many times, haven't you, darling?" he murmured.

Jazz stopped for a paper cone of pink cotton candy then walked to the pier. As she enjoyed her sugary treat, she occasionally took a small bit of the spun candy and tucked it into a large tote bag hanging from her shoulder.

"You two behave," he heard her warn the bag's contents. "I don't want Rex to ban me from the boardwalk too."

"What the Fates?" he muttered then saw a furry ear poke out and the contents of her tote bag shift. He chuckled and settled back. So she still had Fluff and Puff, eh?

"Not wearing the man-eating slippers tonight, Jazz?" Nick heard a grizzled old man tease as he cast his fishing line over the pier's railing.

"No, this time she appears to be carrying them," Nick murmured, wincing at one memorable contact with the bunny chompers. And to think people called *him* bloodthirsty!

"No, I'm not wearing them tonight, Harvey." She winked.

The man glanced at the tote bag that appeared to have a life of its own. "Oh, I see. Well, even bunny slippers need fresh air." His laughter rang out. "I promise not to rat you out to the boardwalk police."

"Thanks." Jazz looked out over the incoming waves. "Having any luck?"

"Nah, I think the waves are too choppy tonight, so the fish have moved out to deeper water." He leaned over. "You wouldn't care to sprinkle some mumbo jumbo on my pole, would you?" He waggled thick eyebrows at her.

"You are a very bad man, Harvey," she chided him. "Fishing is a skill, not magick." She moved on after giving him a one-armed hug. Garbled chatter sounded from her tote bag until she shushed the contents.

Nick sat cross-legged on the roof for the next couple of hours watching Jazz ride the carousel, roller coaster, and Ferris wheel and nibble on funnel cakes before returning to the end of the pier. By this time even the most stubborn of fishermen had gone home.

Nick swore the witch wore solitude like a cloak. He knew she had witch sisters. He had even met a few of them over the centuries. But he always sensed they needed her more than she needed them, that she was the independent one of the group. But he also knew that if any of the other women needed her, she would be there in a heartbeat. His sexy witch was as loyal as they came.

He only wished that same strong loyalty extended to him. Her particular skills and knowledge were just what he needed to uncover the truth inside Clive Reeves Jr.'s mansion. If he managed to stay out of fireball range, he hoped to convince her to help him.

When Jazz left the pier and headed for the board-walk's parking lot, Nick sped back across the rooftops until he reached his building. He stood on the edge of the roof, watching her graceful gait. As she left the arcade area, two pairs of fluffy ears popped above the top of the tote bag and swiveled around like four furry periscopes.

"You take those nasty slippers places, but you don't take me." Irma's whine could be heard from the T-Bird parked at one end of the walkway, conveniently away from a street lamp.

Nick chuckled. "Always good to hear someone else is giving you a little trouble," he whispered toward Jazz, knowing there was no way she could hear him.

As Jazz reached the end of the boardwalk, one arm shot up, the middle finger extended. She continued walking, not looking back.

Nick's chuckle deepened to full blown laughter. "No, fuck you, darling. As soon as I can."

Five

"I'm too mercenary for my own good."

Krebs lifted his head at Jazz's announcement and let out a low whistle of male appreciation.

"Lady, that is one hot outfit. What rock star are you driving tonight?"

Jazz curled her upper lip in a less than ladylike snarl as she adjusted her black leather bustier designed to show off her "charms." Body-molding leather pants and boots made dangerous by razor-sharp four-inch stiletto heels completed the sexy picture. She left her hair loose in a riot of copper waves and kept the eye make-up smoky and bee-stung lips a deep glossy red. She carried a knee-length black leather coat. "I wish. Even the gnarliest rocker would be better than what I've got tonight. But the pay was too good to turn down." She blew him a kiss. "Don't wait up for me, baby."

While they were merely roommates, Jazz and Krebs always made sure the other knew when they were going out. She was touched by his insistence on protecting her even when she could easily disable anyone with a word. Well, anyone but the Witches'

High Council. They were in the "knows all, sees all" category no matter how hard she tried to fly under their all too keen radar.

She grabbed a bottle of water from the refrigerator on her way out the back door and froze the moment she hit the first step. She knew the magickal wards surrounding the house and property were up to date, so nothing dangerous should have gotten past them. Actually, nothing preternatural, either innocent *or* dangerous, should have gotten past them. Yet something had. A hint of thunder rumbled overhead. She really had to focus on not allowing her temper to take charge again or she would end up with decades added to her punishment instead of months. Mother Nature was a good friend with most of the members of the Witches' High Council.

"You may as well show yourself," she called out. "I'm on my way out for the night and I don't want to think someone's going to be hanging around here waiting for me to come home. That or I may as well zap you now since I don't like uninvited visitors."

A shadow separated itself from the carriage house and stood off to one side.

She released a deep sigh as Nikolai moved toward her with that sensual grace innate to vampires. She so did not need this tonight. Still, the man was a pleasure to look at, damn him.

"Get out. Or if you need to hear it in your original tongue," she uttered words in her version of Russian.

He winced. "Your pronunciation is atrocious." His eyes bored into hers, not with the vampire's way of seducing his prey, but with the glow of a man who knew her intimately.

Certain timbres in a man's voice always revved Jazz's engine. This man slash *creature*—an important distinction and she needed to remember it—had them all and then some. It pissed her off that she still felt the power that flowed off him.

"I don't have time to trade words with you, Nikolai," she said.

If his voice tipped her world, his faint hint of smile rocked it. "Some things you never forget. Your beautiful face contorted with frustrated anger is one of them."

She should be furious with him, but anger wasn't what ran through her blood right now.

Why did he have to be the one to affect her like this?

In the wink of an eye she had herself under control again. She took a deep breath to keep that control alive because down deep she felt the faintest quiver running through her system. Something that suspiciously felt like tears threatened to bubble up. He was stirring up memories she refused to revisit.

"How did you get past my wards?" Tiny sparks of light appeared over her head. She had worked hard on those wards, damn it! Any unwelcome predator that entered the property was quickly encouraged to leave or be turned into a toad. Vampires were predators of the first order. He shouldn't have made it past the first ward. When she returned home she planned to increase the protection tenfold with the consequences even worse than before.

She refused to visit the idea that somehow or other her wards recognized him as some kind of welcome predator—pretty much the same way he ignored her question about them.

"Just talk to me then," he spoke slowly and carefully, his Slavic heritage still flavoring his words. "Would that be so difficult? There were many times we talked the night away."

Yes, it would be difficult. To keep anything with him to "just talk," that is. Not that she'd admit it to him. Jazz always had the snappy comeback and could hold her own, except where Nick was concerned. Her hormones always seemed to get in the way and before she knew it, she was kissing him, he was kissing her, her clothes were torn off, and they were doing the horizontal tango. Oh boy, she could already feel her blood warming at the thought.

New life, good. Old life, aka Nikolai, bad, very bad.

"As I said, I'm on my way out."

His gaze traveled over her "sex on the hoof" outfit. "Is that what you wear now when you eliminate curses? Or is that what all drivers for All Creatures wear? If that's the case, I may have to call up and request your services." He grinned.

She wasn't surprised he knew about her job. Cop or lover, Nikolai had always been very good at his profession. "What are you really trying to say, Nikolai? That you've come to realize the error of your ways? That you can't live without me? Oh wait, that's right. You're already dead." She held up her forefinger to make her point.

He cocked his head to one side, gazing at her as if she was something he couldn't fathom. "Do people truly laugh at your idea of humor?"

"More often than not. But enough about me. Tell me what you've been doing— who you've been putting in jail when I'm not around to arrest?" *How many other witches you've seduced over the centuries.* She so hated it when jealousy reared its ugly head.

"You have skills I need," he said in the low voice that thrummed hot along her nerve endings.

A flash of memory slammed her brain like a freight train. A candlelit room highlighting silken sheets and tumbled pillows, the feel of his bare skin against hers, and the incredible power of his body as they mated with the ferocity of creatures whose survival depended on it. She ruthlessly tried to drive the tremble from her body before he noticed it, but she wasn't quick enough. Damn him for evoking the past with a double entendre! At least he didn't acknowledge it or she would have snapped the stake back into her hand without a second thought. She hated to be reminded of past failures. Nikolai was her biggest.

"I need your help, Jazz," he persisted, totally serious.

Her heart went nearly as flat as her voice at his words. "You have a curse that needs eliminating?" Damn, he really was here on business. How could she be crazy enough to think he was here for her? "I didn't think your kind could be cursed."

"Our kind is a curse," he said quietly.

She stepped back. "Uh, look, you, of all people, know I don't do the Buffy thing. You'll have to go elsewhere if you want that kind of curse eliminator."

Nikolai smiled and shook his head. "My form of humor."

"If that's the case it needs serious work." She tucked her thumbs into her pants pockets.

He inclined his head. "Then meet me at my office when you are finished with your work tonight."

"You have an office?" she blurted out. She knew vampires owned businesses, but Nikolai had always chosen to work outside of an office environment. He claimed he hated the idea of walls around him and the Protectorate was only too happy to give him a free rein with his work. True, it was dusk to dawn, but he preferred actively hunting down rogue vampires instead of sitting behind a desk filling out paperwork. He also usually managed to insinuate himself with local law enforcement, which never failed to put a crimp in her lifestyle.

He went on, ignoring her outburst. "Yes, near the boardwalk. It's the two-story building just before the Midway. Number 2200. You can't miss it. The sign reads Gregory Investigations. I go by Nick Gregory. Could you be there at one a.m.?"

"We have nothing to say to each other."

"We have much to say if you would allow it."

"Because of the missing vampires."

He nodded.

"I still don't see why you think I can help you."

"Just because vampires are the victims this time doesn't mean it couldn't happen to other non-humans or even humans in the future, too," he told her. "All of us have some sort of power. Who says what has happened to members of my kind will not eventually happen to witches or Dweezil's kind or any creature that is out there? Sometimes you have to plan ahead, Jazz."

She knew he was right.

She sighed. "All right, but you come here tomorrow evening at seven." If they were going to talk she wanted it done on her turf.

Nick started to take a step forward but one look from her had him remaining in place. She knew it had to be difficult for him. Vampires were arrogant bastards, but she wasn't having him crowd her space for anything.

"Are we going somewhere or not?" a high-pitched voice whined from inside the carriage house.

Nikolai's head then body whipped around to face the carriage house door. He grinned as he called out, "Hello, Irma."

"Nicky, honey!" she trilled. "Is she still giving you trouble? It's the lack of sex in her life. It clogs up the body something awful. I should know. After all these years I am so clogged it would take a marathon of good hot sex to clear out the pipes. Not that I'd want Harold anywhere near me after he cheated on me, but that doesn't stop the body from wanting some loving. Jazz, honey, open the door so I can see Nicky."

Jazz closed her eyes. "I so did not need the image of Mrs. Loose Lips Sink Ships having non-stop monkey sex," she muttered.

Nick grinned at Jazz's World War II reference to people giving away secrets.

"Let me give you a word of warning, *Nick.* The next time you try to enter this property uninvited the wards will be set up to repel you in a very nasty way."

She knew she was in trouble the moment the words left her lips. In the blink of an eye, Nick was standing in front of her. So close she felt his power wash over her like a warm blanket. It would have been so easy for her to zap him back ten feet. Instead, she breathed in the earthy scent of his skin and stared into eyes she swore belonged to another, centuries ago.

"Do not do this, Nick," she whispered.

"We are like two magnets, Griet," he whispered back, using the name she had shed centuries before. "When you put two sides together they push away, but if you turn one of them around so the opposite ends face each other," he moved even closer, "they meet." The words drifted across her lips just before his mouth claimed them.

There was nothing to compare to the dark smoky taste of Nikolai Gregorivich. She was forced to hold on to his waist so she wouldn't fall to her knees and bring him with her. She knew if that happened she would be a goner for sure. As it was, she seriously thought about ripping his shirt off then working on those pesky jeans.

The leather bustier that took a good thirty minutes to wiggle and slither into was undone in seconds. The cool touch of his fingers against the lower slope of her breast sent shock waves through her system. Who needed magick when Nick was around?

"I have missed the feel of your skin," he murmured, trailing his lips across the curve of her jaw and down her throat, "the taste of your skin." His mouth settled near her ear.

Jazz swallowed. She knew there was no way for her to fight the sensations rolling through her. Not that she wanted to. Nick had a way of jumpstarting her hormones.

"If I see even a flash of fang, you're toast," she managed to groan. "Literally."

She felt his smile against her skin. "I would never mar such perfection. Not when I would rather taste you another way." His mouth moved back to hers and covered it, his tongue thrusting inside.

Images flickered behind Jazz's eyelids. Nick's body doing to her what his tongue was imitating now. The way he could make her body sing. She may have been born with magick in her blood, but Nick's magick was purely the carnal kind and she reveled in it.

She inhaled sharply when he rolled her nipple between his fingertips.

"Such a shame to cover so much beautiful skin." He kissed the corner of one eye. "You should be clothed only in moonlight. Forget what you have to do tonight and come to my apartment." His mouth moved back to her lips.

Jazz gave herself up for one more intoxicating taste. Temptation stood in front of her in a fantastic six-foot-two-inch package.

"The night will again be ours," he whispered before uttering carnal words that had her body throbbing with an arousal that threatened to overwhelm her senses.

And then morning will come, the snarky gargoyle in her brain intruded. She gritted her teeth and pushed both Nick and the mental gargoyle away. The edges of her bustier hung open, the cool night air swirling around her nipples.

"I want you to go now," she said slowly, even though she would have preferred dragging him upstairs to her bed.

Nick's eyes were dark with the same fervor that mesmerized her own.

"Jazz." His voice promised what his body was fully prepared to deliver.

She shook her head. "If we have sex now you'll decide I'm pliant and ready to hear whatever you have to say." She fumbled with the buttons, swore under her breath and flicked her fingertips down her front. The buttons fastened with an ease she didn't have when she first put it on.

"I wasn't trying to seduce you into …"

"I know." She refused to look at him as bitterness traveled up her throat. "Like I said before, come back tomorrow night at seven. I promise I'll listen to you then."

"No fireballs?" He eyed her hands.

She so did not want to smile, but couldn't help it. "Only if you really piss me off."

"Are we going anywhere or are the two of you going to stand out there talking all evening?" Irma's plaintive voice broke the last bit of the spell lingering between Jazz and Nick. "Of course, if you're *doing something else* I'll wait."

Jazz sighed. "Too bad a fireball won't take care of her."

"I'll be here at seven, Jazz." The instant the words left Nick's mouth he disappeared right in front of her.

She took a swig of water and several deep breaths to calm her raging hormones before activating the carriage house door. It silently slid to one side and the interior lights came on.

Irma swiveled around in the seat and stared at Jazz.

"I don't understand why the two of you don't kiss and make up," Irma said, as Jazz climbed into the car.

Jazz wasn't about to tell her that she and Nick had, not two minutes previously, far more than covered the kissing part of that request. "There are things you don't know, Irma," she said wearily. "Just let it go. Please."

The ghost looked startled by Jazz's lack of sass. She smiled and reached over, patting Jazz's arm.

"He's a man, honey. You have to put up with their oddities at times. I should know after my Harold betrayed our marriage vows."

Jazz uttered a short laugh. "Except you didn't forgive him, did you? Instead you got even by killing yourself in his brand new T-Bird and cursing your spirit to stay in that damn passenger seat for eternity, and damning me with your presence in the process," she pointed out.

"Oh honey, Nicky isn't like Harold, damn his cheating soul. He really cares for you. Why if I were five years younger I'd show you what it takes to keep a real man."

Jazz shook her head. Thanks to Irma, she felt her equilibrium returning. "You know what, Irma?

Since you adore Nick so much, why don't you go haunt *his* car? Why, you would be the perfect pair. You're both dead!"

Irma narrowed her eyes and lifted her hand, a lit cigarette balanced between her fingers. "This is exactly why you can't keep a boyfriend."

∽

Piloting the sleek black limousine up the narrow two-lane winding canyon road devoid of all streetlights wasn't easy, but it was nothing Jazz hadn't done before. While she enjoyed the funky town of Sierra Madre that lay nestled in the foothills, she didn't enjoy this part of the journey or the destination. The only good thing about having to concentrate on the winding road was that she couldn't think about Nikolai Gregorivich, correction, Nick Gregory.

On either side of the road small houses were set against the mountains, the dwellings boasting elaborate stained glass windows alive with jewel tones and homey plants hanging from rafters set over the doorways. While many of the residents here were known for sneering at the establishment back in the sixties, the rustic façades of their homes now hid expensive art and designer furniture inside. And every driveway seemed to boast a high-end Mercedes, BMW, or Porsche. She continued driving until she reached the end of the road. She parked in front of a series of stone steps leading up to a rounded earth-house that Bilbo Baggins would have envied. She climbed out and went around to stand next to the rear passenger door. One trip up the steep steps had cured Jazz of ever climbing them again. They were, simply put, hazardous to anything without built-in cloven hooves or something equally billy-goat-like, or perhaps sucker-footed since they could stick to the stones. High-fashion stiletto heels—however much the client liked them—were an absolute no-no on Foulshadow's steps or she'd be falling on her ass.

Not that she had to even honk the horn or wait long for him anyway. This particular client always seemed to know exactly when she arrived.

As she stood there she again felt the pull of the waxing moon. She was glad she would be heading for Moonstone Lake soon. She needed the chance to spend time with her witch sisters and center herself. She sensed parts of her world were ready to turn upside down and she feared she would need more strength than ever to handle it.

She tipped her head back and noticed the other-worldly lights drifting out from the half-moon shaped windows in the dwelling.

"Why do I feel as if the dirt used to build that place was not originally from the good ole U. S. of A.?" she muttered.

A portion of the base of the hill rolled upward like a garage door and her client moved toward her on short spindly legs that seemed to allow him to glide more than walk. The opening slid shut behind him with the same low hum of magick.

Jazz kept her features impassive. The last thing she wanted Tyge Foulshadow to know was just how much she detested him. She sensed he would enjoy her disgust more than any form of fear she might display. Whenever she was forced to spend time with this creature she felt the dark power of an ancient and dangerous magick seep out of his skin the same way a gelatinous substance seeped from his pores. But his magick's origin eluded her. It was more like a tainted odor than the comfort offered by the magick within her. She had a strong feeling that there was more to Tyge Foulshadow than met the eye. She couldn't stand him, but she never wanted to find herself on his bad side. She was positive he would be a very formidable enemy if he chose to be. There was no doubt there was an exceptionally sinister side to the creature, which was why she made certain to keep her loathing for him well hidden.

"Prompt as always, my beautiful Jazz." Tyge Foulshadow's voice was more an echo inside her head than any sound coming from the tiny round dark hole that was his mouth.

Even without streetlights, Jazz could see him clearly as if his skin was illuminated from the inside.

She privately described the barely five-foot-tall creature as Jabba the Hutt with legs. Tyge's immense teardrop shaped body was covered with oozing grayish green skin that resembled million-year-old algae. As he moved toward her, multi-colored bursts of noxious gas burst out of his rear end. She mentally damned Dweezil for refusing to allow her to wear a gas mask when dealing with his biggest client. While the gas was dangerous to some and lethal to many, her kind only ended up with a mild nausea and headache. To her regret, Tyge had taken a shine to her after the first time she drove him. After that night he requested her as his driver every time he went out. And every time Jazz refused, Dweezil offered her more money. If she weren't so greedy at times, she'd have an easier time turning him down.

Tyge had tried to hire her away from Dweezil to work full-time as his personal driver. The money may have been tempting, but working for the smelly creature was not. Dealing with him once or twice a month was her limit.

"You look gorgeous tonight, my Jazz," Tyge's voice rumbled in his chest, as he held out his short, pudgy, long, three-fingered arms as if to embrace her.

Jazz deftly sidestepped his maneuver by opening the door for him. No way she wanted those suction-tipped fingers anywhere near her skin.

He glided to a stop by the door. Eyes the color of anthracite swept over her with a thoroughness that Jazz feared meant he could see clear to her bare skin. She steeled herself not to retch when his long purplish-black tongue appeared to wet non-existent lips. Venomous hot-pink gas shot out of his ass exuding a smell strong enough to instantly kill any vegetation unlucky enough to grow within one hundred feet. It took some time for Jazz to figure out that hot-pink meant the creature was slightly aroused. She was just glad it had never grown darker than a pale-red. If she ever saw a dark-ruby shade, she would zap that ugly bastard right on its slimy ass. She kept her gaze determinedly planted on his ugly face. She was soooo glad she hadn't eaten before picking him up. Just being around him was enough to make her lose her dinner.

What she did for the almighty dollar.

"According to your itinerary you want to go to Klub Konfuzion," she said, keeping her features impassive. Yep, she was going to seriously gag if he didn't get in the car right now.

"That is correct. I also hope you will be available to drive me to a private party to be held at Clive Reeves' mansion ten days hence." His face shifted into a smile. Or what his kind might call a smile.

It was all Jazz could do not to flinch. Clive Reeves … after all these years, then twice in one day— and his was a name she never cared to hear again. And now he's haunting her all the time, damn him.

She still had nightmares from that hellish night back in 1932. She had crossed a line that night that, by rights, should have extinguished her life. Only the mercy of the Witches' High Council had saved her body even if her spirit had never felt fully recovered.

She wanted to give Tyge an instant, outright "no," but she thought better of it.

There were less direct, much wiser ways to handle things with certain of Dweezil's top clients, and for once she would use her head, pause, think, and not merely react to the moment. She knew Dweezil would throw a fit when she gave him a flat-out refusal to Tyge's request, but she didn't care. Just because it was the son living there instead of the father, damn his soul to the Underworld, she wasn't crossing that property line for all the gold in the world. Let Dweezil do the driving. Let him go home with a toxic wardrobe for once.

"You would have to speak with Dweezil about that," she said instead. Like D, Tyge didn't appreciate the word no. She was a witch with a strong instinct for survival, and she had no idea exactly what powers Master Foulshadow possessed. For all she knew that noxious gas could turn into something truly nasty if he got riled—as if he wasn't disgusting enough already. But no matter what, the last place she was going was Clive Reeves' mansion.

He inclined his head. "Of course. I will speak to him on the morrow."

She had no doubt that he would. Luckily, he chose that moment to enter the car. She closed the door firmly after him. Once behind the wheel, she turned on the special air filtration system that released Tyge's colorful deadly gas into the atmosphere without harming the driver or turning it into an even nastier form of smog. She was grateful that meant the privacy panel always remained closed. The idea of any form of physical contact with the oozing ugly creature sent her stomach into a tailspin.

Even with the privacy panel up she could hear the high-pitched wailing sounds of Tyge's favorite music and the muted rise and fall of his voice as he chattered away on his cell phone.

"There is no way I can believe he has even one friend to talk to," she muttered, making her way down the narrow road to the freeway.

Traffic was on her side as she headed for San Pedro's warehouse district down by the docks.

During the day the wharf was alive with stevedores loading and unloading the ships that lined up at the port and filled the surrounding warehouses with their goods. The buildings that remained empty and dark during the day teemed with another kind of life at nightfall. They were home to the underground clubs that catered to an exclusive clientele who preferred to live on the edgier side of life. Jazz knew it wasn't just the vampires that enjoyed going out after sunset. But no human with a desire to live beyond that night dared venture into this area.

She resisted an urge to snarl at the creatures lingering outside the club's entrance as she climbed out of the car. The pungent mixture of dead fish, salt air, and diesel fuel burned her nose and eyes. But she knew she would take these smells over what was inside the club any night of the week. Her coat rippled around her body as she moved to the rear of the car and opened the door. Tyge slid out and waddled in his awkward glide close enough that she had to hold her breath to avoid the lingering odor on his skin.

Tyge's eyes glittered with a dark luminance as he stared at her under the red and yellow lights that lined the flat roof of the building. It was the club's only decoration. Jazz knew the symbols surrounding the heavy-duty door were a combination of the club's name and protection wards so no unsuspecting human could accidentally wander in.

"Perhaps you would care to come inside. I can assure you that you would be treated as my most honored guest." His tongue, the color of fresh eggplant, again appeared.

Did he just catch a fly or was he trying to taste her skin? *Eeuuww either way!*

"I'm sorry, but I can't." No, she wasn't sorry at all, but hey, she knew how to lie with the best of them. She refused to spend an extra second with Tyge if she didn't have to. "Dweezil has a strict non-fraternization rule where the clients are concerned." She already knew he didn't have any such rule. Dweezil believed in doing whatever was necessary to keep the client happy and damn his employees' sensibilities. Some drivers didn't care what they had to do to keep the client happy and pick up big tips. Jazz was a hell of a lot more discriminating.

Tyge smiled as if he knew she didn't speak the truth, but he was willing to forgive her transgression. For now. "If you would only be willing to take the time to truly get to know me. I know that we would spawn beautiful offspring together, my lovely Jazz. I could give you riches you can only imagine. I have much to offer a beauty like you."

She felt her smile tremble on her lips, then lost her hard-won control. "I would rather eat dead rotting flesh," she replied, her disgust winning out over her fear of insulting him.

His eyes lit up at her words and bright-red gas literally crawled up his back making the dead fish scent of the wharves smell like French perfume. "You do not know my kind as well as you pretend to, my sexy Jazz. You just spoke of our most popular aphrodisiac." He glided toward the entrance where the burly ogre standing in front of the door nodded him through while others waiting in line snarled and growled their displeasure. One look from the ogre shut them up.

Nursing a stress headache, Jazz moved the limousine to the rear section of the parking lot and backed into a slot so that she was facing out. She privately thought of the music pumping out of the club as a combination of ear-bleeding electric punk with a smidge of New Age thrown in for respectability. She pulled a portable DVD player out of its case and popped in one of her favorite movies. She settled back in the soft leather seat and inserted her ear buds. She knew she would have more room if she went into the back of the car, but no way would she punish herself that way. As it was, her evening would end in a long hot shower she called extreme decontamination while her clothing would go into the biohazard materials bag kept on hand for these occasions.

She sighed. "I should have brought popcorn."

The movie couldn't hold her attention for long, though, since Nick was still on her mind. For a moment she wished Irma were here with her to provide a distraction from her scattered thoughts. She reconsidered the idea quickly. Irma's presence would mean cigarette smoke, whining about Tyge and his smells, and constant chatter about what she should do to bed Nick … nope. She could definitely live with her own ill-timed reflections for a few hours more.

She'd actually reached the six-month mark since she last thought about Nick. It was a milestone for her. Was it too much to ask that a few more decades pass before she ran into him again? She could eliminate curses with the snap of her fingers, but no spell could eliminate the vampire from her thoughts and, if she was honest with herself, her heart.

She didn't understand why he had sought her out. Her reputation had been hard-earned over the years as a high-quality curse eliminator. She didn't have the investigating skills Nick had. She met with the client, gauged the depth of the curse, figured out what it would take to get rid of it and zapped it back to wherever it came from. Then she collected her fee and went on.

Now this.

She didn't think he was using his reports of missing vampires as a ruse to see her again—especially not since they were showing up on Krebsie's radar, too. For one, Nick was too direct in his dealings with everyone. For two, refer to number one. She stared at the small flickering screen and tried desperately to let the movie take her thoughts away. But even Sandra Bullock and Nicole Kidman's magick was flat tonight.

Six

Nick sensed magickal turmoil in the air the moment he rang the doorbell and the door opened with a creak worthy of a Halloween haunted house.

"Forget it, D. I am not working tonight no matter how much money you offer! I'm sick, damn it! All I want to do is stay home and suffer."

Nick followed the raspy voice toward the rear of the house and found Jazz in the kitchen standing over a steaming black iron pot on the stove with another pot set on a back burner. He inhaled the scents of ginger root, licorice root, and astragalus with lemon. He stood there for a moment enjoying the sight of his sexy witch looking less than attractive and doing something domestic. Purple cotton sleep pants echoed the amethyst winking at him from her ankle bracelet while the long-sleeved t-shirt sported a colorful pattern of Tootsie Roll Pops. Her hair was pulled up into a messy ponytail with ends sticking out every which way. And if he wasn't mistaken her nose rivaled Rudolph's on Christmas Eve. She sneezed and the contents of the pot on the back burner immediately bubbled up over the edge.

"At least that one did some good," she muttered, grabbing a dishcloth and mopping up the mess. "Damn thing would have taken another five minutes to boil. Not fair I can't do this in the microwave."

"Good evening."

Jazz spun around and collapsed against the counter. "Oh damn. Oh shit." Her expression warned him she was going to be less than receptive tonight. "I did say tonight, didn't I? Fine, come in. Just don't expect me to be entertaining." She quickly whipped a tissue from her sleeve as a sneeze overtook her. A piece of toast promptly flew out of the toaster and across the room. If he hadn't had preternatural reflexes, it would have smacked him right in the face. "This really isn't a good time," she muttered, wiping her nose.

Witches didn't get sick often, but when they did it was with a magickal vengeance, and provided entertainment to boot. He was fully prepared to sit back and take in the show.

"On the contrary, this might work in my favor." He noted the filled coffee pot and helped himself. While he couldn't assimilate mortal food, he could drink liquids, and coffee was his favorite. He knew Jazz's coffee would be the way he liked it. Hot and strong. He glanced at the black and gold mug and chuckled as he read aloud, "*Vampires are a ghoul's best fiend.*"

"It was a Christmas gift." She poured the contents of the first pot into a mug that read *Witchful Thinking.* She leaned her hip against the counter as she sipped the hot liquid. When she lifted her head her eyes were as red as her nose.

"*You little shits!*"

Nick's head whipped around at the sound of a man's fury-filled voice, but Jazz didn't turn a hair.

"Oh dear, what have they done now?" she murmured with a soft sigh. She looked up at Nick. "Now you'll see the life I lead and why it would simply be wrong for me to turn myself into some big bad witch just to help you with your missing vampire problem when there are days there's so much going on around here."

High-pitched squeals and noisy chatter reached the kitchen at the same time two bunny slippers dashed across the floor. In the wink of an eye, they slid themselves onto Jazz's feet.

"Do you know what those furry little bastards did?" A red-faced Krebs raced into the room, skidding to a stop when he realized Jazz wasn't alone.

"Don't worry, he knows what they are." Jazz blew her nose, tossed the tissue into the trash and pulled a fresh one out of her sleeve. "Nick, Krebs. Krebs, Nick."

"Hi." Krebs remembered his manners before turning to Jazz. "I thought you were going to keep them locked up."

"Yeah, like that can happen."

Krebs started for the slippers who promptly snarled their version of "back off."

"Do you know what this is?" He held up a tiny scrap of black cotton while keeping his distance.

"It's a trifle small to be a handkerchief and I have this bad feeling you're going to tell me what it used to be and I won't like what I hear." She looked down at her feet. "What did you do?"

One of the slippers flashed a toothy grin and cooed up at her while its mate released a discreet burp. Ears rotated like an antenna, then the head whipped around. The bunny reached out and snatched up a piece of licorice root that had dropped to the floor while his buddy growled and promptly grabbed the other end, setting up a game of tug of war with the root. Killer bunny growls and snaps filled the room as they battled for control of the herb, their antics throwing Jazz off balance.

"Bad bunnies." She turned toward her roommate. "Krebs, the veins are sticking out on your neck. You'll give yourself a stroke if you don't calm down," she advised.

"This…" he took a deep breath, "this *was* my Grateful Dead t-shirt. The one Jerry Garcia signed after their '72 European tour." He glared at the unrepentant slippers who chewed on their now individual pieces of the licorice root. "Do you know how much I paid for this shirt on eBay?"

"And here I thought it was bad when they ate my favorite boots," Nick murmured.

"They ate my rubber ducky slippers because they felt they should be my *only* slippers," Jazz said.

Krebs continued breathing heavily through his nose. "I have a shredder and I know how to use it," he threatened Fluff and Puff. Entirely unrepentant and unperturbed, one merely yawned while the other blew him a raspberry.

Jazz barely grabbed her tissue in time for her sneeze. The blender whirred merrily before the top flew off and landed on the counter.

"I will talk to them," she promised. "Again." She held up her hand for silence as he opened his mouth. "Give me a break, Krebs. You know very well they can't *be* punished because they have that crazy protective shield around them that protects them from being harmed. Plus, even if I tried to punish them, they would only take it out on you. Do you really want to chance losing half your computer equipment or at the least the contents of your closet?"

He glared again at the slippers. "The Dead will be avenged."

"Just go to Vegas and enjoy yourself," she urged.

Krebs shot Nick a curious look. "Are you sure?"

Nick smiled at the idea of the human protecting Jazz against a vampire even if said human didn't know he was one. He liked it even more that Krebs's protective gesture was more that of a brother than a lover.

She nodded. "I have a cold. Do you really want to be around me?" Her next sneeze activated the garbage disposal and easily made his mind up for him.

Krebs glanced at Nick again. "No offense, but exactly who are you?"

"Someone who's looking for a curse eliminator," Jazz told him. "Drive safely, have a good trip, win at the craps tables, and find yourself a hot blonde to share your winnings with."

Krebs disappeared long enough to get a small suitcase, muttered a good-bye and left after shooting a murderous look at the happily shameless slippers who had finished their licorice root and were looking around for something else to nibble.

"Some things never change," Nick commented, getting up to refill his cup. When the nearest slipper snarled at him, Nick flashed a hint of fang. The slipper wisely backed off.

Jazz set the mug on the table then moved the second pot over there. Fresh thyme and peppermint scented the air as she picked up a towel and draped it over her head, leaning over the pot, and inhaling the nose-clearing steam. She sniffed loudly.

"I may not be a healer like Lilibet," she released a sigh, mentioning one of her witch sisters, "but I know my herbs. So why can't I cure a simple cold?"

Nick smiled. "It's still safer than when you go through PMS."

She shuddered. Her nasal tones were muffled under the towel. "Those times are scary even to me. The last time I had PMS a roast chicken popped out of the oven and danced the *Macarena*. Krebs had walked in just as the chicken started dancing. By then he was pretty much used to anything and only asked if the chicken shouldn't be doing the *Chicken Dance* instead." She peeked out from under the towel for a second. A smile tugged at the corner of her lips, just as he had hoped. "But you didn't come here to watch the house overreact to my sneezes, did you? I know I told you to come back tonight, but why are we bothering with this? You'll tell me your problem and I'll tell you there is no way I can help you. End of story." She breathed in deeply, allowing the steam to make its way through her sinuses.

"Clive Reeves." She froze at the mention of the name. If she looked pale before, she now looked the color of new fallen snow. "*You know* vampires are disappearing and *I know* that Reeves has something to do with it. But I need a strong witch's magick to help me get onto his property without him knowing it's me. I tried to get onto the grounds not long ago and was rebuffed. He obviously set up a ward specifically to keep me out of there." He could see the hint of old pain in her moss-colored eyes and hated that he was the one to cause it. He resisted the urge to reach across the table and cover her hand with his. He doubted she would appreciate his sympathetic gesture.

"I have been hearing that name way too often lately." It took an effort of will, but Jazz managed to keep her voice steady. She paused for a long moment, measuring her thoughts, her reactions, the extent of her cold, and her unwanted past against Nick here and now. "Look, Nick," she said finally, "Clive Reeves is dead and there are no rumors that his son has gone over to the Dark Side like his father did." Her gaze on him suddenly narrowed and sharpened through her cold fog. "Come to think of it why do you think Junior has something to do with the disappearances? And why would he set up a ward to keep you out?"

"Because of what happened in 1932."

Her hands trembled so badly she had to set the towel to one side. She looked up from her herbal steam, showing a rare vulnerability that worried him. She didn't believe in revealing weakness to anyone. Not even to the one who knew her best.

"Clive wanted to be like us," Nick pressed. "He wanted power and he wanted immortality. He wanted to be the characters he played in his films. When he discovered what you and I were, he sought to find a way to gain what we have."

"That wasn't all he sought," she muttered.

"Jazz…." She waved off whatever he was about to say.

"All he had to do was ask for a vamp hickey." She pushed her mug and the pot to one side, rested her clasped hands on the table and closed her eyes. Nick remained silent watching her gear up for the coming conversation. When she opened her eyes, they were so dark they looked black. "Tell me why you think Clive Reeves Jr. has something to do with the disappearances."

"I believe that there is no Clive Reeves Jr.," he stated and waited for her reaction. She stared at him in disbelief. "Somehow at the moment of his death," Jazz's lips moved in a silent curse as he continued, "Reeves managed to transfer his life force into his son's body. The man everyone thinks is the son is actually the father. He hasn't left the estate grounds, much less the mansion, in decades. It's thought his magick is more powerful there and he feels vulnerable away from his base of operations, so to speak. He has slaves to provide him with anything he needs and a selection of vampires for everything else." His lips twisted in displeasure.

"That isn't possible." She shook her head to further underscore her denial.

"It's more than possible if you use the right spell."

"Do you realize what you're saying? If that's the case then he used…," Jazz took a deep breath and leaned across the table as if afraid of being over-heard, "the man used the black arts to accomplish the unthinkable. No one dabbles there unless they wish to lose all that makes them who, and what, they are. It makes them unclean." She hissed out the last sentence with distaste turning her lips into a sneer.

"And it can make them very powerful," he pointed out.

Jazz looked away. "He couldn't have accomplished such a thing. He was dead. I literally buried that piece of the bottle into his heart. The blood spilled everywhere." She shuddered at the memory. "There was no pulse. The only reason I even touched him was to assure myself that he was dead! Yes, I know I was in and out of consciousness afterwards, but there was no way I could have been mistaken." She rubbed her temples with her fingertips.

Nick understood her anguish. It had gone against her code to kill another. The act had even damaged a part of her. By all rights, Clive Reeves was the weaker one—a mortal. Except somehow he had managed to overpower, assault, and almost kill Jazz before she managed to defend herself. By the time Nick arrived, Reeves' dead body lay sprawled on the floor and a weak and blood-covered Jazz was trying to crawl out of the room. The only reason the Witches' High Council hadn't sentenced her to death back then was that she had been forced to defend herself against dark magick. They ruled she acted in self-defense and should not be punished for the deed.

He wondered if the Council chose that road since they knew Jazz would punish herself harshly enough. After all, living with blood on your hands was more difficult than being granted a swift death. He knew that more than anyone.

"It was a known fact back then that Clive was searching for anyone who dealt in the darker side of the occult," she continued. "He was convinced that with the right kind of help he could live forever. As you said he wanted to be his characters for real. Some mortals echoed his beliefs and latched on to him in hopes his power would become theirs. Others treated it like a joke or a game or even thought he'd lost his mind. Clive sought out anyone with a hint of magick in hopes they could grant his wish. It seems it happened after all." Her voice quivered with old pain that still hadn't been wiped away.

Many times Nick thought of that time and regretted not giving in to his darker side that night and obliterating the man because he had almost destroyed this magnificent woman's spirit. It would have been so easy. He could have carried the body up into the hills and let the wild coyotes and bobcats take care of Reeves. Instead, like Jazz, he thought it was all over. Clive Reeves' widow took her baby son to Europe to escape the scandal, and Jazz took off for parts unknown before Nick could see or talk to her again. He didn't run into her again for almost forty years. It was only because of a vague rumor surfacing that Clive Reeves wasn't who he was purported to be that Nick returned to L.A. The man who claimed to be Clive Reeves' son returned to Hollywood to build a new film empire focusing on stylish horror films that catered to the cult market.

Clive Reeves Jr. was also well known for flamboyant parties, where the preternatural were more than welcome. That was when Nick first heard that party-going vampires may have gone in as guests, but not all of the guests left.

He knew Jazz would fight him when he asked for her help, but if he wanted to conquer Reeves he needed her help. He hoped that her desire for vengeance would outweigh old fears. He only had to look at the pain on her face to know she still hadn't moved past that time. He wanted to see her work on closing up old festering wounds. He waited quietly watching her mull over his words. The only sound in the room was the soft chatter between Fluff and Puff.

Jazz sneezed loudly. The bright red poppies on the dishtowel suddenly burst into full bloom—for real. She wiped her nose with a tissue retrieved from the never-ending supply stashed in her sleeve.

"I don't like hearing this, Nick. That monster's not supposed to be alive and walking around all these years as if nothing ever happened. He's supposed to be dust in his crypt in a mausoleum at Hollywood Memorial Park. Do you know that the night of the funeral I almost went to the cemetery and scattered salt around the entire burial chamber? I didn't want there to be any chance he would try to rise again, let alone be able to …," she muttered in a broken voice. "And now I find out he's not even in there and he's out inflicting pain on a new generation of suckers." As she realized her unintended insult, she muttered, "Sorry. You know what I mean."

Nick nodded. "The worst part is we don't know if it will stop there. If he feels killing vampires no longer works toward whatever goal he's seeking, he will look further into the magick community. He has to know you're living here and that you're more powerful now than you were seventy-five years ago. Not to mention payback." She winced at his reference to her killing Reeves. Or thinking she did.

She pulled the pot back in front of her and picked up the towel. "I hate you." Any heat in her words was neutralized by the atomic power sneeze that overtook her. Water from the pot sprayed outward and over Nick's face. He growled his displeasure as he wiped the hot scented water off his cheek. A tiny smile tipped her lips. "You should be grateful I left out the holy water this time."

Jazz should have known that Nick wouldn't let her comment go. If her head hadn't felt so stuffed up she would have known what was coming next.

What she called his Cossack soul came out as he got up and walked around the table, pulling her up into his arms and capturing her mouth. She was swept up into the darkness that surrounded him and only felt the hard muscles of a man in perfect physical condition.

Some things can't be ignored. You can only conquer your past if you choose to face it.

But she didn't choose to face it. Not here and not now. Not like this and not with him. Furious, she practically threw herself backward. She grabbed hold of the table's edge so she wouldn't fall down. "Don't ever do that again!" she shouted. "You know I hate you bouncing around inside my head! Why can't you take it slow for once? Just give me a chance to take all of this in. You've told me shit I so didn't expect to hear. So let me think it over and I'll stop by your office tomorrow night if I feel up to it." She pulled another tissue out of her sleeve for emphasis.

Nick inclined his head. "I think you're already feeling better." And like that he was gone. Jazz frowned at his words until she realized that her head didn't feel as stuffy as it did before nor was her nose still running like an open faucet.

"Who knew all it took to cure the common cold was a vampire's kiss?" she muttered.

Her attempt at humor fell flat as she thought of the task in front of her. She may have told Nick she'd discuss it further the next evening but both of them knew that in the end she'd agree to help. It was proof she'd lost her mind. Only an idiot witch would be willing to face the man who'd been heavily featured in her nightmares for the past seventy-odd years. Except it wasn't the horror of his raping her or beating her to a bloody pulp that haunted her nights when her subconscious took over. It was the image of her picking up a chunk of glass from a broken champagne bottle and plunging it into his heart that fueled her nightmares. She'd been so weak after the attack she couldn't even call on her magick. All she could do was crawl across the blood-slick floor, palm the shard, and when Reeves went after her, confident she wouldn't fight him any longer, bury it in his chest to the point his heart exploded. So if she had killed him that night, how, at the point of his death, had he managed to transfer his spirit to his son's body?

She only knew the bare basics of the kind of magick that was required for such an evil deed. It wasn't a subject they cared to teach at the Witches' Academy except to warn the witchlings that baneful magick was forbidden. She knew that utilizing such power took one's soul and all of one's humanity. The thought was repugnant.

But it also meant that because of what Clive Reeves had done in the past, Jazz would have to enter the devil's lair once again. Every ounce of what she was demanded it.

Seven

Jazz tossed the tightly closed bright orange plastic bag marked Hazardous Waste behind her and slid into the driver's seat. With her cold gone and feeling more like herself, she woke up ready to do what she'd hoped to do the day before.

"Whatever you have in there smells disgusting," Irma groused. The cigarette between her fingers disappeared as quickly as it had appeared. "Just for once can I choose where we go?"

"What does it matter where we go? You can't even leave the car." Jazz zipped out of the carriage house garage and sped down the road. She would be happier when the bag was in Dweezil's possession and out of hers. After that, she intended to spend the day gearing up for her visit to Nick's office tonight. She vowed to keep the conversation strictly business and herself out of his reach. Not that she could remain out of his reach for long when he could stand next to her before she could blink. All she had to do was make sure he didn't kiss her. She usually gave in when he did that. And giving in on anything to do with Clive Reeves would not be good.

"One of the local cable channels aired a commercial for a drive-in theater that airs classic films every weekend," Irma informed her. "If we go there I could see a film on the big screen again. They're having a Humphrey Bogart film festival this weekend and showing Robert Mitchum the following weekend. I always thought they were two sexy men," she said with relish.

"I know the theater you are talking about and it's all the way out in the Valley. No way am I going out there." Jazz knew she should feel guilty that she didn't do anything special for Irma, but more often than not the woman was irritating as hell. She'd never asked the ghost to keep her company all these years, and she resented her bickering attitude. However, while Irma hadn't realized what she was doing when she cursed herself into the car, Jazz had known what she was getting herself into when she agreed to take the T-bird and its snarky baggage. All because she knew how sexy she looked behind the wheel. Remorse snuck in and suggested there was no reason why Jazz couldn't pick up *The African Queen, The Maltese Falcon,* and some Robert Mitchum films at Blockbuster as a peace offering.

Irma sulked for a moment more then looked over her shoulder and wrinkled her nose. "That revolting smell is getting worse."

Jazz had double-bagged the clothing and sprayed the exterior with an odor killing spray, but apparently it hadn't helped if the stench threatened to overpower even her ghostly passenger. "Never mind, it'll be gone shortly," she said. At least she *hoped,* she amended; because the reek was rapidly endangering her own sense of smell.

The T-Bird shot forward. She vowed the first thing she'd do with her Foulshadow pay was to buy another leather bustier and coat to replace the ones she'd had to throw away. Her boobs had never looked better than in that sexy top and the coat was just plain sinful. She had thought that if she looked dark and dangerous Tyge would finally back off. She should have known better. The pervert had invited her up to his house for an early morning drink. She declined with no lack of regret.

Nick seemed to like it a lot, too, whispered the voice inside her head.

No wonder she got sick. Even that short time with Tyge would turn anyone into a plague victim.

Mindy didn't even try to stop her as Jazz swept through the reception area to the back office. It might have had something to do with the bright orange Hazardous Waste bag exuding an odor that wouldn't easily leave the reception area without some major magickal fumigation.

Dweezil looked up from the pile of paperwork on his desk. "Well, look who the black cat dragged in. You were too sick to work last night, but I see you're well enough to come in to pick up your pay."

"The wonders of modern medicine, D. And this is for you." Jazz deposited the bag on his desk and dropped into the chair opposite him.

"What the fuck?" He took one sniff and used his pen to push the bag off the desk. It thumped and rolled across the carpet. "Mindy, get this outta here!"

He waited until the Elven-blonde walked in wearing a heavy leather glove. She used two fingers to pick up the bag and held it a far distance from her body. She carried it out the back door and then returned to the reception area. "What're you trying to do? Asphyxiate me?"

"Wow, Dweezil, you're using words that comprise more than four letters. I am so impressed." She tossed a slip of paper on his desk. "Here is the receipt for everything I wore the night I drove Tyge. You can just add it to what you owe me."

His eyes bulged as he stared at the total. "You bought all new shit? I figured you'd just wear something old and I'd depreciate it from the original cost."

"I like the clothes in my closet. No way did I plan to ruin any of them. Better I buy something I haven't had a chance to form an attachment to. And you know Foulshadow. He likes his drivers to look good. You told me to do what it takes."

Mindy swept past again, pausing only to pick up the receipt. "I'll have it ready in just a minute," she said.

"I will not drive him anywhere, anymore," Jazz told Dweezil once they were alone again.

"Hey, no witchy tantrums here. You're the only one I can trust with him. He's a valued client who spends a lot of money here. Besides, he likes you." He leered at her, his gaze drifting down to her breasts.

"Eyes up, D. Eyes up. He is a total pervert." She leaned forward. "Did your cleaning crew tell you what he did in the back of the car that night? His kind can have sex with himself and I don't mean a hand job either. It's sick, D."

"Give me a break here, Jazz. You make good money driving for me. More than you'd ever make with your little curse eliminating business."

She narrowed her eyes. "Maggots, D. Lots of them. Crawling in places you can't even reach, much less imagine. It would take you months to get rid of them."

He reared back.

Jazz smiled. The bullying creature always backed down when he was given a bit of his own medicine.

"You can't go in there!" Mindy's sounds of horror were their first warning. Dweezil's door flying open was their second. It was what followed that had Jazz sitting up straight.

"Dweezil Quix…" The heavyset man wearing a dark suit with a gold detective's shield secured to his jacket pocket frowned at the paperwork he held in one hand.

Jazz helped him out with the correct pronunciation including the clicks and whistles.

"This is a search warrant for your premises." The man slapped the paper into Dweezil's hand. A faint look of revulsion crossed his face as he stared at the two long green fingers that curled around the sheets.

"For what?" Dweezil fairly popped out of his chair, waving the paper around.

"Look, buddy, if you don't cooperate with us you could find yourself shut down so fast you won't know what hit you." The man glanced at Jazz then took a second look. "Are you human?"

She issued a bright toothy smile. "Me, mom, and apple pie."

She knew Dweezil wouldn't give her away. Having a human in the office could save him a lot of aggravation if the cops decided they didn't like Dweezil any more than she did. Plus, her plans for the day didn't include spending time in a jail cell. Another bustier and leather coat were calling her name.

"May I ask what you're looking for?" Jazz asked, continuing her friendly female façade.

"You an attorney?"

"Not in this lifetime." Little did he know she spoke the truth with that statement. "It's just that I've worked for Dweezil for some time now and he's always been aboveboard with his dealings." *So she lied. She couldn't receive more penalties for lying as long as she didn't use magick.* She had a sick feeling that Dweezil had been involved in something that was less than legal. She'd always sensed he had his fingers in a variety of slightly shady pies, but as long as it didn't spill over into her life she didn't worry about it. A tickle of worry creased her forehead. *What the Fates could he have done to bring the cops down on him?*

"Well, sister...." *Sister? Did he just call her sister? What Raymond Chandler book did this guy step out of?* "Seems your boss here has been dealing some illegal drugs to his customers. Plus we've got a good idea he might have something to do with vampires disappearing." He did not look all that unhappy about fewer vampires in the city. Jazz had heard that tax-paying vampires owned many of the underground clubs. The mayor wasn't about to lose those additional city funds plus it made him look good to placate the preternatural community. "He cooperates with us and we'll get out of here as soon as we can. He doesn't …," his voice trailed off, but the threat hung in the air.

"Dweezil dealing drugs?" she laughed. "You have so got the wrong guy. He gets the hives just looking at an aspirin."

"Yeah, says you." The cop squinted at her as if he was trying to figure out if she really was human or not.

"Dweezil! They're taking all our files!" Mindy ran to the doorway. Her blue eyes glowed with fear and a golden unearthly sheen now covered her skin. Even the tips of her ears looked more prominent.

The detective stared at her as if he was unsure just what she was and at the same time didn't want to know. He took a few steps back.

Jazz learned forward and plucked the paperwork out of Dweezil's hand. She quickly perused the contents. "It says here they have the right to take all your business records."

"How the fuck can I do business without my records?" Dweezil jumped up and down like a demented elf.

"You keep that up and we'll shut you down for good." The detective's warning wasn't an idle threat.

Jazz stood up. Something about this situation didn't smell right to her. Although after spending time around Tyge, her sense of smell might not be back to normal yet.

"So which is it? Missing vampires or drugs?"

The detective scowled at her. "Are you sure you're not a lawyer?"

She rolled her eyes. "I just had a question about the procedure. I am only here to pick up my pay."

"Trust me, sweetheart, you won't be seeing any paychecks for awhile."

Now Jazz was mad. Both at his calling her sweetheart and his announcing she wouldn't get her money. That bustier and coat were expensive, damn it! She only chose them because she knew she'd be reimbursed. "You said records. You didn't say anything about freezing his funds," she argued.

"You can't freeze my fuckin' funds!" Dweezil shrieked, his face now a combination of its normal olive-green shade mottled with red. Jazz stared at the detective who looked as if he wouldn't mind pulling out his gun and shooting Dweezil. Sure, D was a jerk, but this raid smelled like some kind of set-up to her and even D didn't deserve this kind of treatment. She feared she was going to end up in the middle of a situation she had no desire getting involved with. Suspicion flared up big time. She silently vowed if she discovered a certain undead person—correction, creature—had something to do with this she was marching over to his boardwalk office so she could drive a stake through his non-beating heart.

"Detective Larkin, we found this out back in one of the Dumpsters." A uniformed officer walked in carrying the orange hazardous waste bag.

"Open it up," he ordered. He glared at Dweezil and Jazz. "A pretty clever way of hiding drugs. Hell, the smell alone would probably drive off any drug-sniffing dog."

"No!" Jazz sprang out of her chair but not in time. She dreaded to think what it was like in there since she'd secured the clothing in the bag the minute she got home and undressed.

The officer opened the bag and an ugly grayish-green vapor floated upward. The man's eyes rolled backward and he dropped to the floor.

"Oh shit," Jazz muttered, managing a sickly smile at the detective who didn't look too pleased at seeing his officer stretched out cold on the floor.

"Maybe we need to have a talk down at the station."

Eight

"I told you not to open the bag," Jazz reminded Detective Larkin. The man turned out to have absolutely no sense of humor. After his announcement back at Dweezil's office, she had no choice but to be escorted down to the police station. She now sat in an interrogation room whose décor and stench she dubbed Early Gross. She didn't know who or what had been in here before her, but whatever it was it needed a serious amount of deodorant, soap, and water. "And may I remind you I was able to revive the officer? He won't have any ill-effects from the gas other than a bad headache for a week or three. And since you didn't read me my rights I gather I'm not under arrest for getting rid of a bag of totally disgusting trash."

He shot her a *shut the hell up* glare and she obliged by doing just that. He set a foam cup of coffee in front of her and took the seat across the table, flipping through the contents of the thin file folder set in front of him.

"For a smartass you sure manage to stay out of trouble."

"I do my best." She wondered what his reaction would be if he saw her actual police files, plural.

She estimated they would fill more than a few moving vans. But first they'd have to track down her past identities.

He stared at her. "I asked you if you were human and you said yes."

She waved off the accusation. "No, I only said me, mom, and apple pie. Besides, I am human." She thought she'd forgo the explanation that she was much older than the totally ugly tie he wore loosely looped around his thick neck.

"And a witch."

Jazz ignored the scowl on his face. "Yes, well, that type of accusation died down centuries ago in Salem. Look, we both know you dragged me down here because of the bag, which I can explain."

He leaned back in his chair and crossed his arms over his chest. "So explain."

"One of Dweezil's clients has a...," she searched for the right description and settled for, "hygiene problem."

"Bad hygiene doesn't cause fumes like that to come out of a bag of clothing. And just where did you get a biohazard bag?"

"It does if it has to do with Tyge Foulshadow. Dweezil keeps the bags on hand because of Foulshadow." She ignored his skepticism and reached for the coffee cup. She sipped the lukewarm liquid and found its only saving grace was the knowledge that caffeine lurked somewhere in the murky depths. She ignored Larkin's snort of laughter. "He emits really nasty odors that can make people sick and sometimes, much worse. Your officer passing out is proof of that.

Witches are immune to the gases, which is why I drive him. The clothes in the bag were the ones I wore two nights ago when I drove Master Foulshadow. As you can see, there's no way I can wear them again after I've been around him, so I have to secure the clothing in a biohazard bag. Who knew you guys would show up at Dweezil's and you'd order your officer to open it."

"Man, what you witches do for money," he muttered. "Any more of you work for him?"

She shook her head, taking another sip of the liquid they passed off as coffee. She silently vowed if she had to come down here again, she'd make them stop at Starbucks first.

"Why not?"

"I don't know."

He glanced at his notes again and then looked up. "So what kind of witch are you?"

"You mean am I a good witch or a bad witch?" She could see flippancy wasn't working with him. "I'm a curse eliminator."

"Meaning?"

"Some people will curse an object and the curse sticks with it. They hire me to come in and take off the curse."

"Are you saying people really believe that shit and pay you money to boot?"

"This is L.A., Detective Larkin. Anything goes."

"Like some creature that farts gross gas and a guy that looks like a stretched-out olive?"

She nodded. "What? You think all witches have warts and long chin hairs and cackle when they laugh? Honestly, Detective, I haven't stirred eye of newt, toe of frog, and bat wings in a bubbling cauldron for years." *Not since Potions 101.*

He shifted uncomfortably.

"Okay, I've explained the origin of the fumes from the bag and we have discussed my job, so are we through here?" she asked.

He looked as if he was settling in for the duration. "Just trying to get a little background. So let's talk about your boss now."

"You're out of luck if you're hoping I can tell you anything about Dweezil's illegal activities. There aren't any. That's the funny thing about him. He likes to make his money the legal way. That way he doesn't worry about losing it. As I said before, drugs aren't his thing."

"What is?"

She placed her hands flat on the table and leaned forward. "Did you get a look at his bookcases?"

His face remained as impassive and noncommittal as possible. "The warrant only covered his paperwork."

"Yeah, like you didn't look all around anyway. I refuse to believe you didn't notice that Dweezil collects vintage erotica and antique sex toys."

He uttered a disgusted sound as if she had waved one of Dweezil's prize antique vibrators or penis pumps in his face.

"What exactly is he?"

"We've never discussed politics or religions."

Larkin growled a few words under his breath. "No, I mean *what* is he?"

She started to touch her moonstone ring for comfort then held back. She doubted he would appreciate the stone responding with a soft glow even if it soothed her. "I don't know."

"You're a witch."

"That doesn't mean I know everyone's family background. For all I know, Dweezil is the last of his kind." One could only hope.

The detective sat back, drumming his fingers on the tabletop. Jazz thought about telling him it was annoying. Except she was positive he already knew that.

"Your boss is in big trouble."

"I figured that out when you stormed into his business and carried off all his files. But I can't see why you think he deals in drugs or has anything to do with missing vampires." *Or how you found out about the missing vampires.*

"How often do you drive vamps?"

"Not very often."

"How often?"

Jazz shrugged. "Vampires don't like witches and the dislike is pretty much reciprocated. So I only drive them if there isn't another driver available and the vampire is willing to put up with a witch for a driver."

"That doesn't tell me why they don't like witches." He narrowed his eyes. "Or is it just *you* they don't like?"

"Are you kidding? Everyone loves me! Okay, except for vampires. They don't like any witch. We have sort of a truce. They don't bite us and end up sick from our blood. We don't zap them with flesh-eating spells."

He winced. "You're kidding, right?"

"Are you truly interested in learning more or just hoping I'll say something stupid that you think you can use against Dweezil?"

"Both," he said it unwillingly then looked half bemused to find he'd admitted the fact.

"Witches' blood is poisonous to vampires. At the very least, it can give them a nasty case of heartburn, and at the worst it can kill them."

Disgust crossed his face. "I thought vampires went to clubs for their blood now."

"They do, but sometimes one will have partied too much and be a little too eager, so things might get out of hand. That's why they prefer to stay away from us." *Except for one.*

"Do you know Clive Reeves Jr.?"

She didn't bat an eye at his question even if her stomach twisted itself into a million knots. Obviously her shudder and gag reflex was getting used to hearing the name again—however disturbing it was to her. "I watch his father's movies every Halloween."

"So you don't attend his parties up at his old man's mansion?"

"No." That was one destination she preferred to avoid at all cost.

"Ever been invited to one?"

"Again, no."

"Have you ever driven anyone up there?"

"Third time, no." She figured as long as he didn't ask if she were ever going to drive anyone up there she'd be fine.

He remained quiet for a moment, staring at her and idly drumming his fingers against the tabletop.

"So tell me about your clients. Anyone with strange habits other than the one with mega-strength farts?"

"I never talk about my clients, Detective Larkin. Discretion is my middle name." She grinned. "Well, not really, but I've always wanted to say that. Look, you bringing me here is nothing more than harassment. You know it and I know it. Someone doesn't like Dweezil and sicced the police on him. You didn't like what happened to your officer, so you're now coming down on me. Why don't we agree I don't know anything and I get out of your hair?" She pointedly didn't look at his receding hairline.

A tap on the door brought a scowl to Larkin's face and a smile to Jazz's lips. She was getting to the point where she was ready to use some magick to end this pointless conversation. She knew the detective was going the roundabout way in hopes of trapping her into saying something against Dweezil. Except she knew anything she might say against her boss wouldn't help the cop at all. Dweezil was a sleaze and walked a fine line, but he tended to stay on the right side of that line, so he wouldn't have to worry about police raids. Unfortunately, someone must have decided D was due some harassment.

Her eyes glittered dangerously when two men walked into the room. One of them she instantly dismissed. The other usually meant some time spent in a jail cell.

"Guy's come to pick up Ms. Tremaine," the detective announced.

Jazz saw the subtle interaction between the three men. Cop acknowledging cop. The words "he's a vampire!" rested on the tip of her tongue, but she left them there. She was hoping Nick truly was there to pick her up. She didn't want to think he'd try something that would get her thrown in jail after all. If that happened there was no way in this millennium she'd kiss him again.

"Nick Gregory." Nick held out his hand to a now smiling and affable Larkin.

She figured Nick was using a bit of vamp hypnosis on the detective. Larkin sure never smiled at her like that and she considered herself a hell of a lot cuter.

"We're about through here. Ms. Tremaine's been very cooperative." His gaze flicked over her. She flashed him her best "I'm just an all-American girl" smile as she rose to her feet. While she hated the idea that Nick was rescuing her, she'd eagerly accept his help in getting out of there. Plus she wanted to find out what was going on at Dweezil's office. While there were times she didn't like the creature, she wasn't going to see him railroaded by the police for something he didn't do.

So for now, she would accept Nick's help. She could go her own way once she left the building and returned to Dweezil's for her car. She only hoped the police hadn't towed it—even if the idea of Irma spending a couple hours in an impound yard brought a spring to her step.

"Don't look too happy about leaving here. They might think you're guilty of something," Nick murmured.

"Isn't it a little early for you to be out, Nick? Aren't you afraid of getting a nasty sunburn at the very least?" She followed him through the bustling station. She was finding it easier than she thought being polite to him. Or perhaps it had something to do with all the uniformed officers milling around. Ironic that the last time they'd been surrounded by the police he had been putting her in jail and now he was getting her out.

A faint smiled touched his lips. "How long do you think you've been in here?"

"You know very well I have no sense of time." She held up both wrists showing the lack of a watch. She had learned long ago that witches and time-pieces didn't work well together.

Nick pushed open the front door and allowed her to exit first. She looked up, stunned to find it was past sundown.

"I usually at least feel the shifts in time," she murmured.

"Detective Larkin must have been a fascinating conversationalist if you didn't sense the hours passing." Nick held out a hand toward the visitor's parking lot.

"They like you to wait around in a disgusting little room until they are ready to come in and talk to you about absolutely nothing," she grumbled. "And they make really lousy coffee. I bet they do it deliberately so the suspects will confess in hopes the coffee in jail is better."

"Throwing a biohazard bag filled with deadly smelling clothing into a Dumpster isn't exactly nothing."

"It's not like I can throw the clothes in the washer then give them to charity. Dweezil keeps a Dumpster out back just for those bags, so they don't get tossed out on the landfill where the fumes add another ten layers to the smog." She walked slowly, content to enjoy the cool night air that was considerably fresher than the recycled air she had inhaled for the past number of hours. "There is a good reason why the creature is called Foulshadow. Thank you for getting me out of there, however you did it."

Nick chuckled. "That didn't hurt so much, did it?"

Jazz picked up her pace. Once she reached the edge of the parking lot she stopped short.

"You drove my car?" Thunder briefly rumbled overhead.

"Have you ever thought of taking an anger management course?" Nick asked and then walked ahead of her to the passenger door and opened it. "Irma, my love, we will have to do some shifting around."

The ghost held onto her pocketbook as if her life depended on it. "I'm not moving."

"And I'm not sitting in the passenger seat of my own car." Jazz headed for the driver's side. She peered inside and noticed the seat was shifted further back. "How did you get it here? If you hotwired my car ..."

"I gave him permission to drive the car," Irma informed her. "It was mine before it was yours. And if I give someone permission the car will start up for them without a key." She looked up at Nick with a saucy smile. "Let her drive. You can sit with me, pookie."

Nick moved around the car, smoothly blocking Jazz from sliding onto the driver's seat. While he didn't touch her, she still felt the force of his power. She could have pushed past him, but she didn't dare lay a hand on him. Touching Nick always got her into trouble.

"A few days ago I would have accused you of setting the cops on Dweezil to get even with me," she murmured.

"You know better than that, Jazz. I don't use third parties to achieve my goal." For a moment his eyes seemed to glow with the same life as the moonstones in her jewelry. "I'm a very direct person."

"Yes, I know, and the thought faded as soon as it bloomed." She purposely tried to forget the last two times they were together. Recalling his kisses tended to make her mind wander into forbidden areas.

He blew out a breath and looked around the parking lot. "I suppose now you will put me off for tonight. Tell me something, what will your excuse be tomorrow night? A headache?"

Jazz's snarl was worthy of his.

"Just do whatever he says, honey, so we can go home," Irma whined. "I don't want to miss *House, M.D.*"

Jazz blamed the turmoil bubbling away in the pit of her stomach on not eating anything for most of the day and drinking bad coffee while waiting for the Sam Spade wannabe to get to the point.

"You won't be coming by my office tonight, will you?" He gave away none of his feelings.

"I have to prepare for my trip to Moonstone Lake," she said, not looking at him. "And right now, I have to get her highness home for her Hugh Laurie fix."

Nick straightened up to allow her to get into her car. Once she was settled behind the wheel, he closed the door and leaned down.

"You can't ignore this in hopes it will go away, Jazz," he said. He leaned in and brushed a light kiss across her lips.

A few days ago, Jazz would have seriously thought about zapping him again even if it meant an additional sixty days tacked on to her punishment. Right now, she only resisted the urge to touch her tingling lips.

"Come on, Nicky, we can squeeze in together!" Irma chirped up.

He looked up and grinned as the ghost shifted over in the seat an additional inch or so.

"I'm fine, Irma." He looked back down at Jazz. A heat flared in his eyes that she felt clear down to her toes. Luckily, before she could do something stupid, like drag him into the car, he looked at Irma, blew her a kiss, turned, and walked off.

"You didn't have to be so rude to him," Irma sniffed. "It doesn't take you all that long to pack for that trip up to the lake."

Jazz started up the car and put it into gear. "I thought you wanted to get home to see *House, M.D.?*" She took a quick look around, but as expected, Nick was nowhere in sight.

She told herself that she wasn't going to be able to put Nick off forever. It wouldn't solve a thing. Still, helping him would give her the chance to settle things between them and, as he said, she would face her past. If she could face Clive Reeves and not want to kill him, she was sure that action alone would take a hell of a lot more than sixty days off her banishment. More importantly, she would feel whole for the first time in a long time.

Fine, she would talk to him when she got back.

Then she would tell Nick it was best they never see each other again. She needed to tell him there could never be anything between them.

She looked down the length of her nose. She was positive it had just grown a fraction of an inch.

Nine

The three women wore pale blue robes that moved with the night breeze as they walked along the lake's edge until they reached a flat-topped boulder that jutted out over the water. They walked with sure-footed grace along the length of the large stone's surface until they stood on the tip of the rock. They presented an ethereal picture as the full moon cast silver rays over them.

"May our sanctuary provide us with continued protection and strength," Stasia Romanov intoned, taking multi-colored dust out of a gold mesh bag and sprinkling it over the water. The breeze caught up strands of her sunny brown hair, giving them a life of their own.

"May our sanctuary give us sustenance and nurture us." Blair Fitzpatrick followed with a pinch of silvery dust. Her own darker brown hair with auburn lights displayed the same sense of life.

Jazz was last with her copper hair hanging past her shoulders in loose waves. "During this full moon we ask that our sanctuary always be there for us in our time of need." She opened her bag with its dust spilling forth the color of creamy pearls.

As it touched the water, the color of the lake turned the rare translucent color of a moonstone, which echoed in the gemstone pendant each woman wore. At that moment, all three women's moonstone pendants and rings glowed bright. When a star shot across the velvety night sky, the three women looked at each other and burst into joyous laughter.

"And thank you for making sure the lake monster didn't rise up and eat us!" Jazz shouted across the shimmering water as she spun in a tight circle.

"That's right, Jazz, encourage it to seek out a late night snack," Blair chided her.

As they later retraced their path along the lake's edge, Stasia looked out over the water. A faint ripple appeared in the center, the watery rings moving in ever-increasing circles toward the water's edge.

"Do you think it's true?" she asked.

"What's true? That we have a monster living in the lake?" Blair followed her gaze. "You've been reading too many of those fantasy romances you sell, Stasi. All you'll find out there are fish, pieces of broken boats, and miles of snarled fishing lines caught in the weeds."

"That doesn't mean there isn't something living in the lake," Jazz said, pausing to look out over the lake, which now remained quiet other than a few lingering ripples. "Has there ever been a sighting of anything strange and unusual?"

Stasi shook her head. "High school kids like to come out here at midnight and claim they see a creature's head pop up in the water, but nothing has ever been verified, so everyone assumes they'd been drinking or something."

"At least no one comes out on the nights of the full moon. If they knew we were out here and why, they would probably expect us to be dancing naked around a bonfire," Blair joked.

"Oh right, on a night like this?" Jazz groused, shivering under her thin robe. "It's got to be twenty degrees. I've got long underwear on and I'm still cold!"

The other two laughed and bumped shoulders companionably as they hurried along. They didn't notice the faint outline of a scale-covered head popping out of the water and looking in their direction.

Following their own time-honored custom, the women arose to watch the sun greet them with colors of red, orange, and gold. This way they enjoyed the early morning hours together before Jazz returned to her city life.

When Stasi and Blair stumbled onto Moonstone Lake in 1854, the mining town was aptly named Last Chance. It slowly died when the mines played out and some residents moved on in search of wealth, while others remained because they desired stability. Stasi and Blair stayed, working as waitresses in the small café and eventually purchasing it. By the time they left the town, claiming family matters, they also owned the building the café was housed in. Over the years, Stasi and Blair took turns returning as a grand-daughter or grandniece to make sure the building was kept up for the times they wished to return.

Two years ago, they decided to return to the small town where they renovated the building and opened businesses to cater to the tourists who stopped off on their way to the ski resorts further up the mountain. They also joked they were there to watch over the lake and the mystical monster that supposedly inhabited it. Stasi and Blair took it one step further by sprinkling "not interested" spells throughout the forest that partially surrounded the town. Many developers had visited the area with thoughts of building resorts there, but they always left deciding it wasn't for them. But since the two women were also aware there could always be someone who might slip under the spell's radar, they took further precautions by purchasing the land around the lake under a false corporation's name. This was their own little paradise, and they intended to keep it that way.

For now, Stasi enjoyed running her lingerie boutique that also offered romance novels, while Blair utilized her playful side with a shop specializing in retro—whether it was a Madame Alexander doll from the 1940s, chrome tables from the 1950s, or tie dye clothing from the 1960s. It was easy for Blair to keep a varied inventory when every sister witch had storage units all over the country filled with personal treasures and liked to clean them out every so often.

During the winter, the town was busy with tourists heading up the mountain to the various ski resorts, while the summer season attracted trout fishermen and hikers.

Stasi and Blair never lacked for male company if they so wished, but out of self-preservation they kept their secrets close and deliberately cultivated no long-term relationships. Jazz came up every month for the moon ceremony along with any witch who might be in the area. For the last few months, it had only been the three visiting the lake the first night of the full moon.

Each holding their morning macchiatos, the three sat in comfortable chairs on the building's flat-topped roof, a pair of binoculars within reach on a nearby table.

As Jazz related the events of the past few weeks, she prepared herself for the worst when she mentioned Nick's name. She wasn't disappointed.

"Wait a minute. You used witchflame and missed him? Girlfriend, you have lost your touch if that happened." Blair shook her head. "The fangy sleaze at least deserved singed eyebrows."

"Except he'd end up looking more like a sparkler on the Fourth of July than a man with no eyebrows," Stasi said softly. "Vampires and fire don't go together very well."

"There are ways," Blair pointed out. As one gifted with some pretty nifty revenge spells, she should know. "Do you want some help cooking something up?"

"No, thanks, right now we sort of need each other," Jazz admitted reluctantly, although the idea of picking up a few revenge spells from Blair was a good idea. She wished she hadn't mentioned Nick's return to Stasi and Blair. Now that they knew he was back in her life, they would demand all the gory details. They knew something bad had happened to her back in 1932, but she had never told them the whole story. That was a night she preferred not to discuss with anyone, not even those closest to her.

"I guess I don't need to ask you if Nick has changed," Stasia said with her gentle smile. "He's still gorgeous and all coplike, right?"

"I don't think he would change much even if he wasn't a vampire," Jazz said, sipping her macchiato. "His wardrobe is more updated, but he's still a cop at heart—even if he left the Protectorate."

"You are kidding! I thought he was surgically grafted to that group. Darth Vader with fangs." Blair snickered. "*Nick, I am your destiny,*" she intoned in a deep voice that had the other two laughing.

"Great, now I snorted my macchiato!" Jazz wheezed, rocking back and forth in her chair, accepting the handkerchief the always-prepared Stasi carried on her person.

"We had a *Star Wars* marathon a couple weeks ago. Easy to think Vader when you've seen him in four movies," Blair explained.

"Ha! Don't believe her. She was too busy ogling Han Solo in those tight breeches," Stasi teased.

Jazz looked at her sister witches and felt warm and soothed. She had needed this. She needed the ceremony at the lake to center herself and her power, and she needed to be with those closest to her for emotional centering.

She liked to act the part of scary witch or smart-ass witch, but here, she could be herself. A witch who was still in the process of finding her true self. Who knew? She might even impress the Witches' High Council so much they would lift her banishment. Yeah, that'll happen. The same day the earth rotates in the opposite direction.

She stared out over the wooded area and thought of a life beyond that of an outcast witch.

But then what would I do?

"Come on, Jazz. Give us small town girls news of the big city." Blair's words drew her back to the present. "How is sexy Krebs doing? You need to bring him up here again."

Jazz smiled. "He's still designing websites for the Undead and recently set one up for a jazz club that caters to weres." She went on to talk about her own latest clients. Stasi and Blair laughed at her story of the college girls turning the school jocks into pigs and begged for more stories.

"There was a very nice woman who needed to be rid of a curse placed on her by an ex-boyfriend," Jazz said. "He was convinced she made a major mistake in breaking up with him and he set up a curse where she saw his image in any man she dated. He was convinced this would bring her back to him."

"That's just sick!" Blair sputtered.

Jazz nodded. "It wasn't long before her nerves were shot to hell. She took a leave of absence from her job and hid out in her apartment. Luckily, a friend of hers knew about me and called. The poor woman was almost physically ill from the stress." Her delicate features darkened with the memory.

"That's not love. That's disgusting." Stasi shuddered.

Jazz agreed. "I could feel his obsession tainting everything, as if he'd come into her apartment and coated the walls. I think that's what was making her ill. So I decided he needed a taste of his own medicine." She grinned.

"Good!" Blair shouted, saluting with her macchiato cup. "Warts, boils, or oozing sores?"

Jazz shook her head. "Every time he looks at her, he feels something dark and nasty hovering nearby. It isn't anything he can see. Just that sense of something there. It will wear off in about six months and I think by then he won't even be able to think of her with affection. My own brand of aversion therapy."

"People have no idea what harm can be done in the name of passion," Stasi said. "Love shouldn't be binding but freeing."

"Says the resident romantic," Blair teased.

"That's why we love Stasi." Jazz smiled warmly at the woman she considered closer to her than blood. "Yet, what some think are curses turn out to have nothing to do with magick. One man was convinced his dog was cursed because the dog constantly chewed up his clothing and shoes and even pretty much destroyed his furniture. He said his wife had a curse put on the dog because he won custody of the animal in their divorce. Turned out that wasn't it at all. The dog was just stressed out about the divorce and they needed more quality time together."

"Canines are so easy to understand—almost human," Blair mused.

"Yeah, this was a sweet little pup. Except his idiot owner didn't think he'd need to pay me since there wasn't a curse to eliminate. I explained to him what would happen if he didn't and he happily ponied up." Jazz grinned.

Stasi idly turned the pages of the latest *Allure* magazine. "We wish you would come up here to live, Jazz. It isn't as if there's not enough room here for you."

"I'm happy in L.A. Between the curse elimination and driving for Dweezil, I keep busy." Jazz straightened out her jean-clad legs. Wearing black high-heeled boots, black slim cut jeans, an emerald green silk t-shirt and a black leather jacket along with a black Stetson shading her eyes; she looked like a sexy version of the Marlboro woman. She would have preferred wearing Fluff and Puff, but her slippers were banned from Moonstone Lake since an unfortunate episode with a squirrel.

"I don't know how you can be happy working for that ghastly man." Blair shuddered.

"Dweezil might be disgusting and …"

"Scary looking," Stasi added.

"And a total perv." Blair's lip curled.

"Not to mention having a third arm and second dick," Jazz reflected to a double set of shrieks. "But he does pay well."

"He should." Stasi pulled her legs up onto the chair so she could wrap her arms around her knees. Her skirt drifted down over her legs. "By working for him you have to drive all those disgusting creatures."

"Someone has to do it and I'm better qualified than most." She sipped her triple mocha macchiato thoughtfully. "Some of them even tip well."

"Considering what they look, and smell, like they should." Stasi wrinkled her nose. "You even have to drive that disgusting creature who requires a special car."

Jazz nodded. "Tyge Foulshadow is about as gross as you can get."

"Foul everything from what you've told us," Blair said.

"The man farts smells that are unimaginable and in color, no less. The air recirculation system in the limo is top of the line, but my clothes still end up stinking like something horrible. Dweezil likes to remind me that the gas won't hurt me, but he forgets I can still smell it." She mimicked a gagging sound. "At least he's a big tipper. He sort of reminds me of the Earl of Brambleton." All three women shuddered at the memory of the man who was the cause of their banishment.

"For a member of royalty he was beyond repulsive. He never bathed, there were bugs in his beard and hair." Blair wrapped her hands around her macchiato to keep them warm in the chilly morning air.

"That was nothing unusual back then. As I recall, we weren't into baths all that much either until we entered the school." Stasi propped her feet up on the railing and studied her toenails while looking at a magazine lying open in her lap. She waved her hand across her toes. The bright pink nail polish promptly disappeared. She looked down at her magazine, touched a nail polish bottle in an ad and in turn touched each of her toenails, promptly coloring them a rich shade of coral that matched the squiggly design on her knee-length flirty skirt and her coral sweater. An intricate gold chain circled one ankle, a tiny broom hanging from it. The same anklet graced Blair and Jazz's ankles at all times, except hers displayed a creamy pearl while Jazz's sported a deep purple amethyst and Blair's a rich blue topaz.

"Honestly, Stasi. You do know you can actually go into a store and buy nail polish and manually apply it to your toes, don't you?" Jazz asked. "Or you can go wild and even go to a salon where they'll do it for you." She held up her hands and wiggled her scarlet painted nails.

"I know, but sometimes it's fun to try something out ahead of time." Stasi did the same to her fingernails and sat back to admire the effect. "That way I don't end up with something I don't like."

"Jake is late." Jazz picked up the binoculars resting by her chair and brought them up to her eyes so she could scan the landscape. Several houses were set nearby.

"Only by about five minutes." Blair sipped her vanilla caramel macchiato. "He's not known to oversleep. It is so sad I've never had the pleasure of personally discovering if that little piece of information is true. More's the pity."

"He better get his cute, tight denim-clad butt in gear and up on that roof soon because I have to be on the road in the next half hour." Jazz kept the binoculars trained on a cabin set a short distance away.

"Mrs. Benedict jokes that the minute the coffee is brewed and her first batch of biscuits come out of the oven, he's on her back doorstep ready to work," Blair said.

"Does she still make those incredible sourdough biscuits?" Jazz asked settling back in her chair with her leather-booted feet still propped up on the railing.

"Like clockwork every Thursday morning and sometimes she sends a batch over here. With *him*." The *yummy* was unstated, but the image of hungrily licked lips fairly layered itself over the blonde witch's provocative mouth. "The last time she sent him over with a jar of homemade raspberry jam along with a plate of biscuits," Stasi said with a sense of reverence for a sexy male bearing home-made biscuits and jam.

"There he is!" Blair snatched the binoculars out of Jazz's hands almost strangling her with the neck strap as she brought the lenses up to her eyes. "Good morning, sunshine," she purred. "They are so right—a tool belt does make the man."

"I want to see!" Stasi leaned over to grab the binoculars.

"No, me!" Jazz said, sliding her head out from under the binocular strap even as she reached from the other side. "Besides, I had them before you stole them!"

Blair kept one hand on the binoculars and the other batting back and forth at the women's hands. "Three minutes," she sang out. "The rule is three minutes each. And that means three minutes viewing time without any interference."

Stasi collapsed back in her chair. "Whoever made up that rule was seriously disturbed." She absently fiddled with the delicate coral hearts that dangled at the end of her gold earrings.

"You were the one who suggested the three minute rule. I voted for a five minute viewing time," Blair felt obligated to point out as she settled back in her chair to enjoy the view. She set her cup on the small glass-topped table next to her chair.

"Bandanna?" Stasi asked. "Jeans or cut-offs? Is he wearing a shirt?"

Blair nodded. "Red. Tied neatly around his forehead with that one lock of hair draped artfully over it. Cut-offs and a dark green t-shirt." Her shoulders rose and fell in a sigh. "Think it will be hot enough for him to take his shirt off today? How long do you think it will take before he gets all sweaty?" She looked up at the dim morning sun as if she could use her magick to heat up the orb.

"Never fool with Mother Nature." Anticipating Blair's wish, Stasi shook her head reprovingly. "She doesn't have a sense of humor." Her bare foot gently nudged a small ball of fur lying by her chair. A tan-colored head raised and looked up with canine delight. She leaned over and picked up the small dog that uttered a high-pitched yip and covered her face with Snausage-scented kisses.

"Okay, your three minutes are up. My turn." Jazz twiddled impatient fingers in front of Blair's magnification-enhanced vision, demanding her shot at the binoculars. She settled the lenses in perfect viewing position. "Oh my, almost as good as a nice hot cup of coffee for a wake-up call. Have you seen what incredible hands the man has? And doesn't that give the imagination a lot to work with."

Stasi counted off the seconds to three minutes. As she handed over the binoculars, Jazz plucked the dog out of the other witch's lap and cradled the small canine against her breasts.

"One day, you need to get a real dog," Jazz said, handing the little beast over after Stasi reluctantly passed the binoculars back to Blair.

"Bogie is a real dog," Stasi said, stroking the dog's head and scratching him behind his ears. "He's a Chihuahua/Yorkie. Both are very old and respected breeds."

"Just because the AKC says those are dog breeds doesn't mean this critter is a dog," Jazz said.

"Stop making fun of my Bogie!" She hugged the small canine against her chest and received a sloppy kiss. "He's a wonderful dog!'

"Is not a dog."

"Is so."

"A dog barks. That thing yowls like a scalded cat. A dog licks its ass. That critter licks his paws as if a speck of dirt on them was something downright disgusting. Only cats do that. Do you think he can land on all four paws too? Let's see if he can." Jazz plucked him out of her lap and held him a small distance above the ground.

"Not nice!" Stasi snatched him back.

"He is more like a doggie dust ball than a real dog," Jazz argued.

With a regretful sigh at the distant male figure walking the length of the sloped roof with sure-footed grace, Jazz pushed herself out of her chair. "I need to be off."

"We mean it, Jazz. Move up here with us. Work would be no problem." Stasi said, following her down the stairs that led from their flat-topped roof to the ground. Her small dog trotted happily at her heels, but if anyone looked closely they'd realize the dog's paws never touched the ground. "There's plenty of room in the building to open any type of business you wish. Think how wonderful it would be if more of us settled back here."

"You'd be amazed at all the cute guys that stop by on their way to the resorts," Blair tempted.

"While I enjoy visiting Moonstone Lake, I like where I am now, and I'm doing well there," Jazz assured her. A faint image of Nick lingered in the back of her mind before she ruthlessly banished it. "Who knew there were so many curses in the L.A. area that needed to be eliminated." She chuckled, as they stood near the small parking area behind the building. "Especially in Hollywood."

"It's about time you showed up! A body could die of old age waitin' on you!" A woman's querulous voice drifted toward them.

Jazz rolled her eyes. "Your watch stopped working in 1956!" she snapped.

"You should be nicer to her," Stasi said under her breath. "She hasn't had it easy all these years what with being unable to leave the car."

"*Her? I'm* the one stuck with her." Jazz glared at the gray-haired woman. *Ghost,* she amended irritably. *Ghost, ghost, ghost!* Irma's flower trimmed hat bobbed up and down with her head as she continued criticizing Jazz's social skills and lack of concern for others. Jazz stamped her foot. "You're dead, Irma! Time is not a problem with you!" She muttered a few choice curses under her breath but nothing magickal. Not that any spell could have affected the victim in mind.

"You've been able to eliminate every nasty curse thrown your way," Blair said. "Why haven't you been able to zap Irma out of the car?"

Jazz shook her head. She pulled her keys out of her jacket pocket. "I wish I knew. No other curse gave me this much trouble. It's as if she's under some damn spell that keeps her safe. I've gone through so many spell books and I've never been able to find anything that works."

"Are we leaving or not?" Irma shouted. A stream of cigarette smoke floated out the window.

Jazz cast her eyes upward as if seeking help and then hugged her friends.

"Safe journey," Stasi murmured in Jazz's ear. Blair repeated the same words when the two women hugged.

Jazz smiled at both of them and then turned and stalked toward her car. "I told you no smoking in my car!" she shouted.

"It's not as if I have to worry about lung cancer." Irma held her cigarette to her Tangee-colored lips and blew out a perfect smoke ring. "And you forget, it was my car first, which is why I don't see why I can't have a pet to keep me company when you leave me alone here. It could also protect me."

"No pets allowed," Jazz insisted. "And the only reason you consider the car yours is because you died in it."

Stasi and Blair stood shoulder-to-shoulder watching the snazzy T-bird roar out of the parking lot. The two women walked around to the front of the building to their shops.

"If Irma wasn't already dead, I fear Jazz would gladly accept any punishment as long as she could zap her somewhere unimaginable," Stasi said.

Blair chuckled. "If Irma wasn't dead, Jazz would just turn her into a seat cushion and put it in that special limo for Tyge Foulshadow to use."

Stasi looked over her shoulder in the direction the small car had taken.

"Did you notice something when Jazz told us what's been going on with her lately?"

"Nothing new, other than she still isn't dating, why?"

Stasi shook her head. "She may have thought she made us think she told us all, but I could tell she didn't. Our Jazz kept something back and if she did…"

"That can only mean one thing," Blair finished for her.

They faced each other. "It has to do with Nick!"

Ten

"**W**hat do you mean you haven't stopped by there yet? You promised me you would go by the shop and pick it up for me. They'll be closing in a couple of hours!"

Jazz winced at the accusation in Krebs' voice. She really should have checked caller ID before answering her cell phone. Krebs in a snit was not easy to deal with. And her Witch's Code wouldn't allow her to conjure up a harmless li'l ole spell to allow him to forget her promise. A promise, mind you, she'd given when she was desperate for coffee that morning and he was holding the pot hostage until she agreed to pick up some computer equipment he'd special ordered.

"A promise you extracted from me before you told me exactly where I had to go. They don't like me coming in there."

"That power outage wasn't your fault, so don't use it as an excuse. Just run into the store, tell them you're there to pick up my order, sign the paper, and get out. They'll even load the boxes in the car."

Jazz's mouth opened then closed when she realized he'd already hung up.

"Fine," she muttered, dropping her cell phone into her jacket pocket. Her boot heels clicked loud in the almost empty parking garage. She frowned as she passed a large number of parking spaces devoid of the minivans and SUVs she was used to seeing when she came here. With it being a mega sale day at the mall she would have expected the garage to be filled by this hour. Numerous cars rolled past, the drivers each looking for that all-elusive parking spot closest to the store entrances, but they ignored the nearby empty slots. Echoes of traffic sounded muted in the concrete structure.

Her T-Bird was in sight when an overpowering wave of a suffocating sensation engulfed her. Her footsteps faltered for a moment. She instinctively knew that increasing her speed would only slow her down as she crossed through an invisible threshold that felt like a gooey sticky barrier.

As she stared at her car parked at one end of the deserted section, she knew exactly why drivers subconsciously left this part of the garage alone even if they would have been only a few steps away from the parking garage elevator. She wouldn't have wanted to park here either.

As she walked forward with her eyes trained on her car, which any mortal would see as a dingy sedan, a tall figure separated itself from the shadows near the front bumper and now stood near the taillight. There was no doubt the man had been waiting for her. Irma sat frozen in the passenger seat wearing an expression Jazz didn't think she'd ever seen on the cranky ghost. *Fear.*

Jazz didn't blame her. She wasn't feeling too brave at the moment either. Not that she'd admit it. She had a sick feeling this was one time she would have to rely on her wits more than her gifts.

"Good afternoon." The man flashed a smile that looked about as threatening as a glass of milk but under the surface a promise of something dire lurked. If she read auras, she knew she'd see something as dark as the clothing he wore. Dressed in black slacks and a black polo shirt with an embroidered emblem over his heart that would not be found at Ralph Lauren or La Coste, he looked like any other man. With a full head of salt-and-pepper hair professionally styled and his dark tan, he would be the kind of wealthy retirement-aged man found on any country club golf course. Jazz sincerely doubted he'd been walking the links for the last seventy-some years. "Nice little car you have here," he said, flashing her a warm smile that chilled her to the bone.

Fine, she could play the game he started. "I like it." After all this time, she could role-play with the best of them. Today, she was your typical single working girl enjoying a leisurely afternoon at the mall where *40 percent off* was any red-blooded woman's, and witch's, siren's call. As much as it galled her, she had no choice but to follow his lead. One misstep could lead to her downfall. She'd played that game once and lost. Never again.

She kept her eyes on an ornate gold ring on his right hand as he trailed his fingers along the T-Bird's rear bumper. A fine mist the dark rainbow color of fresh oil rested briefly in the air before it settled on the shining metal. His concentration was centered on the car and he acted as if Irma wasn't there. While humans couldn't see the ghost, Jazz knew the man standing before her was very aware of Irma's presence. If she wasn't mistaken he was even feeding on the spirit's distress as if it were a sumptuous banquet. Once more, she tamped down the fury rising up within her. This was not a time to give in to her temper. It was a time she needed to think way long before she spoke.

"You've kept her in beautiful condition. Any chance you would care to sell her?" He cocked an eyebrow and kept the easy-going smile on his lips. To an outsider, he would still have appeared as nothing more dangerous than an admirer of classic cars. To Jazz, he was about as bad as you could get. "I'm prepared to offer a very good price for this beauty."

The sound of Irma's emotional pain tore through Jazz's body like a cold sharp knife.

"No, I would not." Acting polite tasted harsh on her tongue, but she was determined not to do anything to create a problem. She wasn't sure if the gooey barrier she'd stepped through blocked anyone from seeing them, but knowing the creature she faced, she was certain it would offer an illusion for mortals. She hoped any innocent who might not sense the darkness and happened to walk by would see nothing more than two people having a polite conversation. Yet, she was positive one wrong word could spiral things downhill fast, and she couldn't afford collateral damage among humans who had no idea what stood there contaminating this dimension. "The car holds sentimental value."

He kept his eyes, a flat black color, centered on her face. She kept her features impassive even as she felt something tiny crawl across her skin, mapping it, looking for a spot to burrow in. Gauging her true feelings. Anger and hatred drifted up inside her, but she tamped them down before they erupted and mentally turned the microscopic being to a magickal crispy critter. If it continued on she *would* do something to it. "So you enjoy things from the past?" He remained by the rear bumper, with one hand resting against the metal. The back continued to shimmer with the same rainbow black shade of oil as it flowed across the sides of the car.

"I value some things." She refused to take her eyes off him. That would indicate fear, not to mention that taking your eyes off a cobra was a very good way to get bitten. What stood in front of her would make a cobra bite seem no more dangerous than a paper cut. She knew the creature masquerading as a man was about as dangerous as they came. Her fingers itched to bring up a large quantity of witchflame, but she knew it wouldn't do any good because what stood before her was nothing more than a malevolent illusion bent on infusing her with terror. "Now if you don't mind I have an appointment to keep and I'm running late."

He didn't move off right away but kept watching her, his gaze dark and probing. Jazz felt as if his stare burrowed down to find and touch a part of her that she'd kept tucked deep inside. A violation she abhorred with all her being.

"You're supposed to be dead," she said in a low even voice. "I picked up that broken bottle and I plunged it into your heart. How did you survive that killing blow?"

His smile never wavered as he glanced down at the car, and then at her, speaking as if he hadn't heard her question. "Yes, very lovely indeed. I would be interested if you ever plan on selling your car." He pulled a business card out of his pocket and held it out. She didn't move to take it. He shrugged and left it on the car. "Good day."

He walked past her, the ringing sound of his footsteps soon growing faint until he disappeared from sight.

Jazz stared long and hard at the rectangular calling card lying on the car. Letters the color of blood spelled out a name she had heard all too often lately: *Clive Reeves.* A narrow coil of smoke swirled upward and the card disappeared without leaving any damage to the car's surface. Unfortunately, the oily substance that had covered the rear of the T-bird now covered the entire surface and wouldn't be as easy to remove. While she knew no mortal being could see the damage done to her vehicle, she not only saw it, she felt it all the way to her bones.

"I feel so dirty," Irma whimpered from her spot in the front seat.

Jazz bent over and vomited in front of the car next to hers. Moving away, she braced her back against the wall and slid down until she sat on the concrete floor. She pulled in a ragged breath.

"I killed him once. No prob in killing him again. And this time I'll make it stick."

~

That evening, Nick followed the sound of bells to the back yard. When he rounded the corner of the house he noticed the spotlights set above the carriage house door, which were illuminating the scene before him. Krebs, beer bottle in hand, slouched in a chair on the edge of the lawn watching Jazz pass a wet cloth over the side of her car, which was parked in the driveway in front of the carriage house. What appeared to be some sort of dark viscous oil slowly disappeared from the vehicle's surface and transferred itself to the cloth she wielded with such fury it could have been a weapon. Temple bells sounded from a small boom box sitting on the ground by Krebs' chair. Nick sensed the music playing was not the man's choice.

"Light covers dark, so it will never return," she murmured as she ran the cloth over the metal. "Light gives us life."

Jazz's movements were slow and graceful, that of a dancer as her lips moved, uttering words in a long forgotten language. The sound of her words cast a golden glow over the car and the temple bells created a musical counterpoint to her actions and the fury that transferred to shimmering shades of red, gold, and purple around her. The rich scent of cedar drifted through the air even though he knew there were no cedar trees in the area. Nick realized the scent came from Jazz. She was using water charged with cedar and oils. A large cauldron rested nearby with an unlit white sage smudge stick propped inside; a large quartz crystal lay close beside the pot. Several other crystals were placed around the car. He knew the broom propped near the carriage house door was not there for decoration. It was an important part of Jazz's ritual. She was casting a cleansing spell. She was invoking a strong magick—cleansing the car of something so dark he could sense it like a putrid substance.

He had a very bad feeling he knew where the foul substance came from and it was not good. He stepped closer while remaining out of the circle Jazz had cast around herself and the car.

"What happened?"

Jazz spun on her bare heels. Her tank top and denim capris were soaked from the charged water and sweat. The look on her face boded ill for anyone who stood in her path. Right now, Nick was that obstacle. Nothing like a six-foot plus target to get a witch's back up.

"You bastard, you told me he couldn't leave his estate. You said he hadn't left the mansion in years! But you didn't tell me he had mastered astral projection!" Her accusation sliced through him like a well-honed blade. It didn't take magick for the wet cloth in her hand to score a direct hit against Nick's chest—just Jazz throwing it at him like a fast-pitch baseball the way she'd throw a fireball. The moment the fast-moving cloth broke the circle, she had it sealed again. The cloth slid down his front, landing on the ground with a wet plop. She glared at the cloth, turning it to ash within seconds.

Her words rocked him back on his heels. Jazz zapping a wet cloth to powder was nothing new. The information that she had obviously run into Clive Reeves was. He hadn't expected the man to confront her openly.

"I didn't know." His stunned gaze whipped from her angry features to Irma huddled in the passenger seat, tears streaming down her paler-than-usual features.

Jazz glared at him again and then spun around, sending a fireball straight at the smudge stick. It flamed to life, sending out the scent of white sage.

Nick had a sick feeling that the fireball could just as easily have ended up flying right at him. "Oookay." He turned back to Jazz, ready to face her wrath. He understood her anger, and he was willing to absorb it and take full blame for what had happened. He accepted that Clive Reeves' confronting her outside his estate was his fault and his alone because he hadn't ended this disaster back then. "There's never been any intel that he had the ability to leave his body. No one has reported him leaving the mansion grounds in decades. He even built his offices and studio up there since the property is so extensive."

Jazz's eyes glowed a dark green that seemed to take on a life of their own and snapped with more than their usual share of witchy temper. They looked as if they could invoke a dangerous spell on their own. "Guess again, Fang Boy. Your *intel* is wrong, because he sure as Fates was standing by my car two hours ago." She swept her hand backwards toward the T-bird.

Nick stared at the vehicle, still seeing faint traces of the black and foul substance smeared across the usually immaculate aqua and white exterior. He knew Jazz never went anywhere without powerful wards protecting her car, but it was clear that even they hadn't been enough to defend the vehicle from this particular evil. No wonder she was seriously pissed and looked ready to zap him into powder right along with the befouled cloth.

"What happened, exactly?" he asked again.

Jazz returned to casting her cleansing spell. She picked up another cloth and soaked it with the charged water, running it over the metal surface.

"I was at the mall. When I got back to the car I found some sort of strange thick barrier in front of it. It felt like some weird, really…," she reached for an adequate description, failed to locate one, and so used what came to mind, "revolting goo as I passed through it. He was standing by the car." Her words were jerky with emotion while her movements remained graceful. "He tried to act as if he was some stranger interested in classic cars. He stood there smiling and friendly as if…." Again speech failed. "While all I wanted to do was…." She crushed the wet cloth in her fist. She shook off her thoughts and returned to her task.

Jazz picked up a large quartz crystal that lay near the cauldron and dunked it in the charged water before walking to the car and placing it in Irma's lap. "For you."

"What?" Irma yelped as the crystal promptly fell through her to rest comfortably on the seat.

"It will help calm you," Jazz explained.

"I can't even hold it!" Irma looked down at the crystal that she was "sitting" on.

"Even if it's under your ass it can still calm you," Jazz snapped, going over to pick up her broom.

Nick watched her end the spell by sweeping round the car, casting out the last of the evil.

"Let this be gone and never return. Let this be gone to where it will forever burn," she muttered. "Because I say so, damn it!" Jazz's form of "so mote it be" was more direct, and Nick had to admit it suited her.

The darkness melted away.

Even though the evil was now cleansed from the car, Irma still looked traumatized.

Nick remained in his spot watching Jazz open the circle, clear away her tools, and turn off the boom box.

"I need to relay this sighting to the Protectorate. The Elders need to know what happened to you and Irma."

She straightened up, "You will relay them *nothing*. They haven't done a thing for you in the past, why bother with them now?" She caught his expression. "Give me a break, Nick! They've led you around by the fangs for the past thousand years."

"Fangs?" Krebs muttered, looking from one to the other. "Who has fangs? *He* has fangs?"

"The Protectorate and their damn Elders have their own agenda, which has nothing to do with you and definitely has nothing to do with me," she went on, ignoring Krebs.

"It has everything to do with us. They asked us to help deal with Clive," Nick pointed out. "You know what they are like. If they didn't think we could do the job, they wouldn't have requested our help."

Her smile wasn't the least bit pretty. For a moment, thunder rumbled overhead. "The only reason the Elders thought it was a good idea for me to help you is because they hope if there are any casualties, it will be me instead of you. You're more valuable to them than I am. You may have left the Protectorate, but they still consider you one of their own." She stalked toward him. An angry witch was a dangerous witch. Right now Jazz was practically nuclear.

"Uh, guys," Krebs ventured, but he knew enough to stay out of the danger zone. He'd seen displays of Jazz's temper before. "FYI, we're not totally alone around here. Let's think about the neighbors who might look out their windows or over the fence. We don't want them seeing anything that would prompt them to call the cops, or worse, get us kicked out of the neighborhood, do we?"

Nick stood his ground as the air swirled around them, kicking up tiny dust devils. When what felt like icy daggers hit his skin he hissed in pain and flashed his fangs.

"Holy shit!" Krebs practically climbed up the back of his chair until it fell over, pitching him backwards. He scrambled to his feet and quickly scrambled backwards on all fours.

Jazz glanced at him and realized how far she'd almost gone. She walked around in a tight circle, her arms wrapped around her middle as she pulled in deep breaths to calm down and push her anger away. The colors that reflected her fury slowly subsided.

Nick, likewise, took the time to cool down. "I apologize." He bowed deeply to a shaken Krebs.

"It was just that I—hell." He ran his hand over his hair. He held his hands up, palms out toward them. "You know what? I'm going inside now and pour myself a really big drink. Maybe I'll just drink straight out of the bottle. All I ask is that you do me a favor and don't blow anything up." He backed his way toward the house.

Nick ducked his head, releasing a soft sigh. "He didn't know?"

"He didn't know." Jazz took several deep breaths, calming the snarling beast within her. "It's not exactly something you bring up in a conversation. "Oh, by the way, Krebs, Nick, that guy who's come around? He's a non-living, non-breathing vampire. Krebs deals with vamps in his website building business, but all his work is done over the phone or online. I begged him to do it that way for his own protection, and he thinks he's humoring me by honoring my request. Sometimes, I think he feels they're like some underground club, wannabes and not the real thing."

"And definitely not the same as facing one." He gazed at Irma, huddled in her seat. "You're sure it was Clive?"

"Just because he didn't look the way he did before and it's been more than seventy years doesn't mean I can't recognize the devil." Her face tightened with inner pain. "Do me a favor and just please, go away.

I am not in the mood to discuss strategy right now. I do not want to discuss intel or what needs to be done next or even what an asshole you still are."

Nick wanted to tell her they needed to do just that, but he mentally agreed this wasn't the time. Plus, he wanted to make a few calls. He inclined his head in a brief nod.

"I will contact you later." As he walked away he saw Jazz in his mind's eye. Anger and fear warred in her eyes and her skin was as pale as parchment. Once, he would have remained and done his best to comfort her. Now, he knew it was best if he left and allowed her to cool down on her own, no matter how badly he wanted to stay.

No woman ever made him feel as alive, well, as alive as he could be, the way Jazz did.

❧

Jazz didn't think anything unusual when she heard the faint sound of voices coming from the carriage house as she crossed the back lawn. Since she didn't require sleep, Irma spent many a night watching television, and Jazz kept her well supplied with DVDs. Except… she picked up the pace and used the door at the side of the building. Two heads swiveled to face her. One was gray-haired, the other dark. It was the dark-haired one that captured her attention.

"What are you doing here?" Okay, her less than polite greeting would boot her right out of Miss Manners' class, but *she* had come out here to comfort Irma, since she figured the woman was still upset over the day's events. Considering this was pretty much the worst magickal situation Irma had ever had to deal with, Jazz felt she should come out to make sure she was all right. Except right now, she felt something that suspiciously felt like jealousy.

Nick rose from the chair he'd set next to the car's passenger door. "I thought I would come by and see Irma. I wanted to make sure she was all right."

Jazz shot a quick glance in Irma's direction. When she last saw the ghost, Irma had been a weepy mess. Now, obviously thanks to Nick's attention, she was downright perky.

"Wasn't that nice of Nicky to stop by?" Irma chirped. Now that Jazz had cleansed vehicle and ghost, Irma's gray curls were back in beauty shop order and her white-gloved hands rested lightly on her navy handbag. There was lingering sorrow in her blue eyes, but she looked loads better than she had a few hours earlier.

"Oh yeah, he's a prince." She held up a DVD, a large bucket of buttered popcorn, and a jumbo cup of Diet Coke. A box of Milk Duds was tucked in her jeans pocket. Irma couldn't eat the junk food that went with the movie watching experience, but that didn't stop Jazz from imbibing. "I thought you might like a movie."

Jazz set her booty down on the nearby work-bench, walked over to the television, and popped the DVD in.

"It's probably not your style of film," she warned Nick.

He smiled. "I'm sure I would like anything you'd choose." He leaned back in the chair with his arms crossed across his chest, the gesture of a man prepared to stay for the duration.

She really wished she'd chosen a really good and soppy chick flick instead of a comedy. She and Nick had taken in their share of movies over the years. Judging by the expression in his dark eyes, he was recalling the old days when theaters offered nice, dark, and sometimes deserted, balconies.

Irma's face lit up and she clapped her hands in delight as the screen lit up. "*Arsenic and Old Lace!*" she uttered with a soft sigh. "Cary Grant is one of my favorite actors. Harold never liked him. He always said John Wayne was the only actor worth watching."

Jazz opened the driver's door and slid inside. She pushed the bench seat all the way back in order to stretch out her legs, placed the bucket of popcorn in the middle, and held her Diet Coke in one hand. She loved her car, but she wished it came equipped with cup holders. She was tempted to reach over and give Irma a hug, something she hadn't thought of doing in all the time Irma had been an unwanted passenger. But then, Irma hadn't been tainted with black magick before either. But Jazz knew there was no way to touch the spirit and give her any form of physical comfort. Her hand would only go through her. But she could give the ghost her time. For a moment her gaze collided with Nick's as he watched her with an emotion that made his eyes glow with dark lights.

Irma turned her head from side to side making sure she had both of their attentions. "I have seen that man before, but it doesn't make sense. Of course, it was many years ago and he looked different back then."

Jazz straightened up. "When did you see him, Irma?"

"On a poster at the Excelsior Theater in our town." She tapped her chin with her forefinger in thought. "It advertised a movie that had something to do with night in the title."

Jazz traded a telling glance with Nick.

"*The Midnight Man,*" Jazz whispered, memories swamping her of a movie about a horror actor obsessed with a minor actress in his film and how he destroyed her in the end. At the time, she had no idea that truth would so closely mirror fiction.

"Yes." Irma shuddered. "It was a very frightening poster. I didn't like frightening movies and Harold thought they were a waste of money. My land, that was ages ago."

Jazz had to force her lips to move. "1932." Even more difficult was keeping emotion from her voice.

"Then I couldn't have seen Clive Reeves today," Irma argued. "He died a long time ago. Some say that was why his movie did so well—because it was his last." Since she had swung her attention toward Nick she missed Jazz's instinctive flinch. "But he wasn't a ghost, was he?"

"No, Irma, he wasn't," Nick said.

Eleven

A cigarette appeared between Irma's fingers and just as quickly disappeared. Her usual Tangee-colored lips appeared bare. "Then he is some kind of monster, and that was how he did something horrible to me."

Jazz didn't make a snarky comment about anything being done to Irma as she would have in the past.

Irma took a deep breath. "Please tell me you two are going to do something about this creature. That you will destroy him." She swung her gaze toward Jazz. "That's what you do. You get rid of disgusting things for people. Just because I'm dead doesn't mean I don't have feelings." Her voice rose a few notches. "He made me feel dirty and I hurt inside. And I know it won't go away soon."

If Jazz didn't know better, she'd swear Irma's blood pressure was shooting through the roof. "I eliminate curses. I'm not allowed to take a life." She forced down the old memory that burned through her like acid.

"And he is a curse! Make him go away before he does something else!"

Jazz gave her cup of Diet Coke a magickal push so it landed safely on the workbench.

"We plan to take care of him, Irma," Nick said quietly. "Clive will never come near you again."

Irma's gaze swept from one to the other. "So he is that actor that everyone thought died in 1932. Is he a vampire or a werewolf or just a mad scientist who thinks he can live forever? Because if he's still alive now, he can't be human, and there is no way he is anything like me." She looked incensed at the idea Clive Reeves could be a ghost.

Jazz dry scrubbed her face with her hands. "Let's just say he's something we're not entirely sure about since Nick's intel isn't what it claims to be." She kept her own stress level under control as she glared at Nick. Considering the day she'd had it wasn't easy.

"Then you both intend to do something about destroying him."

"That's the plan." Jazz hoped she sounded more positive than she felt. That afternoon Clive Reeves had revealed magickal talents she hadn't expected. Talents she feared even she and Nick couldn't best.

"I want to help." Sorrow etched new lines in Irma's face. Jazz had no idea ghosts could still age, but at the moment, Irma looked a good ten years older. Her lips tightened with resolve. "I want to see him suffer." She rushed on before Jazz could reply. "But I need to leave this car to do it." She pounded her thigh. Her fist went through her body and the car seat, but her fury made up for the lack of substance in her gesture. Jazz found no humor in the action when she saw the anger and pain that accompanied it. "Please, find a spell for me to leave this vehicle! I want to be with you when you destroy that evil creature!"

Jazz was speechless. Irma had been petulant, even downright sarcastic, but never had she heard the woman plead, much less with such passion. She doubted anyone could understand Irma's need for justice as she did. She only wished she could grant the ghost her request.

"I've never been able to find a spell to release you from the car, Irma," she said gently. "I don't think you need a spell to leave the car, just your own determination. You need to let go of the past, forgive Harold, and in your own way, move on. That may be the only way you can leave the car."

Tears streaked through the layers of Coty powder and rouge Jazz knew Irma was never seen without, while the floral woodsy fragrance of Evening in Paris wrapped around them.

Irma appeared to take several deep breaths, not easy when you've been dead for more than fifty years, and then she turned back to watching the movie. Her voice was raspy with tears when she finally spoke. "Perhaps you're right."

Irma remained quiet throughout the film, although she smiled a few times.

When the movie finished, Jazz and Nick left the carriage house. Jazz looked up at the sky. Nick followed her gaze.

"Remember that night we drove up into the hills to sit on the Hollywood sign?"

She smiled at the memory. "Back then it said Hollywoodland. We sat on top of every letter just because it seemed like the thing to do. I thought I would have a glamorous film career, and instead I couldn't get further than credits like 'second chorus girl' or 'red-haired girl.'" She grimaced.

Nick's shoulder bumped companionably against hers. "That was only because you couldn't act worth a damn regardless of whether it was silent movies or talkies."

"I was not that bad!" she protested, swatting at him.

"A Raggedy Ann doll would have done a better job." He grinned.

"You were just jealous because they thought Bela Lugosi made a better vampire than you."

"My accent was better, but he had the cape."

"Yes, but you had the actual fangs. You should have shown them off. You might have been the cult figure instead of him. And at least you didn't have to avoid casting directors who expected more than a reading." Jazz's laughter stilled as quickly as it began. Recalling what happened to one member of the film community by her own hand tended to dampen the mood.

It also reminded her why she had heaped more mental abuse on Nick's head. She had thought he would rescue her. That he would destroy a mortal monster that was just as bad as the immortals he hunted down. But Nick didn't show up like a fanged knight on a white horse. Instead, Jazz was left to fend for herself as she had so many times before.

And just like so many times in the past he had pulled her in on whatever case he was working on, let her feel the magnetism that was his alone. She wanted to hate him, but she never could. And she hated herself for being such a wuss where Nick was concerned.

Why couldn't she have fallen for a nice were-wolf? If she dated a were she could take him with her to Moonstone Lake, and he could roam the woods hunting rabbits while she performed the monthly ceremony. They both would have enjoyed the full moon.

She glanced at the house and saw lights burning on the second floor. Since the Beach Boys were rocking the place, she guessed Krebs was working on something that needed more upbeat background music.

Recalling the past wasn't a good idea. Like Irma, she took several deep breaths to bring her back to the present.

"I need to find out how he managed what he did today," she said, reverting back to her cooler, and saner, self. "I know of a place that might have the answers we need. I'll go there in the morning."

Nick glanced at her sharply, but she refused to look at him. The fact that she was going during the daylight hours meant she didn't want him accompanying her.

Before Jazz could blink, he stood in front of her.

"This is a joint venture," he said harshly. "And if he can do astral projection, from now on where you go, I go."

"Not where I'm going—just because you still wear that mantle of the Protectorate." She waved him off when he started to speak. "Don't tell me again you left them, Nick. You will always be one of *them*. They might as well have put their brand on your ass."

If he wouldn't have risked slashing his mouth with his fangs, he would have ground his teeth. "Then wait until after sundown."

"I just told you. Where I'm going tomorrow you are definitely not welcome." She moved to step around him, but he easily blocked her in.

"Why do you always have to make things so difficult?"

She prided herself on not backing down, on meeting his gaze full on. And she hated herself for wanting to lift her hand and press it against his cheek. She knew she would find the slightly rough skin cool to the touch. She used to tell him she had enough warmth for the two of them. "Fine, if you want to try to get in and get your ass singed for even trying to cross the threshold, so be it. Because I'm going to The Library and you, of all people, know that vampires are not welcome there. Rumor has it The Librarian has turned your kind into bookends placed all around the reading room. Do you honestly want to chance that?"

Nick winced. He knew all too well she spoke the truth. Jazz throwing witchflame at him was minor compared to what could happen to him at that place. Any place that catered to the wizard and witch trade pretty much effectively posted *Vampires Need Not Enter* over their doors.

"Do you think you will learn anything there?"

"There is a section that might have the right information if I'm allowed into it. Unfortunately, The Librarian and I never got along well and there is no way I can go into that room without his permission." She looked him square in the face. "I want the past to die a vicious horrible death. I want blood to flow and pieces of that monster to be scattered to the four winds." As she spoke, an icy wind wound its way around the couple, touching Jazz's exposed skin with arctic fingers. She didn't flinch from the harsh chill that she knew came from the Witches' High Council. It was a warning she would heed their admonition or face their ire.

Jazz was smart enough to back down.

She looked up into Nick's face, noting how the moonlight slashed across his sea-green eyes. *Eyes that echoed the shades of green found in the Emerald Sea.*

He felt the last threads of her retreat even if she didn't move a muscle. And whatever he saw in her face had nothing to do with him. Anger coiled deep inside.

"What do you think of when you look at me, Jazz?" he asked. "*Who* do you see?"

She felt the pain like the flick of a knife across her flesh. In all the years she had known Nick he had never asked her that. It was as if he never wanted to know there might have been another.

She dug deep within her, finding the strength she needed to keep the truth buried so deep she hoped even she would never find it. Once she found it she forced herself to meet his gaze. She wanted there to be no doubt in his mind about what she was about to say.

"Nothing. I see and feel nothing."

"Liar," he murmured, with a faint smile touching his lips. "We share too much of a past, Griet." She really hated it when he used her birth name. "Over the centuries we have shared many adventures. So many nights we have shared our bodies." His voice lowered to a sensual purr that flowed over her nerve endings like tiny electrical currents. "I remember nights when we were so eager for each other we didn't wait even to find a bed. Remember that night in Venice when we stopped on that deserted bridge and I lifted your skirt and pulled you back against me." His eyes glowed with black light. "When I touched you I found you so wet for me my cock slid in easily, and you felt so good. We wanted each other so much it only took you seconds to orgasm."

She inhaled the musk of his skin and fought the memories that brought further heat trailing along her nerve endings.

"I'd had too much wine that night."

He ignored her fib. "Be honest with yourself. It was the hunger that constantly flowed between us. We've never been able to ignore each other long. Even now our bodies call to each other because they know they belong together." He moved closer until the soft cotton of his t-shirt brushed against her chest.

Jazz felt her nipples tighten and the ache below intensify, moisture pooling in her panties at the memory of what pleasure Nick could give her.

"Why do you deny us, Jazz?" he whispered, allowing the darkness to slide along his voice in a way that she knew would send most women to their knees if not flat on their backs. She was determined to not be one of those women.

"Because this is not the time." She injected steel into her voice just as she injected it into her spine. She stepped around him. Before she could move away from him, he took her arm and spun her toward him. "Don't! Just don't!" She slid out of his grasp and held her hands up to ward him off. If magick had sparked her palms he would have been tempted to push her, but there was nothing. This time it was Jazz, the woman, who rejected him, not Jazz, the witch. She kept shaking her head. "I'll let you know if I find out anything at The Library."

"You'll come to my office," he pressed.

"I'll come to your office," she replied, continuing on to the house.

She was relieved he didn't again try to detain her as she entered the house through the rear door.

Seeing Nick treat Irma with such gentleness disarmed her just as his gentle teasing a few moments before touched her.

As she opened the back door, she heard the sigh of the wind and she knew Nick was gone.

Jazz stopped long enough to snag a glass of wine before climbing to her third floor retreat. She ignored the elegant scroll on the wall that proclaimed *You've Got Mail.*

She undressed, changing into a teal long sleeved v-neck knit top and teal and purple print pajama pants.

Jazz looked at the wall and knew she couldn't ignore the message much longer.

"Message open."

The announcement faded away and other letters appeared.

Please tell me you had a wild exciting evening out clubbing or something because my evening here is enough to put me into the same coma a couple of my patients are in. Write me the minute you get in.

Jazz smiled, knowing who sent the message even if it was unsigned. There was only one witch sister who always sensed when she felt unsettled and needed to talk.

"Message to Lili. Not as exciting as you would like," she said, watching the letters form across the wall. "I was thinking back to when we lived in Boston."

And here I was hoping to hear something fun. So which time in Boston are you thinking about?

Jazz, who always appeared so tough and resilient to her friends, wanted to sink to the floor and cry like a small child. Instead, she dropped in a boneless heap on the black and white toile print chaise and fell back against the red plump pillows.

She didn't want to say the words. If she did, the memories would flood her. But if she didn't, they'd fester like an untreated wound.

"Leroy Biggs of Cotton Holler, West Virginia. A proud member of the West Virginia 15th Infantry," she whispered, watching the name form on the wall. Instead of the letters remaining a deep gold color like the rest of the sentence, they turned black, the color of mourning.

As far as I know the last time you said his name was the night we saw Gone with the Wind *in Boston.*

"He told me he planned to go back to West Virginia and marry Annie. He couldn't even write her a letter to tell her he loved her because she couldn't read and he didn't want the town preacher to read something so personal. He lost a leg and half his chest in that battle. At the end he was choking on his own blood and all I could do was sit there with him and watch him die."

We didn't have the medical knowledge we have today and even with all the advances of today we still couldn't have saved some of the wounded back then. It's just the way it works, Jazz.

"You could have saved him, Lili." She couldn't hold back the bitterness she still felt more than 150 years later.

And you still refuse to understand that it has never been my choice what patient I am allowed to fully heal. This gift of mine is also a curse. So many I wanted to heal and wasn't permitted to.

"If it really was a curse I would banish it and you'd be free to heal anyone you wished," Jazz murmured, aware the wall would hear her no matter how soft her voice was and her words would appear to Lili.

She remembered the days and nights of 1865 as easily as if they had been yesterday. Her name had been Jessie then, and she and the healer, Lilibet, traveled from camp to camp soothing the wounded and doing what they could to make a dying soldier's last moments more comfortable.

There was a reason why litter bearers set him with the dying, Jazz. Just as you've always known there were some things we weren't allowed to do. Interfering with a Higher Power has always been the most sacred of rules.

"I know," she said sadly. "But all he wanted to do was go home and marry Annie and raise kids and farm the land. For all we know, Annie never knew what happened to him. She might have thought he found someone else."

Just remember this. He didn't die alone as so many did. But that was not why you remember him. You remember him for the color of his eyes. The words disappeared and the wall remained blank for a moment. *You've seen Nick again, haven't you?*

Jazz winced as she stared at the words scrolled across the wall. "He has an office just off the boardwalk."

And?

"And he's working as a private detective. He claims he left the Protectorate, but we both know no one leaves them except in death."

Do you want to know what I think?

"Am I going to like it?" She grabbed one of her pillows and hugged it against her chest. The velvety texture didn't comfort her as much as she would have liked. She looked over and noticed the tips of four twitching ears appearing over the side of the chaise. A second later, Fluff and Puff's heads appeared, their expressive faces alight with concern.

The slippers scooted upward and slid their way onto her feet.

I'm sure you won't like it, but I feel it needs to be said.

Jazz couldn't help smiling even if her stomach was doing a rollercoaster dive. Her normally gentle-natured friend was showing a hint of snark.

"Then say it."

When you have comforted men over the centuries, you claim it's because the color of their eyes reminded you of your first love in your village. I don't think that's the case. I think they all are a reminder of Nick, and that even if he is an immortal being there is still a chance he could be destroyed. I think you sit with these men at the end of their time, because you secretly fear you will not be with Nick if something happens to him. That if the time ever came you would not have the chance to say good-bye to him and at least there's someone to say good-bye to the others.

Jazz felt her stomach free fall all the way to the ground floor. Hearing the truth was bad enough. Seeing it written so starkly made it too real.

"Psychology is not one of your strong points, Lili," she said harshly.

The first time you comforted a dying man with eyes the color of the Irish Sea was after that time Nick battled that Mongol demon. He would have died if he hadn't fed off a dying soldier. Two months after that, you went to a battlefield with me and helped nurse the wounded.

If she shut her eyes very tightly she would not see the damning words on the wall. If she screamed *delete!* they would disappear. Except it wouldn't be that simple to erase them from her memory. "Nick is more a thorn in my side than anything else."

And yet you always welcome him back into your life, and your bed, no matter how many times he's hurt you in the past. Considering everything that's gone on you've still never hit him over the head with a sledgehammer when he truly deserves it.

Be honest with yourself, Jazz. It all has to do with Nick.

"Does not."

Does so, so stop fibbing to yourself. I have to go. Be safe and I will talk to you soon.

"Be safe," Jazz echoed, watching the words fade from the wall.

She sat there for a long time, listening to Fluff and Puff murmur to each other. Every once in a while one of the slippers would swivel its head in her direction to glance at her and then turn back to talk to its buddy and continue its chatter.

She plopped her head back against the chaise and groaned.

"Why does everything always have to come back to Nick?"

Twelve

*J*azz bent over the sink to get a better look in the bathroom mirror. What she saw wasn't a pleasant sight. She made a face at the close-up view of her bloodshot eyes and pasty-looking skin. The weariness in her bones confirmed her sleepless night.

"It could be worse," she murmured, casting a minor glamour spell that took the red out of her eyes and added brightness to her skin. Considering what she was about to face this morning she would need all the armor she could conjure up.

Krebs was in the kitchen nursing a cup of coffee when Jazz walked in. She picked up one of her favorite mugs and pulled a couple of peanut butter cookies out of the cookie jar. He looked up, cocked an eyebrow in surprise at her sedate—for Jazz—skirt and sweater, and then returned to staring into his coffee.

"So Nick's really a vampire? Those fangs he flashed are real, as I don't suspect he had cosmetic dentistry. Drinks blood, is a total night person? Working on a tan would literally turn him into a crispy critter?"

"He's been one as long as I've known him." She inhaled the rich French vanilla fragrance as she poured the brew into her mug.

"Which is?"

She took a few cautious sips to jumpstart her system. "Too long."

"I get it. If you tell me, you'd have to kill me."

"No, your coffee is too good for me to want to kill you, but you really don't want to know." She settled in the chair across from him and took another sip. She closed her eyes in bliss as the caffeine flooded her system.

He reached across the table and covered her hand with his. "Talk to me, Jazz."

She thought it over for a few moments before replying.

"Remember the notices posted online about missing vampires?" She waited for his nod. "Nick has been hired by a vampire organization to investigate the disappearances."

"Even with the news about the disappearances online, it seemed kinda low key. Why would anyone want them investigated?"

"More like kept quiet for good reason." Jazz didn't want to go into much detail if she didn't have to. If Krebs was going to deal with the vampire community, she preferred he remained on the fringes as much as possible and she was pretty sure the vamps he dealt with would agree with her.

"C'mon Jazz, there's more to it than that. You forget, I work with vampires all the time." He sprinkled brown sugar over his oatmeal. "What is really going on?"

Jazz momentarily closed her eyes and tried to recall if she'd ever tried to explain her life to someone who wasn't a part of her world. In a word, no. "You work with vampires via email or on the phone. You've never met any of your clients in person and that's by *their* choice and one, if you remember, I agreed with," she pointed out. "The real thing is different than emailing someone whose screen name is *Suck You.* We're not talking about people who dress in black and wear fang prosthetics or see a dentist to have their canine incisors filed to points. We're talking about big bads who prefer an all-liquid diet that just happens to be your blood. Creatures that literally can't get a natural tan, where a heart attack means a stake in that body organ, and believe me when I tell you that garlic does not do a thing to them except give them bad breath. I should have talked you out of it when Leticia first approached you about designing her site and then started referring new clients to you, but you enjoyed doing something different and they all liked your designs. And their websites were a whole new challenge for you."

"Okay, I get the point. I have to keep in mind they're for real and not role-playing creatures of the night. Which, I confess, I have been doing maybe because it was easier than admitting they actually existed." Krebs looked a little green around the gills. "But why couldn't you tell me what he really was? I've never told anyone about Leticia and her crowd. Did you think I'd tell the world I saw a real living vampire?"

"Nick isn't exactly living," Jazz gently pointed out. "I know you can keep secrets. It's just that I didn't want you pulled into something you don't need to be a part of. Something that is dangerous and nasty and … sick," she whispered. "What you read about in books and see in the movies isn't even close to their reality."

"Okay, now you're scaring me. If it's that bad then even you shouldn't be involved. Did that Nick get you messed up in something that has to do with his world?" he demanded. "I know I couldn't see whatever nasty magick stuff was on the car yesterday that upset you so much, nor can I see that ghost you told me is in there, but you have taught me enough over the past few years that I can figure out that whatever happened was not good. And if it's that bad, then you need to worry about yourself, not bother about them."

She raked her fingers through her hair. "You are right, Krebs. It wasn't good. The absolute worst slasher movie would be a picnic compared to what is going on." Jazz finished her coffee and cookies and got up to refill her mug and top off Krebs' mug. "That's why I need to find a way to make sure what happened yesterday never happens again, to me or to anyone else."

"Give me a break here. Tell me everything that's going on," Krebs pleaded, grabbing hold of her hand again. "You know I can keep a secret," he said, once he caught her expression. "It's not that I'm worried for myself. Well, I am when you talk about all these vampires and nasty stuff going on," he admitted with a sheepish grin, "but I'm also worried about you. I've never seen you this stressed. I can't remember ever seeing you actually frightened, but…."

"But this is a hell of a lot more than I have dealt with in the past." She stood behind him and bent down, looping her arms around his neck. She dropped a kiss on the top of his head. "You are a wonderful friend and I love you dearly, but right about now I would be so much happier if you were far away from here in case something happens. Say… Siberia. And I understand Antarctica is nice this time of year. Aren't there penguins there? You love watching *March of the Penguins* and *Happy Feet*."

"Jeez, Jazz, why not send me to the North Pole to meet up with Santa Claus?" He still looked a little green around the gills. "Look, I know you are not one of those witches that dance naked by the light of the moon—damn—and that you are obviously someone who holds a lot of power li'l ole unmagick me couldn't begin to understand." He reached back and took one of her hands that rested on his shoulder. "And while I don't know what's going on, I would say you are going up against the Big Bad in capital letters, so I am here for you, kid. Sometimes we mortal humans can come in handy."

It took Jazz a moment to realize the dampness on her cheeks came from tears.

He stood up and turned around, flashing her a crooked smile. For a brief moment, she imagined she saw a hint of Nick's nature in Krebs's warm gaze.

"You have to promise me, Jazz. Promise me that if there is anything I can do, you will let me do it." He made sure she met his gaze.

She stepped in for a hug. "I promise if it's something within your power, I will ask for your help." This was a vow she knew she could easily keep. There was no way poor mortal Krebs could help her defeat a monster such as Clive Reeves.

"So what can I do?" Krebs asked, flexing his fingers.

"Right now, I'm heading out to see if I can get some information to help Nick with his investigation." She rooted around for a travel mug and filled it with coffee.

"I can't believe that with the eight computers I have upstairs, not to mention the laptop I set up specifically for your needs that you feel you need to go out to get information?" He looked amused. "Jazz, anything you need to know can be found on the internet. Unless you need to talk to someone in the flesh." He paused. "The person you're planning on seeing is made of flesh and blood, right?"

Jazz laughed. "I have often wondered about that. Trust me, if I could do it here I would. But what I need to find out can't be found on the Information Highway," she said dryly. "The person in charge of the place I'm going to considers himself above computers." She was so not looking forward to the trip ahead of her. She started out the door, and then paused as something occurred to her. It would have been easy to forget it had come to mind. *Except you made a promise and you cannot break it.* She

mentally damned the little gargoyle inside her head
and she kept on going out the door. While she had
thought of a way Krebs' computer skills could come
in handy, she did not want him looking for any information on Clive Reeves unless she was around. She
had long ago set wards on all his computers, but she
knew it was too easy for something to go wrong,
especially with Reeves displaying powers they
hadn't expected. And she would hate herself if something happened to Krebs and she wasn't there to
prevent it.

"What's wrong?"

She shook her head. "Just one of those random
thoughts. I'll see you later." She left before that
voice piped up again.

∞

"That alcoholic establishment is luxury compared
to this ghastly place," Irma said, staring at the two
storefronts Jazz parked in front of. "You never take me
anywhere nice as it is, but this is downright deplorable.
Why on earth would you come to such a disgusting
place?" She peered narrowly at Jazz. "I can't believe
this has to do with Nicky. Is this one of those vampire
sex parlors in disguise? You don't think I know about
these things, but those little men at the car service talk
about these places all the time. All those perverted
creatures think about is sex." She absently stroked her
purse strap, fingers tightening on it as if she feared
someone would run past and snatch it up.

"It sounds like they're not the only ones with sex
on the brain since you tend to bring the subject up

a lot." Jazz cast the illusion spell for the car and stepped up onto the cracked sidewalk. The two single-story buildings in front of her were not the least bit encouraging. An adult bookstore stood on her right, a boutique that catered to drag queens on the left. Even worse was the dark very nasty-looking alley right down the middle. A mournful whistle from a freight train in the distance enhanced the ambiance of life passing by. When she asked to be guided to The Library, she hadn't expected to end up here.

"Most libraries are designed as nice clean modern buildings or even beautiful historical buildings," she murmured. Old and moldy as time or not, The Library didn't have to bring her to a place that looked every bit as aged, ancient, and unsavory as some of the knowledge it housed.

"Why can't we go to that nice library near the house?" Irma asked. "There's a lovely park next to it where I can watch the children on the playground if you park me under that lovely oak tree. Too much sun isn't good for my skin."

"That library won't have what I need." She heaved a sigh and lifted her right hand, palm out. The moonstone in her ring glowed softly as she sent her power outward, seeking.

"I humbly request entrance to the realm that will offer me guidance I can find nowhere else," she said in a formal voice. She hated the formality required in some aspects of her magick, but when dealing with ones who had been around for thousands of years and believed in proper etiquette, she knew it was vital she behave with appropriate witchy decorum or she'd never be allowed entrance.

When she left the house she asked for the location to The Library and was directed here. Now she had to wait to be guided to the door. She had no idea her choices would end up to be between an adult bookstore and a drag queen boutique.

A tiny bubble of golden light bobbed up in front of her.

"Is that Tinkerbell?" Irma leaned over the car door and stared at the light.

"Not even close. I'll be back."

"What if some depraved individual comes by?" She looked around. "You know, if I had a pet, he could protect me while you're gone."

"You just want to be the only ghost on the block with a guard dog. If someone comes by just flash him your ethereal charms." Jazz watched the light move toward the alley. "I should have known the entrance wouldn't be something sleazy like the adult bookstore when it could be put somewhere even more repulsive." She wrinkled her nose as she passed an overflowing Dumpster that smelled as if it hadn't been emptied in years. The tiny bubble of illumination stopped at the end of the dark alley, blinked three times, and then disappeared.

"They just can't make it easy." She stared at the concrete wall spray-painted with pictures of imaginative sexual positions she couldn't imagine doing if she was double or even triple jointed. "I seek The Library," she said in a loud voice.

The air in front of her shimmered until the concrete wall disappeared and a massive, ornately carved wooden door took its place. She wrapped her fingers around the large bronze griffin-shaped doorknocker and rapped it three times against the door.

The griffin opened its eyes and peered closely at Jazz while its beak widened in a yawn. "What is your purpose here, witchling?"

"I require counsel I can find only here. I ask to be allowed to enter." She wished she could just turn the knob and go in, but the guardian of The Library's door had its own rules. No playing along, no entrance.

The griffin's beak opened in a broad yawn. "Password?"

"Hermione got better grades than Harry."

The griffin squawked. "One day, young witch, your impertinence will be your undoing."

"Maybe, but not today." She waited for the metallic click and then pushed open the door that slowly swung open with the creak of ancient wood and hardware. She stepped across the doorway aware she'd also stepped into a different realm known to no human.

Jazz stood still as the door closed behind her, leaving her in a dim hallway smelling of ages-old dust, leather, paper, and materials that fairly screamed the magick embedded in them. As she ventured into the dim vestibule, torches adorning the wall burst into flame, lighting her way until she reached the end of a passage that expanded into a room that seemed to go on for miles. Rows of intricately carved shelves held ancient grimoires, books, scrolls, and parchments. Rumor had it that a portion of Alexander's library was back among the stacks, but she had never found it.

She knew she didn't imagine she smelled magick in the air. It was well and truly there. Just standing there she felt as powerful as the highest-placed witch. Not that she'd ever say the words out loud. It was a good way for her banishment to never end.

"What do you seek, young witch?"

She looked to her right, finding a man seated on a stool pushed up to a waist-high counter. He wore old-fashioned knee britches in bottle green, a faded waistcoat over a linen shirt the color of old parchment and a bottle green long tailed coat. Ancient scrolls, leather bound books, and what even looked like a few stone tablets were carefully arranged on the counter near his spot of power.

Narrowed black eyes peered at her over the rim of ancient half-spectacles perched on his beaklike nose. His thinning brown hair looked just as it had the first time she entered The Library with her class more than seven hundred years ago, when he had lectured them in the proper use of the facilities. A lot more "don'ts" were uttered than "do's." Even though today she had dressed appropriately in a black calf-length skirt and a roll-neck sweater with a silver belt for accent and black boots, he still looked at her as if she had shown up in a micro-bikini. His rules in The Library were as prissy as he looked.

"The Librarian," she said, knowing if she didn't address him properly and with the correct tone of respect, he would ban her from The Library as he had before. She had been barred from the premises for eighty years before he even deigned to hear her apology. To say she had issues with the prissy wizard was an understatement.

His narrow lips pursed as if he had just sucked a lemon. She wouldn't put it past him to eat the tart fruit as a treat.

"The Librarian," he corrected her, pronouncing the first word with a long "e."

"*Thee* Librarian," she repeated. *Why couldn't all of this be available online?*

He sniffed. "Proper reference material must be read in its original form." He smiled, pleased he'd startled her with his admission that he'd read her thoughts. "What do you wish to find here?"

Oh yeah, not going to be easy at all.

"I require information on astral projection when it is combined with other forms of magick meant to foul an object."

He sniffed. "That is nothing new. Look over there." He gestured to his right with a plumed pen and returned to his task, effectively dismissing her from his mind and his presence.

Jazz shook her head. "Excuse me, The Librarian, but what I seek would be found in a section we were taught not to speak of lightly." She hated having to ask for formal permission, but she knew it was the only way she could cross the portal leading to the room holding the works that had to do with baneful magick.

The Librarian looked up and peered at her over the top of his half-spectacles before he straightened up and returned to the yellowed sheet of parchment before him. "You are not seasoned enough to enter that room. Ask me again in one thousand years. As long as you return any borrowed material in a timely manner, that is."

She swallowed the argument that threatened to erupt. She had known it was going to be rough. She simply hadn't expected it to be this bad. The man just plain didn't like her! Yes, it was a bit late, okay, ten years late, but for Fate's sake, she had returned the scroll eventually. She'd signed out *Fifty Ways to Hex Your Lover* with the intention of using every one of the hexes on Nick. She had even paid the grossly inflated overdue charges without one word of complaint! What more could the strait-laced fossil want? Not that she was about to ask. To this day she was convinced he deliberately inflated the late fee as punishment. She kept her voice level. "Please, The Librarian, I humbly ask your permission to enter the room holding Baneful Magick, because I am positive what I need is in that section." She so hated doing the Miss Manners shtick, but The Librarian could give the diva of proper behavior lessons.

He looked up and stared at her with a piercing gaze. "Why would you think that what you require could be found in the room holding baneful magick? A room that is dangerous to many and only kept intact because the material must be protected from those who would use it for wrongdoing. If I had my way, it would have been obliterated centuries ago."

Jazz resisted rolling her eyes. Where had this man been for the last thousand years? Like wizard guards would have stopped any wrongdoing when people were so inventive. The old wizard needed broadband down here big time.

"A man who supposedly died seventy-five years ago used astral projection along with baneful magick to try to frighten me."

His smile held absolutely no humor. "I did not think you frightened easily, young witch."

She took that as a compliment although she wasn't sure he meant it that way. "Normally, nothing can scare me, but right now I'm facing something I've never dealt with before, and yes, he terrifies the wits out of me. This creep is using dark magick to destroy vampires in a manner that is cruel and wrong for any preternatural being. I need to find a way to stop him."

"That sounds more like someone performing a good deed to me," he said. "The fewer vampires in our world the better." He sniffed and returned to his work.

"But it won't end there, will it?" Jazz fired back. "And once he is through destroying vampires it would be natural for him to feel empowered to move on to others. That's usually what psychotic villains who want to rule the universe tend to do." She stared hard at him with a mental, *Get my meaning?*

Jazz felt the pinpricks of magick swirl around her as The Librarian—with a long *e*—gauged the level of her sincerity. Over the centuries many a student wizard and witch had tried to gain entrance to the room on a dare. There was nothing more appealing, and at the same time daunting, than entering a forbidden area. And a room holding unlimited knowledge of baneful magick was about as illicit as you could get. Punishment for such a deed was not pleasant. The few who managed to cross that threshold without permission never spoke of what they saw and found there. Even the portal leading to that room was not for the faint of heart.

The Librarian snapped his fingers. A high-pitched sound echoed off the ceiling as a dark brown winged creature headed for Jazz. She flinched but stood her ground. She really hated bats! If that thing attacked her hair she was outta there.

"Felix, show the young witch to Section 22F," he instructed. "Be sure she remains on the correct path."

"I can find it on my own if you'll give me directions or draw a map," Jazz said.

"That is unacceptable. Felix will guide you and remain at the portal until you are finished with your research, so that you will have a safe return. Otherwise, it would be impossible for you to find your way back to our realm," he said with a cold smile.

"*Our* realm? I know The Library is housed in a different realm than the mortal world, but are you saying the portal to the Baneful Magick room is in yet another realm?" She so did not like hearing this! Why couldn't she be looking for books on rare herbs or talismans? Those sections had nice plump-cushioned couches, big easy chairs, and excellent reading light. Not to mention she heard rumors cappuccino machines had been put in some of the reading rooms. What she wouldn't give for a high dose of caffeine right now.

He heaved a long-suffering sigh. "Do you not recall anything from your Academy instruction on using The Library? Every section is housed in a different realm. The portal leading to the room holding baneful magick is not only the oldest portal but also the most difficult to find, and with good reason. After all, we cannot have just anyone stumbling upon it, can we? There could be serious repercussions if a young witchling or wizard wandered in there, which is why I must take so many precautions." He picked up his plumed pen. "I suggest you follow Felix quickly. You have one hour to find what you require." He picked up the two-foot-high green marble hourglass that suddenly appeared on the edge of his desk and turned it over. The sand immediately started flowing downward in an off-white stream.

Her jaw dropped. "*One hour?* There is no way I can find what I need in an hour. I'll be lucky if it doesn't take me all day."

The Librarian glanced at the hourglass and at the sand drifting downward. He lifted a brow. "Fifty-nine minutes and counting."

"You could turn it over and it would start fresh," Jazz suggested.

He peered at her over the tops of his spectacles with a look that implied she should have remained silent. He tapped the glass. For a moment, it looked as if the sand flowed even faster.

Jazz muttered under her breath as she took off after the bat that flew off. She slowed down once to glance through one portal. A young woman wearing a medieval-style gown sat at a plain wooden table.

She looked up from the ancient book of spells she was studying and noted Jazz's modern clothing before presenting her with a smile.

Jazz had forgotten that time had no meaning in The Library. It was just as easy to run into someone from the sixteenth century as it was to see someone from the twenty-third. The bat's screech brought her back to the present.

"You know, in some places deep fried bat wings are considered a delicacy," she muttered, knowing the bat's delicate hearing would catch the jibe. She grinned slightly when the responding sound from the creature resembled a sneer. It flew a short distance ahead of her, leading the way.

She felt a distinct damp chill in the air as they walked deeper into the bowels of The Library. She wished she'd worn a jacket since her sweater was proving not to be warm enough in the dank air. She crossed her arms in front of her chest in an effort to keep warm.

"Central heat would be nice," she muttered, glancing here and there at portals displaying ancient bound books and scrolls. Some housed witches or wizards perusing the contents. Others were empty but the hum of magick was strong and every so often she noticed glowing red or orange eyes peeking out of portals bathed in darkness. She didn't want to think what type of creatures might inhabit those areas.

She didn't need the bat to hover about her head, its leathery wings slowing, to tell her they'd arrived at their destination. All she had to do was look ahead at the towering shiny black volcanic-rock entrance with its silvery-black spider web criss-crossing the entrance. She raised her head to stare at the upper left hand corner. The spider, with a bloated belly— no wonder there didn't appear to be any bugs around—seemed to be repairing a tear in the web. Its head swiveled around and peered at her through blood-red eyes as if gauging what kind of meal she'd make. She resisted using a spot of witchflame on it. While she hated spiders with a passion, she also valued her ass and she knew if she turned the portal's spider guardian into a fireball, The Librarian would do the same to her. She was also pretty sure he wouldn't be banished for it either.

Felix hovered in the air, its wings flapping slowly as it directed a high-pitched squeak towards the portal. The cobweb parted in the center and the filmy barrier lifted like a theater curtain, except there was no popcorn, Diet Coke, or even a movie screen waiting for her.

"Maybe I should have let Nick come with me after all." She drew in a bracing breath and stepped across the rocky threshold, feeling a brief sense of disorientation as she crossed into another realm. Her nose wrinkled at the strong scent that enveloped her and burned her throat. Sulfur definitely didn't mix well with her perfume. She doubted it would blend with any scent known to man, including *eau de* skunk. "Oh, gross! A truckload of room deodorizers would be useful here. Whoever said sulfur smelled like rotten eggs was seriously wrong. It's way worse than that." She pressed the back of her hand against her nose. The urge to breathe through her mouth was strong, but the knowledge she would then taste what she smelled kept her mouth firmly closed. Memories of old London, where all sorts of refuse, and worse, littered the dirt roads also helped her take in shallow breaths.

The lighting in the chamber was poor with pitch-covered torches stuck in the walls at random intervals. The cavelike structure appeared endless, with not even a broken-down couch or chair in sight, much less a three-legged stool for the casual visitor to perch on.

"No wonder there's only an hour time limit. That's all anyone could stand to be in here before they pass out from the fumes," she murmured to herself. "And I thought Foulshadow was bad." She cringed at the faint sound of something, or maybe somethings, if whatever it was didn't have many legs, skittering off in the far shadows. Jazz wasn't a total girl when it came to creepy-crawlies, but some sported venom-filled pincers and fangs, so she knew when to be careful and wear heavy boots. She studied the area waiting to make sure the creatures were heading *away* from her instead of *toward* her.

Instead of shelves holding the contents, the stone walls revealed carved-out sections that reminded her of the catacombs in Paris, but instead of human bones, carefully stacked books, parchments, and scrolls were arranged according to size in the hollows. She feared the faint tendrils of smoke drifting up from some of the books had nothing to do with the chance of fire and more to do with the contents of the books themselves. She hoped she wouldn't need to look through any of them.

She stopped at a tall barrel standing by the portal and pulled out a pair of protective gloves that glimmered with a layer of defensive magick. She knew many forms of baneful, or dark, magick could be absorbed through the skin, and she wasn't taking any chances of being infected. She didn't want to discover what The Librarian's methods of decontamination would be.

Jazz hadn't been in the room long before she felt the same overpowering emotions she had experienced when Reeves magickally violated Irma and the car. That identical suffocating sensation seemed to ooze its way over her skin like thick oil. She ignored the feeling as she moved through the seemingly endless room pausing here and there to study titles written or stamped on ancient leather tomes and skimmed scrolls that automatically translated themselves from their original languages to give her a hint of their contents.

"There is no way I'm going to be able to find what I need in an hour," she muttered, experiencing frustration before she'd barely begun her quest. "Even spending a year in here wouldn't be long enough." She spun in a tight circle, allowing her senses to roam freely. She knew it was risky because even the air reeked of something so dark and forbidding that she knew she had to be careful not to get sucked into whatever ruled the room and its contents. So much power hovered here that it would be easy to allow it to overtake her. But she felt she had no choice if she was to discover what she needed. "I ask for assistance. I ask that my questions be answered. Show me what can touch the non-living without fear of reprisal. Show me what one might use to bring the non-living into the light of day without loss of existence," she asked out loud. Then she waited, hoping the answer was there. "I'll even take a hint," she said with a bit of desperation. "A direction to take! A map would be nice!"

A tiny pinpoint of light appeared in the distance. She took it as the first clue that her question had been answered.

The light didn't brighten the closer she got to it, but remained a soft steady glow that beckoned to her. She found nothing comforting about the light that hovered over a stone table. The very old stone table set against a wall with inscriptions in an ancient language engraved along the edge wasn't very reassuring either. A large brown-edged parchment sat atop its rough surface and she had a sick feeling deep in the pit of her stomach that the red ink forming the archaic words and symbols on the parchment wasn't fashioned from a form of colored water. Even with the protective gloves covering her hands it took all of her courage to reach out to the parchment.

"Please let this be really old animal skin or some sort of handmade paper," she murmured, gingerly touching the edges.

The papyrus felt like a living thing under her fingertips. Even through the gloves she felt sullied by the feel, as the letters moved with her touch. Now she truly understood why The Librarian limited her time here. She was convinced if she spent even one minute longer than her allotted hour, she would run screaming from the room. She was almost ready to do that now. Jazz was not known as a coward. But she did have a strong sense of self-preservation. This place dictated she keep that sense as powerful as possible.

"He who feeds on the life force of those who walk in the shadows shall take their strength for his own by taking what keeps them alive," she read out loud. "He who steals the life force of shadow walkers shall require more sustenance as moons pass by. He will rule those he has conquered until the night a shadow sends him to the land of eternal oblivion." She stepped back, resisting the urge to wipe her hands on her skirt. She hoped the icky residue she imagined coated her gloves wouldn't find a way to leave with her.

As she stared down at the letters and symbols on the aged parchment, they took on a life of their own, creating pictures that were repellent, that portrayed creatures and things of a darker nature. Even worse, it felt as if what she saw tried to burrow its way inside her head. For a moment, she wasn't sure if the scream came from her mind or her lips.

An ear-splitting screech abruptly pulled her back to the present. The sound appeared to come from far away and sounded anxious. She started to take a cleansing breath to center herself when the tainted air reminded her it wasn't a good place for deep breathing exercises.

"I haven't found enough," she called out, even though she was more than ready to leave the dark place that enfolded her like a noxious cloak. Judging by the squeaks that increased in volume, Felix wasn't about to argue with her. The picture of the sand running out in the hourglass appeared in her mind. "I told him an hour wasn't enough time!" She was positive if she could further explore the parchment she could find what she needed. And it wasn't as if she was going to sneak it out of there. Knowing The Librarian, there were safeguards everywhere to ensure that didn't happen, plus she couldn't imagine taking anything from this room. But she still felt she needed more time, but she felt so repelled by what she'd seen and found so far, she equally knew she needed to escape this place before it consumed her.

Just before the bat's screeches grew shrill enough to cause her ears to bleed, Jazz felt a shifting in the room as the stone floor abruptly rolled under her feet. The parchment in front of her unexpectedly rolled up and flew back to the crypt it had come from. At the same time, the air grew so close she found it difficult to breathe.

As if that wasn't enough to scare her, she looked toward the portal and saw the cobweb begin to lower slowly to the ground. She just knew if she didn't get to the opening in time she would be trapped here forever. Definitely not a good option for a witch who liked wide-open spaces that offered lots of light and no nasty magick.

"Okay, I get the point! Time's up. Time to leave before I become a permanent addition to the collection." She quickly made her way back to the descending cobweb and barely made her way outside before the web dropped fully to the ground. The spider in the top corner scuttled to the other side and hung there, munching on its latest victim.

It took Jazz a moment to realize that the floor no longer buckled under her feet and the air was now scented with pleasant smelling herbs instead of the reek of sulfur. She took several deep breaths, banishing the nasty smell from her olfactory memory.

She swatted at Felix as he swooped close to her head, almost tangling his claws in her hair. "You touch the hair and I'm feeding you to my slippers," she snarled, picking up the pace. Now that she was away from the room that held so much darkness she was more than ready to get out of there.

She considered it a shame that leaving the building meant she would have to pass by The Librarian, with a long "e." She even went so far as to look for any exit doors on her way back, but no such luck.

As she headed for the main door, she slowed down near a section separated into reading rooms. A group of ten young girls wearing pale blue robes sat in a half circle around an older woman reading a Greek legend to them.

Memories of afternoons spent in The Library hearing old tales had been something she'd stored away for some time. For many years when she was young and afraid she would never be allowed to return, it was easier to forget the pleasant times spent at the Academy. She had wondered how she would survive. But today, seeing the young girls so like her classmates of old brought the memories back and she smiled at the recollections. She thought of the closeness they all had shared back then, that they still shared seven hundred years later.

"Your time is up, young witch," The Librarian's reedy voice echoed in the chamber just as she crossed the threshold to the reception area.

He sat on his stool, the faint sounds of his plumed pen scratching across the surface the only sound that broke the silence in the high-ceilinged room. As she entered the area, the last grain of sand left the top globe of the hourglass and drifted downward. As the last grain topped the bottom pile, the hourglass winked out of sight.

"Did you discover what you wished to find among the crypts of dark magick?" he asked, without looking up from his task.

"All I unearthed were more questions," she sighed. She didn't mention the word pictures that frankly freaked her out. She was convinced that talking about them would only make them real. As it was, she would have enough nightmares from what she saw to last her years.

He barely glanced at her. "You might wish to discard the protective gloves. They are not allowed to leave The Library."

Jazz wrinkled her nose. The last thing she wanted to do was touch them.

The Librarian sighed. "Off," he instructed.

Just like that, the gloves disappeared from her hands.

"Thank you." Jazz headed for the vestibule and the large double doors that would allow her to escape.

"You must remember something, young witch." The Librarian's words followed her. "Each question has an answer, but you may not be the one who is meant to provide that answer."

She spun around. "I don't need riddles. I need solutions. I want to know how to make sure no more innocent vampires disappear."

"Vampires are not innocent," he sniffed with the arrogant disdain only a civil servant wizard could portray. "They are vile creatures that prey on the weak."

"And someone who targets vampires can easily target witches and wizards next," she deliberately talked over him even if it was the highest form of disrespect. Judging by the way his face tightened, the barb hit home, which had her wishing she could click her heels and wish herself home … right now.

"Then perhaps the answer you require is not found here."

"From the time I entered the Witches' Academy I was told any magickal answer I required would be found here," she argued, losing her sense … once again. "You, of all people, know I can't go anywhere else."

His mouth stretched in his version of a cold smile. "Then perhaps what you need is not here."

Jazz silently counted to ten, and then counted to ten in Gaelic and again in Italian, French, and Russian. It helped.

"Then where am I to go? Tell me that," she demanded, even as the gargoyle in her mind yelled *never good to piss off The Librarian!*

"Consider yourself lucky, young witch, that you are still allowed to come here. The Library is for those who follow our tenets. It is only due to the compassion of others that you who were banished are still permitted to use the facilities." He waved his plumed pen like a royal scepter.

Jazz knew the smarmy despot spoke the truth, but if he chose to bar her and her witch sisters entrance, she also knew he had the power to do so. A wizard working in civil service was about as power hungry as you could get.

All she could do was take what she read and saw and hope it would be enough.

"Thank you for your time, The Librarian," she said, not caring if she mocked him. She'd spent the last hour in a dank-smelling chamber where Tyge Foulshadow would have felt right at home. Now all she wanted to do was go home and take a long hot shower with lots of soap and a plethora of cleansing spells.

The door opened with creaks and groans and Jazz exited as quickly as she could.

"Goodbye," the griffin doorknocker called after her. "Come again."

The door winked out of sight and she was left alone in the dark filthy alley that resembled a tunnel out of her nightmares.

"I can't believe you left me here all day!" Irma groused the moment Jazz exited the alley and crossed the sidewalk. "You would not believe the things I've seen. And here I thought those little men at the car service were perverts. Someone actually urinated against one of the tires! Although I'm sure I wouldn't want to use a restroom in either of these establishments. Lord knows if they've ever been properly cleaned. I believed in keeping a bathroom fresh and clean at all times. Harold complained using that much pine air freshener was too much, but I wanted anyone who entered my bathroom to know it had been properly cleaned." Jazz wrinkled her nose against the pungent aroma coming off the front tire. "If you had a dog like you've been bugging me for, *all* my tires would have been marked. " She made a mental note to stop at the car wash on the way home. Then she planned on a shower and change of clothes before she headed to the boardwalk ... and Nick. She really hated puzzles and hoped he was better at solving the riddles she'd found than she was.

Thirteen

Once home, Jazz was relieved to find she had the house to herself. She was still feeling pretty freaked about her time spent in The Library's Baneful Magick section and the last thing she wanted was to have Krebs ask her questions about where she'd been. It wouldn't have been difficult for him to sense her unease and immediately demand an explanation. It wasn't something she could easily explain to him anyway. At least with Nick she could say as little as possible and he'd understand, while she'd have to drag out flash cards and alphabet blocks for Krebs. It seemed her roomie was being drawn into her life more and more whether she thought it was a good idea or not.

She undressed and took the time to center herself with meditation. She needed to rid herself of the sense of wrong she'd felt inside the room that had been infected with so much darkness.

After she felt more like herself she settled in for a relaxing bath, choosing a body wash that left the bathroom, and her, smelling like lemon, following it with body cream in the same fragrance topped with matching cologne.

"Lemon-fresh witch," she proclaimed, keeping with her theme by pulling on a creamy yellow cotton long sleeved hoodie, a pair of faded jeans that clung lovingly to her long legs and yellow flip-flops with a whimsical daisy pattern across the leather bands. To add to the illusion of a girl out to enjoy an evening on her own, she brushed her hair back and up in a perky ponytail decorated with a yellow scrunchie. She studied her reflection in the mirror as she applied coral lip-gloss. "I am so damn cute, it's downright scary."

This time, she left the car, and Irma, home while she walked the few blocks to the boardwalk. So far, she'd managed to avoid coming to Nick's office by using every excuse known to witch. But her excuses were long gone, plus she had promised to come to his office after she left The Library. She still wasn't looking forward to talking about her time spent at The Library, but she didn't want to put it off either. Even now, when she needed to see him and discuss her findings, she still took her time by stopping for a large Diet Coke and a powdered sugar-dusted funnel cake that called out to her. She even considered picking up some cotton candy, except she couldn't figure out how to carry that too. At times like this she wished for Dweezil's third hand.

She hadn't been inside the building housing Nick's office before, but once inside the 1920s style building with its ornate cage-style elevator at one end of the narrow hallway and the shiny black wrought iron railing decorating the stairs at the other end, she knew it suited his love of history.

She checked the directory on the wall near the main door and headed for the nearby elevator.

She was now in his territory.

Unlike the other time, Nick sensed Jazz's presence the moment she stepped onto the boardwalk. He leaned back in his battered leather chair, legs stretched out on top of his desk, ankles crossed. And waited.

He smiled when a slender shadow appeared on the other side of the frosted glass.

"Damn it, Nick! Open the door!"

He resisted the urge to use his mind to open the door and chose the conventional way. He uncoiled his length from the chair and moved toward the door.

"I live to serve, milady." He pulled open the door and stepped back.

Jazz walked in looking like the sunshine he had only seen on television, her hands filled with food and drink. The ends of her hair were still damp as if she'd just showered.

She turned in a tight circle, probably mapping every inch of the office.

"And here I thought the Protectorate paid their people well. What? No 401k or IRA to help set you up something more elaborate?" She set her drink and a plate holding a half-eaten funnel cake on his desk. "No offense, but this place is sort of a dump, in a 1940s gumshoe movie sort of way."

"None taken. I do well enough. I bought the building for the good-sized Civil Defense Shelter under the building that makes for a comfortable apartment." He gestured toward the guest chair. "How was your time spent at The Library?"

"*Augh!*" She flopped in the chair. "The Librarian hasn't changed in the last eighty years. He is still a pompous ass." She took a swig from her Diet Coke and pinched off a piece of her funnel cake scattering powdered sugar everywhere. She delicately licked the powdered sugar from each finger.

He returned to his chair. The lemon scent of her skin tempted him to find out if she tasted as tart as she smelled. He sensed now was not the time to find out.

"So were you able to learn anything in that all-hallowed witches' fount of information?" He regretted his sarcasm when he saw the change in her expression. If his heart still pumped blood he would have said it ran cold. What in Hades' name happened in that place?

Jazz's easy-going smile dimmed. "Just be glad you've never gone to The Library. Dealing with The Librarian is bad enough. But the section holding the dark magick material is, well," she took a deep breath, "dark is an understatement. And it's smothering even though the portal seems to go on forever with no end in sight. What I found in there were books, scrolls, and parchments with contents I don't even want to think about. And objects I am sure would give pretty much anyone nightmares. These past centuries have shown me forms of evil that tears at the soul, but what's housed in that room goes far beyond anything we could imagine. The portal to the room is protected by a big bad spider that would probably consider a dragon nothing more than a light mid-morning snack."

He noticed she did not pull away when he walked over and wrapped his arms around her. The chill in her skin didn't come from the air around them. He lamented he had no body heat to share with her. No way to warm her. All he could do was offer her what little comfort his nearness would afford her.

"Legend has it that deep within the mountains of Carpathia is an endless cave that holds all the true secrets of vampires," he murmured. "There you can find stories of the first vampire and how he came to be, how he came to find out what sustained his life and what could endanger him. Part of the legend is that inside the cave is a vial holding that which can give a vampire a true immortal existence, where the sun would not turn him to flame nor would a stake to the heart end his life. Those are only a very few of the secrets housed there that are known to no one but the Protectorate."

"Oh sure, they would like to claim the first vampire was a man," she mumbled against his shirtfront. "Easy to do when there's probably no one around from that long ago who would tell them that there was a good chance a woman was the first bloodsucker."

Nick smiled. His Jazz was back.

"Come." He stepped back and took her hand, pulling her toward the window.

"You do realize you have a perfectly good door, don't you?" She hung back.

"Yes, but it's faster this way." He opened the window and climbed out onto the iron fire escape and reached up to pull down the ladder that led to the roof. While he could easily scale the side of the building, he knew Jazz would require a more conventional method.

Seeing his intent, she looked over her shoulder and wiggled her fingers at her Diet Coke and funnel cake. The two disappeared from their spot on the desk.

When she was heading to a rooftop, Jazz usually didn't like climbing eighty-year-old ladders that looked as if they'd disintegrate at the slightest touch. Except she didn't need to worry about looking down when she could look up to the spectacular view of Nick's tight butt as he climbed ahead of her. Jeans were clearly designed with him in mind.

The roof had been converted to a patio with two chairs and a small table, now holding her Diet Coke and funnel cake. In one corner, a garden lent a patchwork floral effect and another corner was covered with a large rubber mat where she imagined a stripped-to-the waist Nick practiced his martial arts in the evening.

Nick's refuge.

She walked over to the edge of the roof and looked out over the boardwalk. The tinny sounds of the carousel's calliope mixed with the voices of teenagers waiting in line at the Ferris wheel and the rollercoaster. Carnies along the Midway invited visitors to try their luck and she could see the snack booths doing a brisk business. Further out, a few fishermen lined up along the pier casting out their lines in hopes of catching more than a shoe. The chilly sea air rushed through her, lifting her hair up, giving the still-damp strands a life of their own, and adding color to her cheeks.

"So much life out there," she murmured. "An innocence that has no idea what really goes on in a part of the world they don't know exists. I hope they never find out."

Nick stood just behind her. "Some will remain oblivious, others will discover the truth. The same way it's been going on for centuries."

She turned around.

He brushed his thumb across the curve of her cheek. "Amazing. What in Fate's name did you find at The Library that left you this philosophical?"

She pulled in a deep breath. "Riddles."

"Riddles are not answers. Only more questions."

Jazz nodded. "People think practicing the Dark Arts is easy, but it requires a lot of work, a lot of cunning, and the knowledge their lives will never be the same again. The rewards are short-lived since the price is too high for many, but of course, they don't know that until it's too late. What I found said *'He who feeds on the life force of those who walk the shadows will gain their strength. He who takes the life force of shadow walkers and keeps it as his own will require more food as moons pass by. He will rule those he has conquered until the night one of the shadows sends him to the land of eternal void.'* Then my sixty minutes was up, the parchment shot itself back to its crypt and I made sure I got out of there before I was trapped with a very large man-eating, well, I don't know the man-eating part for a fact, but it was big enough to be one, spider."

"Takes the life force," Nick murmured to himself. "Blood. He is taking our blood." His eyes briefly glowed red. "That can only mean he's taking our blood to sustain his own life."

"Then why does it state it will take a shadow to kill him? Don't you all go poof when you lose all your blood like you do if someone stakes you in the heart or cuts off your head?"

"Something I really don't like to think about since none of those options appeal to me," he said dryly. "Many think that taking a vampire's blood is a cure for disease and even more think it can extend their lives. That appears to be happening here."

"It does if the vampire bites the human first, almost drains them dry then urges the victim to drink from them." Jazz wrinkled her nose. "They wake up as night people on an eternal liquid diet. Personally, the idea of giving up chocolate and coffee for life is enough to keep me out of that non-lifestyle."

Nick shook his head as he searched his memory for whispers of stories told long ago, tales he would not have thought of until now. He would have to contact Flavius. As an Elder in the Protectorate he would know all the legends, fact and fiction. The Elders enjoyed stirring up old tales every decade or so because it kept the mortals from truly knowing what walked their streets after dark.

"We need to speak to Flavius." He felt her withdrawal the moment the words left his lips. "Don't give me that look. He might be able to make sense of the riddle where we can't. He's existed longer than both of us together."

"Really? Then I'm surprised they asked for my help," she said with a touch of snark.

"It doesn't hurt to ask."

"He's an Elder, Nick. He'll only take what I learned and pass it on to the Protectorate. He won't tell us a thing."

"And why shouldn't he do what is right? It's my kind in peril, not yours!" he shouted. "My kind who have vanished while yours have no fear of being hunted like animals and, for all we know, treated like nothing more than a food source."

Okay, now she was mad. "No *fear* of being hunted? What do you call the bloody Inquisition in 1233? How about Salem in 1692? While *your kind* hid in the shadows, *mine* were dragged out into the light, burned at the stake, pressed to death, stoned, tied to horses, and torn apart like a piece of meat!" She advanced on him, her fury a living thing. Thunder echoed overhead. "And along with my sisters were innocents unjustly accused just because they happened to be different. Is that a wart on your nose? *You must be a witch!*" She planted her palms against his chest and shoved. He fell back a step. "You take walks in the moonlight? *You must be a witch!* You have red hair. *You must be a witch!*" She started to push him again, but this time he grabbed her wrists and held them tightly. She struggled but was no match for his superior strength. "While vampires creep along the shadows, preying on whomever they wish, some-times erasing their victims' memories of the encounters. While vampires treat many innocents like a damn *food source*." Her words tasted bitter on the tongue.

"I have not crept in the shadows for over nine hundred years," he said tightly. "You want to compare horror stories? I can do that, too. So let's just agree that both of our kind have had it rough." He tightened his hold on her wrists. "We have survived, Jazz. That is what counts. We have made our way in the world as best we could."

She tipped her head back, inhaling the earthy scent she always associated with him. She looked up into his face that showed arrogance with a rare vulnerability peeking out.

"Why couldn't you stay out of my life?" Her cry carried centuries of memories, centuries of lovemaking, and centuries of pain. "I've made a good life here. I have everything I need." She did not move away as he once again wrapped his arms around her and his hand crept up to curve around the back of her neck, gently rubbing the exposed skin.

"I can't stay out of your life anymore than you can stay out of mine," he murmured close to her ear.

"We are bad for each other," she whispered.

"We are very good together," he corrected.

"For one night, maybe. You rock my world then next thing I know I'm pulled into whatever rogue vampire caper you're investigating, and I somehow end up in jail because you claim you're protecting me even if it sure doesn't sound like protection to me. Like that time I got thrown in a cell with that shapeshifter and almost ended up a full moon snack. There are times I've really hated you." Her anger had been replaced with sorrow for what had been, what she knew would happen if she allowed Nick fully back into her life, and what could happen if they did go up against Clive Reeves and lost the battle.

Even if she didn't have the gift of Second Sight she could see the time coming when the dying man she comforted would be Nick. Except, in the end, all she'd have would be a handful of dust and no chance to say what she truly felt.

She opened her mouth to tell him just that, but he made the first move.

His mouth covered hers pulling her breath from her lungs. Even if his skin couldn't generate heat, hers could and did. The surface of her skin warmed under his touch as her blood raced in her veins, giving him what he lacked.

"Don't say a word," he whispered into her mouth. "Just feel."

And feel she did. Jazz looped her arms around Nick's neck, aligning her body against his when he bent at the knees enough that she could feel the heaviness of his erection nestled in the cradle of her hips. She pushed back, wanting more—needing more. When he straightened up, keeping her in his arms, she lifted her legs and wrapped them around his hips.

No amount of chocolate could equal the taste that spelled Nick in big block letters.

He walked them over to the table and set her down on the top. She didn't bother to unwind her legs from his waist. Having him against her, feeling his desire for her was just too good.

"You are my sun. My warmth," he said against her lips, trailing his fingers along the waistband of her jeans then moving them upward under her hoodie. His fingertips traced her bright yellow bra's lace band then edged under it to trail across the curve of her breast before he pushed up the fabric and covered her breast with his palm. His skin was cool against hers but no less arousing. He pressed his palm over the plump flesh, feeling the increasing respiration. "Your heart beats fast for me, Griet of Ardglass," he murmured, finding her lips again, parting them with his tongue, sinking into her taste, the smell of her skin, the very essence that once foretold she was the woman for him.

For eons, witches and vampires fought each other. Their battles were conducted tastefully with no bloodshed. Never a truce was sought and it was understood among all that never the twain would meet.

Until the night Nikolai Gregorivich attended a party in Venice in the guise of a wealthy Slavic merchant while he investigated an Italian vampire's bloodthirsty reign. With the approval of the Protectorate he had executed the vampire, and then to his own surprise and hers, had swept a saucy copper-haired witch off her feet and into his bed.

Nick had never been a witch's lover before that night nor had he sought another after. He felt it was because Jazz always caused so much turmoil in his usually well-ordered existence that he couldn't imagine having all the ups and downs with someone else. Plus he felt that any other would be found seriously lacking.

He pulled her closer to him, smoothing his hands along her denim-covered thighs until he reached the juncture. She uttered a soft mewling sound as he ran his fingertip up the zipper until he reached the tab. He slowly lowered it, nudging his fingers inside to find silk fabric. He didn't need to see them to know her panties were the same bright yellow as her bra. His sun. His light.

"It is only the two of us here under the night sky." He ran his mouth along the exposed skin just above the hoodie's neckline, pushing her hair aside to kiss the delicate surface along her neck.

He used two fingers to push aside the silk and delve into her, finding her wet and welcoming. Her inner muscles contracted around him.

"It's been too long, Jazz," he whispered, finding the small nub and rubbing it between his thumb and forefinger.

She dug her nails into his shoulders as she lifted her butt off the table to keep the tension as tight as possible, but he felt no pain from the tiny wounds she inflicted. He tore the waistband tab open and lifted her up enough to push down her jeans. A flick of his fingers and the ribbons at her hips were loosened, revealing skin that was now flushed pink with arousal. He dipped his head, finding the small mole seemingly purposely placed just above the crisp red hairline.

"Mark of the witch," he murmured against her skin.

She jerked under his touch and cried out.

"Nick!" She pulled at his shoulders, drawing him back up to her. The moment his head lifted, she reached for his waistband, her nails tearing at the fly.

Not that he was complaining, since he needed her as much as she needed him.

He shoved down his jeans, grasped her hips and brought her onto him.

She cried out in pleasure as his cock stretched her. She wrapped her legs around his hips, arching up as he bore down.

Jazz vaguely heard Nick's rough voice mutter words in his native tongue. No translation was needed. She imagined she could read them inside her mind.

He filled her as no other man ever had, aroused her to the point where pain and pleasure mingled in a rush of heat. She tunneled her hands under his shirt, enjoying the feel of his smooth muscular skin. She felt his muscles ripple and tighten under her palms and his back bow as she lowered one hand to caress the dip in his spine. As she pressed down with her fingertips, she felt his body tighten.

It had been so long for them and she knew they were too close to hold back.

"Show me the moon," she whispered. "And I'll show you the sun."

Nick's thrusts increased their intensity with Jazz arching to meet them. She felt the ripples of her orgasm increase until they shot through her like lightning. As she looked up at the velvet black sky and screamed his name she knew she saw fireworks.

Yet she also felt the tickle of magick being worked around her. She could have sworn she felt eyes watching their intimate activity. She shivered at the thought and Nick misinterpreted her movement as a reaction to their unleashed passion. He swept her into his arms and all thoughts of a voyeur were banished from her mind as he kissed her into oblivion.

Fourteen

The night the lights went out in Georgia." Jazz's smile broadened in a face alight with post-coital bliss. "Look at us. We almost did it again." She rested her forehead against his chest. "Mmm, you don't expect me to move, do you? Because right now I'm not sure I can move a muscle even if this table is really cold on my ass."

"And such a lovely ass you have too." He rested his chin on top of her head, occasionally dropping a kiss in the coppery strands. "So you think that was our absolute best?"

She wiggled her bare butt against the table, smiling as his cock thickened and lengthened within her. There was certainly something about a vampire's recuperative powers that appealed to her love for multiple orgasms. She automatically tight-ened her inner muscles, pulsing around him and urging him for more. His growl of pleasure was all she needed to tighten them again.

When his mouth hovered over the vein in her neck, she automatically moved her face away.

"Why ruin a perfectly good moment? Fangs and witches don't mix, remember?" She buried her face against his shirtfront, inhaling the scent of his cologne mixed with his personal scent.

He settled for pressing a kiss along the sweet spot behind her ear. She shivered under his touch. "I don't know. We seem to mix quite well." He rotated his hips, finding another sweet spot that brought a gasp to her lips. He carefully bit down on her ear lobe, making sure not to break the skin. She moaned, lifting her hips to push back. He inhaled the scent of arousal skimming along her skin, her blood running hotly beneath the surface—and regretfully backed off before he was drawn more to her blood than to her body. Sharing of blood was a potent aphrodisiac between vampires but went the other way when one of the partners was a witch. He and Jazz had treaded that fine line for years and veering off wasn't an option. "I fit so well within you," he murmured, thrusting inside her slow and deep, wanting to savor her every countermovement.

He drove in deep and stilled, feeling her contract around him with a possessive grip.

He leaned back just enough to see her face. A peachy flush lit up her skin leaving her moss green eyes round and luminous with desire. She panted lightly as she looked up at him.

"Don't stop now," she purred, reaching down, her delicate hand cupping his sacs and squeezing oh so gently but with enough pressure to make him hiss. He didn't need any type of reflection to know his eyes glowed a dark red.

He quickened his thrusts, gripping her hips tightly until he felt his orgasm rise up and seem to explode out of his head. If he hadn't held on to Jazz, she would have been pushed off the table and possibly straight off the roof.

Nick lifted his head, blood red eyes glowing, fangs flashing white as he roared with exultation. After that, all he could do was wrap his arms around her as she fought to regain her breath.

So many times their encounters had been hot and fast, the desire between them so strong there could be no leisurely lovemaking, just raw animal mating. This time was no different and no less intense.

Except once their hot blood cooled and reason returned, something always happened.

He never told Jazz nor, it appeared, did she realize that the times in the past when he arranged to have her arrested on false charges were actually for her own good. Each of those times he was involved in cases where his prey was dangerous and insane to the point they would have retaliated by striking back at him through her. Of course, if he had explained his reasons to her back then, she would have accused him of lying and conjured up a stake.

Jazz's personality was one that burned bright and hot. She attracted men to her like moths to a flame. Some of those men had not taken rejection kindly. Others suspected there was more to her than met the eye. He knew she was well able to take care of herself, but there were times he still felt she needed help and he was willing to give it, whether she wanted it or not.

The Protectorate always provided a secure identity for him and his guise as a police inspector or detective from another country allowed him freedom to hunt the ones he was sent to find. The fact that Jazz was sometimes in the same city and they usually managed to find each other wasn't always a good thing because he might not be able to offer her the protection she needed if his work turned more dangerous than anticipated. He preferred to fabricate false charges against Jazz and keep her out of harm's way. He knew his witch too well. She would have been right in the midst of battle fighting by his side instead of retreating to a safe place.

While he would prefer her to be fighting *with* him rather than *against* him, he refused to be the one who would cause any harm to her or worse. The wrath of the Witches' High Council would be minor compared to what he would do to himself if anything happened to her.

He nosed her hair, inhaling the lemon scent. Tart. Like her.

"Uh, Nick." Jazz's voice was muffled against his shirtfront. "While you don't feel temperatures, I do, and this table is bloody freezing. My ass is turning into an ice cube."

He chuckled, but obliged by stepping back. Forgetting his jeans were around his ankles, he stumbled, not displaying his grace in movements. Jazz giggled as she slid off the table and rearranged her clothing. She laughingly flashed him her breasts as she pulled her bra down and then her hoodie. She pulled her scrunchie out of her drooping ponytail, raked her fingers through her hair and secured it again.

She looked over her shoulder at the gooey mess that was once her large cup of Diet Coke and funnel cake that was now splattered on the rooftop.

"I'm not cleaning that up." She heaved a deep sigh when Nick shot her a look. "Sure, let the witch do the domestic work," she muttered, zapping the cup and funnel cake into a trashcan set near the Emergency Exit.

Nick crooked his arm around her neck and brought her back against his side.

"It appears there's a celebration somewhere," he said, pointing beyond the pier. They sat down on the edge of the roof, Jazz settled in comfortably between Nick's legs with his arms looped around her waist, their legs dangling off the building.

Jazz's face lit up as the sky seemed to explode with multi-colored sparkles. The crackling sound of fireworks echoed in the air, prompting people below to stop and watch the show.

"And here I thought I only imagined them," she whispered.

ᑌ

"We need to find a way to get onto the mansion grounds," Nick said as they took the stairs down to his office with the intention of heading to the basement slash Civil Defense Shelter slash Nick's apartment. He still felt the tingling remnants of their lovemaking. He thought about an encore in the large bed that dominated his place. Then he saw the look on her face.

The moment had been lost.

Jazz didn't need to pull away from him physically. She'd already pulled away mentally so far that she might as well have been in another galaxy. He cast a quick look at her hands. So far, no witchflame was in sight.

He quickly guided her into the elevator, but she slipped out before he could pull the grille across.

"Since you know everything I do, I think I'll head on home." She walked toward the large glass door leading to the boardwalk.

"Jazz," he called after her. "Fine! We won't talk about it, how is that?"

She paused with her hands on the door handle and looked over her shoulder.

"One thing that hasn't changed over the years is your timing."

"My timing? My timing was perfect!" He shouted after her.

She momentarily closed her eyes. "Do us both a favor and think with your other brain, Gregorivich." She pushed the door open and walked out.

Nick growled under his breath then reared back when he realized he'd bent the bars on the iron grille. By the time he had straightened the bars and gotten out of the elevator he knew she was absent from the boardwalk.

He was also angry enough to do just what she didn't want done. He went back up to his office and called Flavius.

"We need to meet," he told his sire.

"You've learned something?"

"I'm not sure it will help, since it's more a puzzle or riddle than an answer, but it's a start." They arranged to meet in an hour, which gave Nick enough time to shower and change his clothes. While he would have preferred having Jazz's scent on his clothing and skin for the next few hours, he knew it wouldn't be as welcome where he was going.

∽

Jazz was angry that Nick could go so swiftly from passionate lover to cop.

"Would it have hurt him to just forget about that damn monster for a few hours more? The man has no sense of romance," she muttered to herself as she checked her voice mail. She didn't expect an apology from Nick, but it would have made things easier. She winced at the screeching voice.

"Where the fuck are you? Call me as soon as you get this."

While Dweezil's frantic call for help wasn't appreciated, it accomplished one thing. It took Jazz's mind off what happened on the rooftop of Nick's office building and what the vampire did to ruin the mood.

What surprised her was Dweezil's choice of meeting place.

"I'm staying out of the office until things cool down," he told her when she called him back. "I'll be at Klub Konfuzion. Meet me there at eleven."

"Klub Konfuzion? It's bad enough I drive clients there! Why would I want to go there of my own free will?"

"Because no one will expect me there. Eleven, Jazz."

"I'm on the clock then," she snarled, but she said it to dead air.

Jazz looked at her rumpled appearance. Perky lemon-scented witch with an overlying vamp scent wasn't a good idea in a club where basic black, blood on tap, and fangs reigned.

She was running late by the time she showered, yet again, and changed into something more befitting when visiting the ultimate Goth club.

Once changed, she studied herself in the full-length mirror.

"It's like I've gone from Donna Reed to Kate Beckinsale in *Underworld*," she muttered, smoothing the front of her new leather bustier. "Even if I can't breathe."

Jazz topped her outfit with a black leather coat that brushed the top of her stiletto-heeled boots and headed for the carriage house.

"My land, are you going to a costume party?" Irma asked once she got a look at Goth Witch Chick Jazz.

In defiance of the typical black dress code, Jazz wore a deep purple leather bustier tucked into a black leather micro-mini that barely covered the essentials, which was a purple thong panty. Her thigh high fishnet hose were held up with black silk garters adorned with purple ribbons. One garter held her cell phone, the other her lipstick. All the essentials a witch would need when out clubbing. All visible skin shone with gold glitter, her eye makeup smoky and lips a deep red. She had pulled her hair up into a tight knot and dusted it with the same glitter. In many places, she would be arrested for the outfit she wore. Where she was going, it was a guarantee she'd be hit on at the very least.

"You complain I don't take you out," she said, climbing into the car in a cloud of Michael Kors and settled behind the steering wheel. "Well, tonight we are going clubbing. At least, I am."

"I can't believe you're seeing the alcoholic dressed like that."

Jazz felt a pang at realizing she hadn't stopped by Murphy's Pub since the night Nick came back into her life. She knew tonight wouldn't be a good idea. Murphy would definitely not understand her style of dress.

"No, we're not going there."

During the entire trip, Irma questioned Jazz about their destination, but Jazz refused to give it up.

"What is that smell?" Irma screwed up her face as Jazz pulled the car into the club's parking lot and parked it under a vapor lamp that glowed a strange dark green instead of the usual orange. She stared at the obscene graffiti decorating all the warehouse buildings except for Klub Konfuzion. The only decoration on that building was what the owner wanted there. Music from the club filtered out each time the door opened.

"Dead fish, the ocean, and whatever bodies the police haven't found yet." Jazz climbed out of the car and triple-boosted her wards on the vehicle.

Irma shook her head. "The last time I saw a woman wearing something like that was on one of those cable programs, and she was up to no good."

"Same here."

"How long will you be in that place of debauchery?" Irma called after her. A hint of fear colored her voice.

Jazz turned around and walked back to the car. She rested her hands on the metal, bending down so Irma could look into her eyes. "Nothing will happen to you," she said quietly. "No one, absolutely *no one*, will come within twenty feet of this car. I have made very sure of that. Believe me that if anyone tries they will get a very nasty surprise they won't soon forget."

Irma studied her for several minutes. Satisfied with her statement, she slowly nodded. "Is there a chance you could bring me a Brandy Alexander or perhaps a Pink Squirrel?" she asked.

"I doubt they serve either drink, but who knows." Considering Irma's unease about being left alone here, she didn't want to remind her there was no way she'd allow any drink inside Irma that would ultimately end up on the seat. Jazz straightened up and started for the club.

So much had happened since the last time Jazz had driven Tyge Foulshadow to Klub Konfuzion that she felt as if it had been centuries instead of a couple of weeks.

Jazz flashed a sexy smile at the eight-foot mass of muscle at the door and was instantly admitted even if a growl followed her steps. Witches weren't popular in the club, but money-hungry vampires never turned away a paying customer.

The black and red décor fit everyone's idea of a predominantly vampire club. Jazz knew many considered it sexy. She thought it looked more like a dominatrix paradise.

She winced as what passed for music assaulted her ears until they felt ready to bleed. She conjured up a pair of dark glasses to shield her eyes from the pulsating lights overhead. She wondered how the vampires, with their enhanced sight and sound, managed to stay in here without their heads exploding. She'd barely stepped inside and she was ready to leave.

Knowing she would need something to numb the pain, Jazz wasted no time in heading for the bar.

"JD, straight up," she ordered.

The bartender peered closely at her. "Anything else to go with it?"

She lowered the dark glasses just enough to reveal eyes that didn't show a hint of red. "Just the JD." The last thing she wanted was a Type O chaser.

With her drink in hand, Jazz prowled the perimeter of the club, nodding at a few she knew, glaring at men who wanted to get to know her better, and looking for Dweezil. Her frustration level rose the longer she didn't see him. The club, with its techno rock music, gyrating dancers, and young women looking for a one night hook-up, wasn't her idea of fun, and she wanted out of there as fast as possible.

As she looked over the dance floor, her gaze moved past then shifted back again. What she saw was enough to make her grind her teeth down to nubs.

"Oh for Fate's sake," she sighed, stalking toward the edge of the dance floor until she reached a petite blonde wearing a black velvet dress that could double for a napkin talking to a vampire who looked at her as if he planned on making her his late night snack. As if sensing Jazz's approach, the young woman turned her head, saw one angry witch bearing down on her, blanched, and took a step to the side. Jazz muttered a few words and the girl literally froze.

"What part of *you can no longer use magick* do you not understand?" Jazz growled. She refused to believe her binding spell on the sorority Twinkie hadn't worked. She'd pushed a lot of power into that spell, damn it!

She gave the girl credit. She didn't back off. She tipped up her finely-sculpted chin and glared at her through heavily mascaraed eyes. Jazz wanted to strangle the doorman for letting the girl in since it was obvious she was underage even if she had the other attributes Klub Konfuzion liked: cute, young, and breathing. "I'm an adult. I can do whatever I want. Paris Hilton comes here to party all the time."

The girl's toothy companion hissed a warning at Jazz.

She rolled her eyes and waved her hand in front of her face. "Oh puleeze, would it hurt you to use some mouthwash? Listerine comes in flavors you know. In fact, why don't you hunt some down right now? A lot of drugstores are open 24 hours."

"And maybe you should leave her alone and go on your way," the young vampire male said, positive she'd immediately back off when he flashed a hint of fang and red eyes.

Jazz whipped her head to one side and stared him down. She instinctively knew he hadn't been a

member of the high-iron diet for any longer than a
year. "Do not mess with me, vampire. You will not
win." She deliberately pushed enough power at him
that he was forced to stumble back a step. One more
push of power guaranteed he left them with the girl
whining his name. She turned her pout on Jazz.

Jazz turned her ire back on the hapless college
girl. "If Paris Hilton was ever stupid enough to step
one Jimmy Choo-shod foot inside this club, she
would be devoured before she could utter "this is
hot." As for you, you are barely one-third of the way
into your nineteenth year." Her jaw was so tight it
was amazing it didn't break. "Give me your mirror."
She snapped her fingers when the girl didn't immediately comply. "*Now!*"

The girl dug into her miniscule black velvet bag
and pulled out a small compact.

Jazz opened it with the reflective glass facing the
girl. "Let me make this totally clear so you can go
back to the sorority house and tell the others what
happens to stupid girls who try to break one of my
binding spells."

She knew the moment the girl saw her reflection
and what she saw in the mirror—nineteen going on
one hundred and nineteen with deep wrinkles, age
spots, and a nasty twitch below the right eye, just
because Jazz felt like inflicting one on her. She so
hated it when people didn't follow her rules.

The girl gasped and took off as fast as her four-
inch heels could take her.

"Now you're scaring children? Man, you really
can be a bitch, can't you?" Dweezil looked over her

shoulder. His gaze lingered on her cleavage then slid away before Jazz could witch-slap him.

Jazz held out her palm, watching the mirrored disc spin in a silvery circle before disappearing. "Good to see you too, D. If I hadn't found you in the next five seconds I was leaving."

Dweezil looked around, started to grasp her arm but her expression had him pulling back. "There's a booth over there." He gestured with the hand holding a multi-colored drink that bubbled up to the top of the glass. Jazz had no clue what the contents were and she so did not want to know what comprised something that smelled like gym socks left in a locker for fifty years.

The last place Jazz wanted to be was in a dark corner with Dweezil, but she also didn't want to be here at all and she was curious to find out why he had called her in such a panic. She figured the faster she listened to him, the faster she would be out of there.

"Tick-tock, D. I'm on the clock, remember?" She slid onto the cushioned bench. She glared at his rapt stare centered on her glittery chest.

"Are you bare-ass naked under that skirt? Why the fuck don't you wear something that hot when you're working for me? I could charge triple rates all the time. Maybe more if you would cut holes in that top to show off your tits."

She leaned across the table. "Forget the maggots, Dweez. Let's talk leeches. Guess where they'd head first?"

He held up his hands as he took the seat on the other side. "Sooorrryy."

"Then let's cut to the chase and you tell me why we had to meet here instead of your office."

He looked over his shoulder and leaned across the table to whisper, which wasn't easy to hear with the music blaring overhead. "Someone's out to get me."

She wrinkled her nose against the burnt almond smell coming off him. The creature was seriously stressed. "And that's a new thing?"

If she didn't know better, she would think his skin had turned an even more putrid shade of green. "I'm serious here, Jazz. I think someone put a curse on me. I need you to take it off and find out who did it."

Dweezil acting like a total shit was nothing new. Dweezil acting more than a little crazy, ditto. Dweezil actually begging for help was something new. Jazz sat back and sipped her drink. "Do I look like a Charlie's Angel, D? I eliminate curses. I'm not some preppy private investigator who backtracks to find the originator."

"And without me you don't have a job except for the shit money you make eliminating curses," he reminded her. "The cops coming in and taking my records shut me down for a week before my lawyer managed to get them to give it all back. Then all the fuckin' cops say is there wasn't anything there. But they're still watching me. There's no reason for them to hang around like that without some fucker setting them on me." He sat back and drew in a deep breath. "Okay, I'll pay you."

Now Jazz was interested. Dweezil literally offering to give up cold hard cash meant he was seriously worried.

"So where is the curse? Was something in the office cursed?"

He shrugged. "Fuck if I know. Don't you find that out?"

"If you're actually cursed then it could be anything." She pulled off her dark glasses and stared at him. "I don't see anything about you that would indicate you were personally cursed, so it has to be something around you. Give me a starting place."

Dweezil groaned. "Gotta be the whole fuckin' building then," he groused. "Just clean it, okay?"

"Which includes the garage."

"Whatever it takes." He nodded miserably, picking up his drink.

She named her price.

"Fifty!" Dweezil almost choked on his drink. "Fifty-thousand?"

"Two buildings, a lot of work involved there. Plus I'll have to go through all the cars. Or," she waited until she knew she had his full attention, "I take twenty-five and I never have to drive Tyge Foulshadow ever again."

"He only wants you plus you're the only witch I have driving for me right now," he argued. "And he pays in gold bars!"

Jazz waved him off. "Yeah, yeah, yeah. And I don't care. Take your choice. You can either pay me fifty in cash or pay me twenty-five and I don't have to drive Foulshadow ever again." She picked up her drink and sipped the whiskey, enjoying the bite along with the look on Dweezil's face. There was nothing he hated more than giving up money. She just offered him a choice as to how much he was willing to give up. She doubted someone had cast a curse on him, but she wasn't going to tell him that. She would check out the buildings first in case Dweezil was right and someone had cast a curse on him. Not that the idea didn't have merit. There had been many a time she was tempted to throw down something nastier than a bad case of maggots and she'd gladly take any punishment given.

Dweezil picked up his glass and knocked back the last of the foaming contents. If possible, his skin was even greener than before.

"I'll have the fifty K for you tomorrow." He stared at her plumped-up breasts for a moment, realized whatever he thought of saying might not be a good idea and pushed away from the table.

She should have known he would not give in where Master Foulshadow was concerned.

"I will be there at nine."

Dweezil scowled. "How do you expect me to have the money that early?"

"It's called that safe you have in your private bathroom."

He muttered a few choice words under his breath and walked away.

Jazz nursed her drink and watched the dancers. She was tempted to look around for a partner. She loved to dance, but thoughts of Nick soured the idea of prowling the club. Her gaze swung past the dance floor to the bar and across the line of patrons with their own choice of drinks. Some of them drank that special chaser she turned down. She preferred blood running in her veins, she didn't even want to look at it in a glass much less smell it on someone's breath.

She froze and swung her gaze further down the bar to where two men stood resting against it scanning the club's dance floor.

Both tall. One man dark-haired, one light. They were dressed in typical vamp fashion of black shirts and snug fitting pants with black leather dusters hanging open. But it was the dark-haired one that snagged her attention. Many of the male vampires preferred shoulder length hair either kept loose or tied back with a leather thong. Usually it was because the older ones grew up in an era where all men sported longer hair. Others did it because they thought it made them look sexy. On Hugh Jackman, yes, but there were still a lot of vamps that couldn't carry off the look. Nick was one who could carry off either look easily, but he favored shorter hair. He once said something about lice. She inwardly shuddered at the thought.

As if the object of her thoughts sensed her gaze on him, he turned his head, cocked a brow and raised his glass in a silent toast.

"Bloody hell."

Fifteen

"Bloody hell," Nick muttered, echoing Jazz's words.

Flavius looked over his shoulder. "She looks angry enough to call down thunder."

"Been there, done that. Barely escaped the fireball the last time." Nick straightened up.

"What are you going to do?" The other vampire's lips were tipped up in an amused smile.

"Ask the lady to dance."

Flavius scanned the bar and smiled at a sultry brunette. "Good idea. I feel the need of some dancing myself."

Nick made a straight line for Jazz. He noticed her look of surprise that shifted to anger when she saw Flavius was now very neutral. At the moment he wasn't bothering with her face, but with what else he could see above the tabletop. All of it good, very good. If he weren't careful drool would be dripping down his fangs.

"Would you like to dance?"

She silently rose to her feet, giving him a full view of the whole package.

Okay, now drool was dripping. Jazz, the innocent

witch of this afternoon, was now Queen of the Night. Visions of peeling that bustier off and pulling her hair out of that tight knot assaulted his brain. Correction, ripping that bustier off because peeling it off would take too much time.

Perfume that prompted thoughts of Jazz's bare skin and a large bed wafted past him as she walked toward the dance floor. Nick was next to her in a flash, his arms around her body as they moved to music more suited for sex than dancing. He almost lost it when his hands encountered bare skin under the micro mini.

"Fancy seeing you here," he murmured in her ear rotating his hips against hers in a move that was similar to what they had been doing that afternoon. It wouldn't have taken much rearranging of clothing for that to happen here and now. And it wouldn't be the first time that style of dance was done here.

"Yes," she tilted her head back, "especially seeing you with Flavius. Not his usual place, is it?"

"He wanted a change from the usual clubs."

"Yes, I'm sure this is very different than the elegant places he frequents. He used to be good at puzzles. What did he think the riddle meant?"

He kept his arms around her so she couldn't move away. "I haven't told him."

She kept her eyes centered on his face. "Yet."

He loosened his grip enough to run his hands down her arms and lace his fingers through hers which only brought their bodies even closer together. "We can talk about it."

"Or not."

Damn stubborn witch.

Jazz wanted to hate him. She really did. Except it wasn't easy when Nick's body rubbing up against her brought other emotions to the surface that raced even hotter and wilder than her anger ever ran.

His nostrils flared. She knew he smelled her arousal, just as she felt his cock heavy and erect against her. She felt herself moisten and soften, her skin warm under his touch. There were times she wondered if she shouldn't look into vampire aversion therapy. Although she doubted it would help where Nick was concerned.

"I don't want to fight with you, Jazz," Nick murmured in her ear.

"I can tell." Her breath quickened as his hips brushed against hers.

"Wanna go somewhere quiet and make out?" She could feel his smile against her temple.

Jazz had always sensed Nick's emotions when they were together, but tonight their mutual senses seemed somehow headier, more intimate than usual. She knew the sex they shared on the rooftop had been more powerful than it ever had been before. She wondered if that had something to do with it since the sex between them had always been intense, but today had gone beyond that.

Before she knew it, they were out a side door. The heavy iron door barely swung shut before Nick had Jazz backed up against the building and his mouth slammed against hers.

Whoa baby! She should have remembered that there were times Nick could generate heat and this was one of them in spades. Jazz felt like she was ready to go up in flames as he kissed her with the intensity of a man with hundreds of years of experience.

She only took a second to be thankful his drink of choice in there hadn't included a blood chaser. No matter how much she wanted to devour him, she would have insisted on a good dose of Listerine first if that had been the case. Instead, she angled a leg past the folds of his coat and hooked it up against his hip. He grabbed hold of her thigh and kept it pressed up against him.

Stretch with Nick. Have fun with your health.

Jazz felt her sexual beast rise up and roar big time. Their first time on the roof had been fast because it had been so long since they had been together. The second time was slow and just as powerful for that *just because* moment. Tonight was different. Tonight was pure raw lust.

Nick growled as he tore away her thong and delved between her labia, finding her hot and wet. He slowly pushed his fingers inside, finding all the spots that had her rotating against his hand. He slowly withdrew them and brought them up to his mouth. Jazz couldn't look away as Nick slowly licked each finger clean. She rocked against his hand as he cupped her mound, his fingers invading her again.

"This is us, Jazz," he murmured. "But it's more than sex. It's our minds and bodies as a perfect match. No one can give you what I can give you. And no one can offer me what you do."

When he leaned in to kiss her again, she tasted herself on his lips.

She ran a hand over the front of his leather pants, finding the bulge that pulsed under her flattened palm. She pressed inward, rubbing in slow circles.

She saw the fiery glow in his eyes pierce the darkness as his fangs dropped.

The Lady Temptation suggested she lean forward and bite his neck until she broke the skin. Vampires believed the best sex merged with biting and taking blood.

"You're right in one way, Nick," she said softly. "We are a pair. Except we can't share blood without you ending up with a major case of heartburn and the only red stuff I drink are Cosmopolitans." She felt strung so tight with desire she was ready to snap. "You came to me because of Clive Reeves. Not because of us."

It almost killed her then, but she managed to walk away without looking back.

⟳

Jazz carefully handled her triple mocha espresso as she exited her car. Considering her sleepless night she only hoped the triple shot would be enough.

"You never told me what went on between you and Nicky last night," Irma said.

"No, I didn't." She sipped her espresso, savoring the hot rush of mega-caffeine.

"I couldn't see much from the car, but it looked like something nasty was happening." The ghost peered at her. "I guess you didn't realize the two of you came out along the side of the building where you could be seen from the parking lot."

Jazz could feel heat rise in her cheeks. She thought she had quit blushing five hundred years ago. Obviously, that wasn't the case.

"I won't be long. Afterwards, we can drive up the coast."

"Now I know something happened." Irma never gave up easily. Jazz was about to pay for silence quite literally now. "You never do something nice for me unless it does you some good too."

Guilt was something Jazz could easily ignore.

"Dweezil's paying me a nice sum to find the curse and eliminate it. I'll buy a nice safe space heater for the carriage house."

Irma considered the bribe. "I want a new dress."

"You died in that dress. I can't change what you died in."

"I didn't die in this dress. I was buried in it. Harold must have bought it for the funeral, so his clients would think he was a generous man." She sniffed. "I want something hip. I want to look more up to date."

Jazz suddenly visualized spandex on Irma's plump figure and she wasn't thinking a heavy-duty girdle either. It was enough to inspire nightmares.

"I'll see what I can do," she promised, wondering if there was a spell available that could provide a ghost with a new wardrobe and if finding one would involve, gagging here, a return trip to The Library. Still, Irma focusing on her clothing meant she didn't think about the dwarves working in the garage. This could turn into a win-win situation.

At first sight, Jazz thought that Dweezil was back in business, but then she realized that the dwarves were washing and detailing the limousines and town cars more as busy work than getting them ready for clients.

"About time you got here," Dweezil greeted her when she stepped inside the entrance door. He glared at the venti grande Starbucks cup she carried in one hand. "You stopped for coffee? We have coffee here."

"Which is why I stopped for coffee first. I wanted coffee that's actually drinkable. Yours could strip paint."

"It never bothers me," he mumbled, going into his office and closing the door. The loud snick of a lock echoed in the room.

"Hi, Jazz," Mindy greeted her with a sunny smile and a shared look of commiseration. Instead of sitting behind the counter, she sat at a small square table set up near a window. A stack of papers was scattered across the surface.

"How bad has he been since the police were here that day?" Jazz asked.

Mindy picked up a receipt, studied it, and then chose the appropriate pile. Her long fingers topped with shimmering pink-polished nails shone in the sunlight. "The usual."

Jazz sipped her espresso and walked around the reception area. She gestured to banker's boxes set against one wall. "All of D's records?"

Mindy nodded. "The police made such a mess of them it will take me months to get them back into order." She placed an invoice in another pile.

"How is business? Did D lose any clients, or are they coming back?"

"Calls were slow at first," Mindy replied. "Then it seemed everyone learned he was open again and they've been calling in more. But it's not near what it was before and we've been having problems at the bank too."

"Here." Dweezil walked out with a manila envelope that he thrust at Jazz. She quickly moved back before his wandering fingers made contact with her breast. Dweezil tended to cop a feel any time he got a chance even if it meant he'd end up with singed fingers. Literally.

She made a show of checking the contents and amount. "Okay, I'll check the garage first then I'll come back in here."

"Don't let them know what you're doing," he warned. "If those dwarves think there's a curse on me, they'll take off and never come back. Who knows, they might even sue me claiming I put them in danger when I'm the one whose life is threatened."

"You could be right, D. This could be all about you." She cocked an eyebrow. "I'll be back after I go through the garage."

"Shouldn't I come with you?" He asked, clearly hoping she'd refuse. He sighed with relief when she assured him she worked better on her own.

Jazz stopped long enough to drop the envelope in the T-Bird. "Don't even think about a shopping spree," she told Irma.

"Ha ha, the last time I was in J.C. Penney was 1956 and I bought an ironing board for myself and some long underwear for Harold," the ghost grumbled. "Besides, if you're taking me shopping I'd rather go to Nordstrom or even check out the shops on that Rodeo Drive."

Jazz walked on to the garage. Since she had been in there other times, the dwarves didn't think it was odd for her to greet them and start a conversation. With casual dialogue she was able to learn if any new clients had been around—none—and if any cars had been out for repairs the dwarves weren't able to handle themselves. Again, none were noted.

She kept her senses wide open as she walked through the garage, occasionally stopping to touch a tool, finger a piece of equipment, or even place her hand on one of the vehicles. She took her time, and almost two hours later, she left the garage and headed for the office.

"Well?" Dweezil practically pounced on her when she walked inside.

"There is nothing out there you need to worry about, although it wouldn't hurt for you to update some of the equipment and tools they use," she pointed out. "And the restrooms are disgusting. Stock up on some cleaning supplies, will you?"

"I didn't pay you a shitload of money for you to tell me what my business needs," he grumbled. "Just find and get rid of what's trying to ruin me."

He slumped in despair. "I figured if anyone did anything it would be one of them. I think they've been taking booze out of the cars or watering it down."

"No way could they water down the liquor and the clients not notice." Jazz roamed the small reception area. Mindy looked up once and then returned to her task. Jazz studied her for a moment, noticing the sun lighting up Mindy's golden-blonde hair that was pulled back with a mint-green scarf that matched her silky cotton t-shirt tucked into darker green pants. A silver ring with an odd looking stone winked a kaleidoscope of color on her right-hand ring finger. Today, there was no denying the slight points on her ears. When she looked up, a swirl of ethereal color showed in her eyes. Clearly, Mindy had decided it was past time to stop hiding her heritage. Considering what came into this place, showing off her Elven side made her more of an asset than a liability.

"Did you purchase any new equipment in the past couple of months?" Jazz asked, glancing at the flat panel computer monitor on the counter.

"We updated the computers a year ago. The police took them, but they were returned with the files." Mindy was the one to reply.

Keeping her senses wide open, Jazz knew there was something wrong. But at the moment, she couldn't put her finger on it.

The sense increased when she passed by Dweezil's office. She turned around and stepped inside.

Oh yes. Someone had laid down a curse on him and it was a doozey. All she had to do was find out just where.

She remained silent on it for now. She didn't want Dweezil adding his own crazy vibes to the mix.

Something was wrong. There was something here that truly didn't belong.

Jazz trailed her fingers across the top of Dweezil's desk, bypassing pens and a small clock fashioned in the shape of a woman's breast. She wrinkled her nose at the latter.

She sensed the negative energy was nearby—a strong beacon for trouble.

Jazz turned around and faced the shelves housing Dweezil's beloved erotica collection. She hated looking at the pieces, but she was positive what she was looking for was hidden within the assortment of jade penises surrounding a silver dildo.

She walked slowly towards the case and studied each piece.

"Hide in plain sight," she whispered, picking the crystal dildo up by the corners of the small velvet cloth it sat on. She was certain it had been deliberately placed to one side as an afterthought so it wouldn't be easily noticed.

She carefully carried it over to the desk and set it down. "A new acquisition?"

"Yeah, pretty, huh?" He stood in the doorway beaming with pride at his latest treasure.

"Not exactly the description I'd use. Where did you find it?" Jazz bent over, peering closely into the crystal until she found what she was looking for.

"eBay. I heard that some caliph in Ancient Turkey had these crystal dildos made for his harem favorites. Supposed to be shaped just like his cock. I had to pay a lot for it, but it was worth it. Got it about a month ago."

"I guess you can find anything you want there. I didn't see this piece the last time I was in here."

She continued examining the tiny dark speck that barely showed within the clear crystal. She doubted the flaw had been in the crystal when the dildo was first fashioned.

"Didn't unpack it until a few days ago. Before that it was in the storeroom." Dweezil paused. "Is that the problem?"

Jazz continued to stare at the tiny black speck that seemed to pulsate in tune with her heartbeat.

"Someone arranged for you to buy this, because there is definitely a curse embedded in the crystal. I would say it's the kind that invites trouble to your doorstep. And you've sure had your share of trouble lately."

"I got a business to run here. I don't need any fuckin' trouble," Dweezil growled. "Just get the curse out of it."

She straightened up, already anticipating trouble. "I can't just take the curse out of the crystal, D, like you would take a splinter out of a finger. The only way it can be properly eliminated is for the crystal to be destroyed."

"Destroyed? You mean break it? It's a fuckin' antique! There were three made and this is the only one left! It's not like I can go down to The Love Den and buy another one there." He paced the office. "You just have to take the curse out. That's your job."

She made sure her hands were still shielded as she carefully moved her palms over the crystal. The last thing she wanted to do was actually touch it, even with her hands shielded. Major eeuuww factor there.

"If you want the trouble to be gone, the crystal has to go too. Where's a hammer?" She looked around.

Dweezil held up his hands. "You can't break it!"

Mindy wandered in and stood in the doorway. "It's really expensive, Jazz."

"Take your pick, Dweezil. Disgusting dildo in a million pieces or even more trouble coming to your door?" she asked. "Next time around, the cops might close you down permanently."

Dweezil stared at the crystal. Greed warred with lust for his treasure. He dropped into a chair and covered his face with his hands.

Jazz heaved a sigh. "Fine." She went back into the storeroom and rummaged around until she came out with a hammer.

Mindy shifted uneasily in her spot.

"Is that a good idea?" she asked. "I mean, couldn't breaking it make things worse?"

"Breaking it releases the negative energy, yes," Jazz replied, laying the hammer down by the crystal. "But I'm going to bless the hammer first to diffuse the negative energy."

"I can't watch," Dweezil moaned, keeping his hands over his eyes, while Mindy watched with bright-eyed fascination.

"Light overcomes dark. Take away what lies beneath, because I say so, damn it!" Jazz murmured, turning her head just as she brought the hammer down hard enough to break the crystal. Instead of shattering, the crystal broke into chunks and a whoosh of air smelling like rotten eggs escaped.

The moment the smell dissipated in the air a booming sound shook the building hard enough that the windows shattered and a security alarm sent out its piercing sound.

All three ran to the front where they saw heavy smoke and pieces of metal flying through the air in the spot where Jazz had parked. Dwarves swarmed out of the garage, running around the parking lot with fire extinguishers in hand to put out the tiny fires scattered throughout the lot. Mindy ran to the back and silenced the alarm.

Jazz's mouth dropped in shock just before she felt all the air leave her lungs. Her ears still rang from the shrieking alarm, but it was the sight before her that left her stunned.

"My car! That was my car!" she wheezed, gripping the doorjamb. She staggered backward and grabbed hold of Dweezil's shirtfront in a grip that tore the fabric. "Your crystal blew up my car!" She shook him like a rag doll.

"Hey! Watch the threads!" He tried to free himself, but she wasn't letting go. "'Sides, how can you blame the crystal? Maybe you had a gas leak or somethin'. And look at my office! It's a mess! With my luck, insurance won't pay for it!"

Jazz shook him so hard his teeth clacked together. Considering they were an even darker yellow than usual, it wasn't a pretty sight.

"That shouldn't have happened! There should have been no backlash, especially on me! It was *your* crystal!" She looked back outside at the smoke that was still as dense as when the explosion first happened. Her hands dropped and she realized she couldn't breathe. She clutched her throat and looked wildly around. For what, she didn't know.

Mindy took her arm and steered her quickly toward a chair. "Here." She snatched up a sheet of paper, turned it into a cone and pressed it over Jazz's nose and mouth. "Breathe into this."

"My car is gone! Irma's gone! So's my fifty thousand in cash!" Okay, probably should have listed Irma first, but I did think of her before I thought of the money! And she is already dead, unlike my car.

Jazz closed her eyes and breathed in and out until she felt the buzzing leave her ears and she no longer felt dizzy. Even then, she felt so nauseous she feared she was going to be sick. She pushed the paper cone away and lowered her head to her knees.

She loved that car. Loved how the snazzy little roadster made her feel as she drove it around. And while Irma was a complete pain in the ass, she was also sort of comforting in a weird, nagging kind of way.

Irma, who only wanted a pet to keep her company and a new dress because her asshole husband had bought an ugly funeral outfit she was stuck in for eternity. Irma, who constantly told her she drove too fast or complained she never took her any place special. Egads! When had she come to develop a fondness for the recalcitrant ghost? When had she started thinking about her as a friend?

What would Jazz do without Irma?

"Hey, wait a minute." Dweezil plucked at her shoulder. "Look." He pointed out the window.

Jazz turned her head, wincing at the sight of all the smoke that was now slowly thinning. A familiar outline appeared first, and then as the smoke cleared even more, she saw her car, smudged a bit but intact. Irma sat in the passenger seat, coughing and waving at the smoke.

"What happened?" she called out.

Jazz pushed herself out of the chair. Broken glass crunched under her boots as she headed for the doorway and strode outside.

Irma waved her handbag in front of her face. "I told you this was a dangerous place!" she groused. "A body can't sit quietly without something happening. Police swarming all over. Getting blown up."

Jazz realized she was about to make the biggest mistake of her life. She was rushing over there with the express purpose of hugging Irma and telling her she was glad she was all right.

She braked so hard, she skidded back on her heels. She was so not ready for a change in their relationship.

She took several deep breaths and centered herself. "Just tell me the money survived too."

"Money? All you care about is the money? I could have died out here!" Irma yelled, her rouge standing out on her cheeks.

"Not an option since you're already dead!" She turned away to hide her smile even as she muttered, "I will never be able to get rid of that woman."

Oh yeah, things were back to normal.

Almost.

Because now a few things were clicking into place and Jazz intended to get some answers.

She returned to the office, ignored Dweezil's ear-splitting howls about the destroyed reception area, his precious crystal dildo, chunks of asphalt now missing from the parking lot, and that was just the beginning.

Instead, Jazz focused on Mindy.

The blonde elf took one step back.

"Do not move," Jazz ordered, advancing on her like a witchy freight train.

"What good luck! Your car doesn't look harmed," Mindy chirped, but Jazz's hand slicing through the air stopped any more conversation. The elf stood still, her hands clasped lightly in front of her, looking so damn sweet and innocent Jazz seriously thought about dumping mud all over her Barbie-blonde hair. She imagined lots of dark gooey smelly mud that would be impossible for the always immaculate Mindy to wash off.

"Mindy, where did you get the crystal?"

Her Dresden blue eyes didn't veer from Jazz's face. "Dweezil got it."

Jazz kept her gaze on Mindy the way she'd watch a cobra. "Dweezil got that piece because you originally found it and set up the eBay auction in such a way he'd make sure to win it. Embedding a curse in a crystal is a complicated process and smacks of Miranda. Is that who you hired to do it?"

Dweezil paused in his stomping around. "This was some kind of set-up?" Even with the shattered windows and door and smell of smoke and dust, the area was flooded with the smell of burnt almond. "Is that right, Mindy? Did you do this?"

"She just wants to blame someone else since she broke the crystal and it hurt her car."

"One more lie and I will turn your nose into something that will make Pinocchio look like a Pug," Jazz threatened. Steam practically poured from her ears. "You used magick to bring humans in where they do not belong. You used magick to destroy a dwelling."

"It's a business!"

"A dwelling," she repeated. "Yes, humans know about us, but we still *do not* draw unwanted attention to our kind. We do not use magick against each other and we do not *blow up my fucking car!*"

Mindy winced at the level of Jazz's voice that in her fury could have shattered what glass was left intact. To an elf's delicate hearing, it was like an ear-splitting screech. Jazz didn't care.

"Why did you do it, Mindy?" Jazz asked. She put up a hand to stop Dweezil, who looked ready to pounce on the elf.

"Why shouldn't I?" She tipped her chin up, but her sweet baby-doll looks couldn't carry off any form of menace. "Dweezil's a disgusting creature who doesn't deserve to run this business. My family said if I could find the right business I could have it. Well," she propped her hands on her hips, "this is it. I could run it a lot more successfully than he can. All he does is spend the profits on disgusting things like that crystal!"

"You fuckin' bi—." Dweezil stopped just in time to avoid Jazz's ire aimed at him when she was doing such an excellent job with Mindy. "The office is ruined!" He stared at the now destroyed computer that was covered in glass fragments, papers flying everywhere and the dwarves still swarming the parking lot to stamp out tiny fires that popped up in the asphalt. "And my beautiful crystal! How could it get worse?"

Jazz cocked her head to one side. The piercing sound of sirens rent the air and it could only mean one thing.

"It just did."

∽

Two hours later, Jazz decided her new best friend, Detective Larkin, would have preferred if she were anywhere but there.

The blinding colors on his tie resembled a *Rorschach* test and prompted Jazz to slip on her sunglasses.

"So you were just hanging around here, helping them put away their files." He gazed at the scraps of paper that made the carpet look like the aftermath of a wild New Year's Eve party.

"That's me, helpful to a fault." If she had acted any perkier she would have been Mindy without the pointed ears. The moment the sheriff's car rolled into the parking lot along with a fire truck, Jazz grabbed the green scarf so that Mindy's hair fell down around her ears.

"Yeah, a real Girl Scout." He shook his head. "And you have no idea what happened?"

She shook her head. "At first we thought it was a sonic boom or an earthquake. Then Dweezil said maybe a gas main blew."

He looked out at the parking lot that looked like a war zone. Then he looked to the left at a pristine looking 1956 T-Bird.

"Amazing a sweet ride like that escaped any damage."

"It was in the garage when it happened," Jazz lied without batting an eye.

"Uh-huh." He turned to Mindy. "What did you see?"

"She doesn't work here anymore. She only stopped by to pick up her final check," Dweezil said in a flat voice.

Mindy glared at him, but wisely said nothing with Jazz standing next to her.

"Something witchy didn't cause that?" Detective Larkin asked Jazz before he walked back to his vehicle.

"My work never includes explosions," she assured him. "Too messy."

Sixteen

"Don't hang up, Jazz." She was about to do just that when she heard Nick's voice. She remained silent and waited. "Flavius is missing."

"Did you check Rodeo Drive? Maybe he went shopping." She regretted her bitchy witch remark the moment she said it. She couldn't miss the stress in Nick's voice. She didn't think he even knew what that emotion comprised. "He was at the club with you. Maybe he got lucky."

"He left a voicemail last night saying that he learned something and would meet me at the Howling Moon Café tonight. He didn't show up."

Jazz winced at the idea of two vampires meeting up at a café geared for the werewolf clientele, but it was also a good place to go when a low profile was necessary because the weres left them alone and vice versa.

She'd returned home the previous night in such a state of sexual frustration she seriously thought about digging out her handy dandy vibrator, but she knew it wouldn't accomplish what Nick could. Plus, she hated any kind of substitution. Especially when it came to sex.

"Where are you now?"

"My office. I plan to go back to Klub Konfuzion and see if I can find his trail and track him."

"You won't be successful," she said. "The owner employs a very powerful witch to keep not only very strong wards around the entire area but also a barrier even around the perimeter so any creature can't be tracked from the club back to its lair. It's one of the reasons why it's so popular. The patrons feel safe when they leave."

His growl of frustration tugged at her. She had always liked the debonair vampire and didn't want to think the worst.

"What do you feel?" She knew that since Flavius was Nick's sire, the two could easily communicate without having to worry about looking for a cell phone signal.

It was a few moments before Nick replied. "I can't feel anything. I've tried several times contacting him telepathically, but there's nothing there." He paused. "It's as if he's been totally cut off."

Jazz closed her eyes. She knew her senses wouldn't be able to find Flavius, but she knew what would help.

"I'll call you right back." She hung up and dialed another number. When the line on the other end was picked up, she took a deep breath. She so did not want to do this! "D, if Master Foulshadow needs a driver this week I am available." She listened to his excited chatter. "Call it my good deed for the year, but don't expect anything this generous ever again. Since your insurance won't pay for the damage to the office, just charge Foulshadow whatever fee you think you can get out of him."

She hung up knowing she had just offered Tyge Foulshadow a deal he couldn't resist.

She called Nick back next. "Meet me on the pier," she said without preamble then hung up.

She looked down at the sound of animated squeaks and squeals. "Be good and you can come along." She picked up Fluff and Puff and carefully stuck them in her large leather tote bag before leaving the house for the pier.

She stopped for a funnel cake for the slippers to snack on then walked on to the pier.

Nick stood at the end, looking out over the ocean. Jazz knew he was aware of her presence, but he remained standing with his back to her. Trust like that in a vampire was rare and she treasured it. Treasured him.

Too bad witches and vampires didn't mix.

Try telling that to their bodies though.

She stood there a moment, looking at his bowed figure, sensing the sorrow and frustration he felt. Below that she sensed the anger that he was experiencing because he felt helpless in finding his friend and sire.

She ignored the slippers' happy babbling as they consumed their treat. She hated to think what the inside of her bag would look like once they were finished. They weren't exactly the neatest eaters around. She had purposely taken out her lipstick and blush before putting Fluff and Puff in the tote. When they got peckish, they pretty much ate anything and anyone. She walked down the weathered boards. Once she reached the end, she stood next to Nick, bumping his shoulder with her own.

"I gather he hasn't contacted you to say that he's shacked up with some bimbo at a 5-star hotel and forgot about meeting you?" she asked.

Nick shook his head. "Any time I try to contact him…" he paused. "Normally, there is no problem in sensing his thoughts. Now, it's as if there's a wall there." He straightened up, bracing his hands on the railing.

"It's never happened before?" She hoped he would say yes. That Flavius would turn out to be in the mountains of Nepal or something, even though she couldn't imagine him hiring a sherpa and lugging a designer wardrobe up a mountain. Flavius was born and bred a Roman highborn soldier who enjoyed his creature comforts and thousands of years hadn't changed that mindset.

He shook his head, still looking out over the dark sea. "Never. No matter what is going on with our lives we have always responded to each other's call or at least let the other know we were safe." His jaw tightened. "It has to do with Reeves. I know it. I feel it." He closed his eyes in thought. "Some brunette was giving him the eye and he was going to ask her to dance. I lost track of him after that."

Jazz knew exactly what caused Nick to lose track of Flavius. She ducked her head. There was that damn blush again. She absently reached inside her tote and ruffled a pair of soft ears. She wanted to hug Nick, but she wasn't sure he would accept her touch. A hug meant sympathy and Nick didn't do sympathy well.

Before she could come up with anything to say, her cell phone rang.

Nick cocked an eyebrow. "*Ding Dong the Witch Is Dead?*"

She shrugged. "It seemed like a good idea at the time. She dug her cell out, glanced at the caller ID and flipped it open. "Hey, D." Nick turned to face her, openly listening. "Fine, I'll be there." She flipped the phone closed and looked up. She still didn't know what to say, but there was something she could offer him.

"I found a way for us to get onto the estate. No guarantee we'll leave there in one piece. With our luck, we could literally end up *in* pieces, but along the way we might be able to find out for ourselves what happened to all those missing vampires."

A glimmer of a smile lit up Nick's dark features. "It's more fun when the odds are stacked against us."

Jazz grinned back at Nick. "Ready for a fight, are we?"

"I'm a vampire. It's part of my nature." He returned her grin. "Yours, too, as I recall." He looked down at her hands and looked up with a cocked eyebrow.

Jazz jerked with surprise as the image of a fireball appeared inside her mind.

"None of that!" she ordered, but not with her usual heat. The last thing she wanted to do was fight with him. They'd done that so much over the centuries that she knew she didn't want any anger lingering between them before they faced off against Clive Reeves. And considering what little they still knew about him, they were pretty much going in blind. But it wouldn't stop her since she didn't like bullies and Reeves was a bully of the worst kind.

So she'd forgive Nick for showing up inside her head. This time.

Jazz turned around to rest her elbows back on the pier railing. The bright lights from the Ferris wheel and carousel provided a festive picture that belied the dark and fearful thoughts running through their heads.

"In a few days we could be in the midst of the battle of our lives. We could even lose them. Not that I'm planning on it, of course," she said dryly. "I'd like to at least crawl out of there in as close to one piece as possible."

Nick mimicked her posture. "Won't be the first time. Won't be the last."

"Thank you for assuming we'll at least survive." She took a deep breath, inhaling mingled scents of salt air and fish with the sweeter scents of sugary cotton candy and funnel cake. Growing up in a seaside village she had always gravitated to beach towns. She felt the breeze lift up the ends of her hair and then felt a light touch move across her skin under her hair.

"We'll survive. We're the good guys." His fingertips stroked the back of her neck in a slow seductive trail that sent waves of sensation through her body.

She closed her eyes. She wanted to give in to the burn Nick's touch ignited. Except instead of imagining the two of them on a bed somewhere, anywhere, she saw the past unfurl before her eyes. Fear and pain threatened to overtake the lust that simmered deep within her belly. She ruthlessly pushed away the former before Nick could sense what went through her mind and concentrated on the latter. She knew what she needed in order to forget.

"Hide us from the outside world. Let the magick be unfurled," Jazz whispered, holding her hands out in front of her. "Because I say so, damn it!"

The air just beyond them thickened to a silvery mass, turning the boardwalk into a blur of colors and sound. Behind them the ocean suffered the same fate, enclosing them in a magickal bubble.

She then turned to Nick, placing her palm over the spot where she knew his heart lay. She allowed her imagination to believe it beat for her. And for the barest of seconds, she was positive she did hear it. Her lips replaced her hand, feeling the soft cotton, and inhaling the scent that was uniquely his. She drew it deep into her lungs as if to imprint it on her memories and smiled when she felt his muscles tighten in response. She knew if she lowered her hand she would feel another muscle just as taut. Instead she raised her head and stood up on tiptoe to brush her lips against his.

"I remember the first time we made love," she whispered.

"That small village outside of Venice."

"Small? The inn was larger than the entire town. And the bed had fleas." She wrinkled her nose.

"I didn't notice." One hand tunneled under her t-shirt. "I gather from your spell we won't attract an audience?"

"All they'll see is an empty pier and they'll feel no desire to even come down here." She dropped her tote bag to the ground, ignoring the protesting squeaks from inside. Pulling Nick's t-shirt up over his head and discarding it was her next task.

"My apartment isn't all that far from here." Nick growled his pleasure when her bra hooks snapped free. "Lots of privacy, big bed." He used one hand to pull her closer to him as he cupped his hand over her breast, feeling the nipple pebble against his palm.

"I like it here. Fresh air, and even with the spell there's still that sense of being discovered." She made short shrift of his belt before tearing open his jeans, muttering another form of dire curses on men who chose a button fly over a zipper. Another set of words sent the metal buttons flying everywhere.

Nick heard just the faintest hint of desperation in her voice, felt the skips in her respiration, saw the stark color that stood out on her cheeks, and recognized it for what it was. His fearless witch was afraid. So afraid she was ready to indulge in hot primal sex right here so for a short time she could forget they would be walking into an unknown hell in a few days time.

He grasped her hands when she started to pull down his jeans.

"Jazz." She ignored him and continued tugging to no avail. She may have been strong, but she couldn't beat his preternatural strength. "*Griet.*" A muffled sob hurt his ears. Not the sound, but the emotion and despair that overlaid it.

"I want you. What is so wrong with that?" she asked, keeping her gaze on the ground.

"Not that way." He used two fingers to tip her chin up. "What we share is passion. If we have sex the way you want it now, *he* will win." He hurt inside when she recoiled.

She breathed sharply through her nose. He could feel her struggle to center herself. He also smelled the frantic arousal on her skin. He planned to erase the anxiety and intensify the arousal.

"All you have to do is say no." She still refused to meet his eyes.

Nick smiled. "Ah, but I don't intend to say no." He leaned down to whisper in her ear. "I just intend to make this all about us." He didn't bother pulling her t-shirt off, but tore it from her body as if it was paper. Her bra was next. He bent his head and covered one breast with his mouth, taking the nipple between his lips. He ignored his body's clamor to drop his fangs and focused on showing her as much pleasure as their bodies could handle. As he suckled, he drove his hands downward into the sides of her panties, fondling her bare skin as he pulled her fully against him. He slid one hand to her front, finding the nest of hair that tangled around his fingertips. Below he found her slick and moist for him. He delved further, seeking her clit and pinching it between his fingers.

Jazz gasped as the fire tore through her body. She bucked her hips against his hand as she clasped his head, sliding her fingers through the dark silky strands.

This is all for us, Jazz. Nick's voice bloomed through her head.

Magick.

The mental image was so raw and erotic that Jazz reeled from the intense power that slid around her. Her hips rocked as Nick's fingers sped up their seductive rhythm within her core and what she saw in her mind's eye upped the ante to something so strong it was amazing she didn't fall to the ground.

She saw herself naked, kneeling on dark-purple silk cushions. Her hair was loose, a fiery nimbus around her pale shoulders. Moss-green eyes glittered with heat that should have seared the man standing before her.

The Nick in her vision, in all his naked glory, leaned forward, resting one knee on the cushions while Jazz reached up to loop her arms around his neck. She smiled up at him, lips parted, inviting his kiss.

How?

I said this was all about us. The least I could do was add something to go with our privacy bubble. His words growled inside her mind, as they watched Nick's X-rated vision.

Jazz felt Nick's fingers dance another form of enchantment along her labia as she watched the dream Nick approach her dream self with the feral grace of the predator of the shadows he was. And what she saw she also felt.

She felt the hot satin of his erect cock as she circled it with her fingers, stroking the drop of pre-cum glistening on the head with her thumb then lifting it to her lips. She delicately licked the salty drop from her skin. Keeping her hand wrapped around his cock, she slowly leaned back, her long legs bent at the knee. Nick didn't hesitate in following her, settling heavily between her thighs.

Jazz shook with reaction. Every inhalation brought the rich scent of her arousal. Judging from the dark lights in Nick's eyes and flared nostrils, he sensed it too.

She tipped her head back, feeling his hands buried in her hair, fingers digging in her scalp. The sense of feeling what he was actually doing to her and what she saw in his magickal vision had her whimpering with need as her body tightened to an unbearable tension. She felt Nick standing behind her, his cock resting against her ass even as he continued to stroke her damp petals. She closed her eyes against the unbearable pleasure that rolled through her body. Or was it her vision body?

Open your eyes, Jazz. Look at us.

She forced her eyes open in time to see Nick's ass muscles bunch as he reared up and thrust deeply inside her. A primitive snarl escaped his lips as he claimed her while she answered with a feral snarl of her own.

Jazz's hips instinctively rose with vision Jazz's, feeling his fingers strum her ultra sensitive flesh.

Open your mind to my magick, Jazz. See what I see. Feel what I feel.

Her eyes widened with shock as for several brief seconds she was in Nick's mind, looking down at her own face flushed hotly with passion, feeling the heated glove of her body as he thrust deeply within. She felt his power, the bloodlust for her that he tamped down with strength she couldn't even imagine. He offered her the chance to see their lovemaking through his eyes. And as she looked at her face through his eyes she knew at the same time he experienced their lovemaking through her mind.

She should have jerked away from his mental intrusion. Demanded he stop. Instead, she craved more. She felt Nick's body nestled behind her, the coolness of his skin as he inserted his knee between her thighs and nudged them apart. As she flew from Nick's mind and returned fully to herself, he gripped her hips, lifted her up just enough, bent her over slightly and plunged into her damp core with the same ferocity she saw in their images.

Jazz gasped at how deeply he entered her from that position then moaned as reality and the magickal scene she viewed blended into one. It seemed both Nicks thrust in tandem while she and vision Jazz burned with the same desire. All too soon, her body tightened to the point of pleasure pain. As Nick's thrusts increased, so did the fire racing through her body. She pushed back as he pushed forward, rotating her hips and then she was flying.

She didn't know if it was the vision Jazz who screamed Nick's name or if it was she. For all she knew, both of them did as her orgasm ripped through her body with the intensity of a tidal wave. She struggled to breathe, air sawing in and out of her lungs. It wasn't easy to pull in oxygen when after-shocks still rippled through her body.

Jazz's knees buckled and she would have fallen to the ground if she hadn't still been enclosed in Nick's arms. His soft laughter in her ear held the same sense of wonder.

"Wow," she finally managed to get out. "How did you do that?"

"Even vampires can conjure up some magick when they need it. This is why I'm not worried about what we're about to face," he murmured. "Together, we can do anything, Jazz."

Her hands shook so much when she tried to pull up her panties and jeans, she almost twisted her clothing into knots. Nick brushed her hands away and arranged her clothing, then his own. She whispered a few words and the buttons returned to Nick's jeans in a neat row. He picked up his t-shirt and dropped it over her head.

"No reason to have you arrested on an indecency charge," he told her.

She nodded. She knew their time was now over.

"Bring the world back to us and return us to the world," she murmured. The milky bubble disappeared with a soft *pop*.

Nick settled his hands on her shoulders, but she didn't turn around. What happened still had her shaking.

She continued staring at the boardwalk. "The trouble is, the kind of magick we'd need at Reeves' mansion might provide some unwanted attention. I'd rather just blow up the place."

"Let's concentrate on taking care of Reeves, then we'll see what we can do about cleansing the property." He rubbed her shoulders lightly.

No way would Jazz admit that Nick had done an excellent job of taking her mind off her fears and infused her with a new strength.

"Oh yes, by the time we finish he'll be toast."

◇

Jazz moved around her bedroom suite. Even the soft chatter of Fluff and Puff couldn't calm her down. She felt as if the energy simmering within her would break out and create havoc before she was ready to release it.

She and Nick only had three days to complete their plans. She knew he had gone to the Protectorate to inform them Flavius was missing and that he had a pretty fair assumption that Clive Reeves had something to do with his sire's disappearance. She didn't ask about anything beyond that and he didn't offer.

They knew it wouldn't be easy to plan for every contingency, so they did the best they could and hoped for the best.

There was no going back now. Tonight, they would gain access to the estate and the bowels of Clive Reeves' mansion. Her stomach churned at the thought of returning to the scene of the crime. Since she believed she had killed Reeves back then it was all too easy for her to think of the mansion in those terms.

This time, she would enter the house knowing just what she would be facing. And she didn't plan to leave until one of them was dead. Naturally, her choice was Reeves.

So why did she feel the need for more? To find out why that tiny piece of information seemed to flicker on the very edge of her consciousness?

She swung about and stared at the blank wall.

What would it hurt to ask? All they can do is say no. It's not like they haven't done that before.

"No hurry." She glanced at the clock and winced. "Okay, I lied." Jazz slipped off the bunny slippers and set them in their favorite corner with some dog treats. They liked anything crunchy.

Aware she couldn't put it off any longer, she pulled in a deep breath, shook her arms and legs and faced the blank wall. She closed her eyes and bowed her head.

"I humbly ask for entrance to the Great Hall." And then she waited.

In the blink of an eye she stood in the middle of a room that rivaled many a castle's great halls. In place of her cotton yoga pants and crop top, she wore a robe the color of morning lilacs that matched the amethyst in her ankle bracelet—the robe she wore in the Witches' Academy.

"What is it you wish, Griet?" Eurydice sat at the head of a long table carved with elaborate symbols. A large emerald embedded in a gold pendant glowed with green fire against her chest. Two witches sat on either side of her. Jazz was familiar with them all from her days of training.

Jazz waited a second before replying. Showing anything but absolute proper deference to the

Witches' High Council promised a swift exit out of the hall and little chance of returning.

"You were the one to call us," Eurydice prompted with more than a touch of impatience.

"The one I believed I destroyed is alive after all," Jazz began. "He is not only alive but also using baneful magick to extract the life force of vampires in order to extend his own life. Possibly the same magick he used to transfer his life force to his baby son's body upon the moment of his death. He has managed to keep his life that way. It is time to end it."

"There are those who would not miss vampires on this earth," Eurydice commented with a grim smile.

"And if this man decides a vampire life force can no longer extend his life he will move on to others in the supernatural community, such as witches." She slowly raised her head. "I must be assured I can stop him."

"Then seek a fortuneteller."

And this was why she hated coming here. Hated asking.

"You sought your answers in The Library," Eurydice said. "And you continued with your quest without coming here before. Why are you asking us for assistance now?"

Perhaps she should have thought this through before coming here. "All I received for my efforts were more questions. This man needs to be stopped." She swallowed the impatience she knew she couldn't display. "Please tell me that what we plan to do won't be in vain. If we need to know more, please advise me what I need to do. There is very little time left." She forced her head up to stare in the witch's eyes. Jazz didn't bother explaining what the plan was. She knew that Eurydice was aware of everything that went on. She kept up with everything to do with the witches she'd banished to the outside world. Just because they were out of sight didn't mean they were out of mind.

Standing in Eurydice's presence was the magickal equivalent of being sent to the principal's office.

Even if Jazz was no longer a young girl, she still felt the same sting of the authority figure seated before her.

"Why did you not seek the Protectorate's counsel on this? This situation would fall more under their jurisdiction."

Oh yeah, she was not going to make it easy for her.

"Because I go to my kind for assistance."

No emotion showed on Eurydice's face. "If you choose to work with vampires, you cannot expect us to help you. You have always had an arrogance about you, young Griet," the elder witch spoke. "And it appears you have not truly learned humility in the past seven centuries."

Counting to ten or even ten billion wasn't going to cut it. Jazz had asked for an audience because she needed help, damn it! She so did not need this "go help yourself" shit!

"How dare you say what I have and have not learned!" she spat out. "*You* were the ones to push us out into the world before we were ready. *You* were the ones to force us to make our way in the unknown! Only by the grace of the Fates did we not starve those first years." Her fists tightened by her side.

"And yet you survived." Eurydice was unruffled by Jazz's fury. "And you interact with others who are not of our kind. Yet, when you need help, you come to us. The creature you speak of has been victimizing the children of the night for decades. Why do you come to us now?"

Jazz reared back as the revelation sunk in. "You *knew* he was alive? I have lived all this time with the agony of extinguishing a life, even though the one I killed deserved death. At the time, I would have welcomed my own death as payment for the life I took. And now I learn you already knew he survived!" She felt a roaring in her head and forced herself back to the here and now. Passing out in the presence of the Witches' High Council would so not be a good idea. Plus, her temper was ready to explode if she didn't break down in tears first.

She took a step backwards. "You lied to me!"

"Be cautious of your words, Griet." Eurydice's words whipped across her like an icy lash. "You must have known that merely requesting an audience did not mean we would help you."

Jazz shook her head. "This was a mistake. I don't need any of you." Her furious gaze moved from one witch to the other. None looked away. None showed any sense of sympathy. "And this time, I will make sure that Clive Reeves is dead once and for all. I *beg* your leave." As she winked out of sight, the scent of something burning lingered in the air.

"She has found her power," Zafira, one of the other witches, said.

"The true test will be when she faces him," Eurydice said with a soft sigh.

∽

Jazz's anger with the Witches' High Council helped get her through the next hour of making her preparations. She operated on autopilot, dressing in a black silk shirt and black leather pants and pulling her hair back in a tight braid.

Irma watched her place quartz crystals under the car seats. The magick was strong enough that even Irma sensed it.

"Something's wrong," the ghost said as they drove to Dweezil's. "You've never done this before."

"Nothing is wrong," Jazz quietly replied. "I know you've felt a little nervous lately, so the crystals will help you stay calm. I'll park you in the side garage at the car service. The crew doesn't go in there and you'll feel more comfortable."

Irma hugged her handbag against her chest. "You'll leave the lights on?"

"Yes."

Jazz knew Irma was suspicious of her behavior, but she didn't know what to say to her—that things could go so wrong she wasn't coming back? Jazz had already made arrangements for that contingency by leaving a letter behind for Krebs telling him where the car would be if she didn't return by morning and to contact Stasi and Blair. They would know what to do. Anything else, she couldn't think that far ahead.

Once in the garage, she took a small black bag out of the T-Bird's trunk and flicked on the lights to illuminate the one-car garage Dweezil usually used for parking his Jag.

"You're going after that monster, aren't you?" Irma's words followed her. "And you don't think you're coming back. That's why you parked me in here. Before, you didn't care what happened to me. And that's why you put the crystals in the car."

Jazz was tempted to ignore her words and keep on walking, but she found she couldn't do it. She set the bag down by the door and walked back to the car, resting her hands on the door. As she looked into Irma's eyes, she knew there was one thing she could do.

"I want you to remember that you have the strength to do what you want to do most," she said. "What I see, you shall see. What I feel, you will feel. You will be with me. Because I say so, damn it!"

The moment Irma's form shimmered Jazz knew her spell had worked, especially when she felt another presence inside her mind.

I see myself! Irma's delighted laughter echoed inside Jazz's head. *Does this mean others will see and hear me?*

"No, just me." She tapped the metal with her fingertips. "All I ask is no screaming if things get rough. I can't be distracted or I'll have to shut you off."

I'll be good. I promise.

Jazz quickly learned that Irma's version of being good and her own version were two entirely different things. Irma chattered about everything to do with the limousine. *Does it have to smell like this?* to *Where are we going now?*

"No talking or I shut down audio," Jazz warned, pulling into the boardwalk parking lot where Nick stood by one of the buildings. Like Jazz, he wore all black.

Is Nicky going with us?

"I mean it, Irma."

I'll be good. Jazz felt the sensation of Irma zipping her lips shut. If only.

Jazz noticed the weariness in Nick's shoulders, sorrow darkening his eyes. He knew as well as she did that they probably wouldn't find Flavius on the estate, that Flavius was in a place they couldn't follow.

Nick walked over and climbed into the front seat. Before she could say a word, he grasped her by the back of the neck and pulled her towards him, delivering a kiss that was rough with passion and the fear of never being able to touch her again. She clutched his shoulders, needing the sense of touch, the taste, everything that branded Nick on her very soul.

Oh my! She immediately shut Irma off. There were some things Jazz wasn't willing to share.

"I am so scared," she whispered against his mouth.

"Ssh, no talk of fear. Even if I am just as scared as you are," he murmured, mapping her face with his lips. "But we will succeed, Jazz."

"How do you know that? If he's grown too powerful we could be walking into a disaster." She cupped his face with her hands, stroking the hair-roughened skin. "Let's just leave here, Nick. We could go to Europe. Go anywhere where he isn't. Let the damn Elders and the Protectorate take care of him." She continued running her fingertips over his face, reading him the way a blind woman would. "Why should we do their dirty work for them? I can drive us to the airport and we could get on the next plane." She choked up, feeling the fear and pain building up inside her like a time bomb. "Scandinavia has long nights."

Nick pulled in a deep breath, and rested his forehead against hers. He stroked her arms with his palms in a slow soothing gesture.

"I know where your words are coming from," he said softly. "And I know that you truly don't mean it because the Jazz I know doesn't run from a fight. She wades in with fireballs flying," he smiled at her soft laughter, "and curses raining on the bad guys until they end up as wart-covered toads."

"And then you make sure I am thrown in some disgusting jail cell and I hate you all over again," she whispered, swallowing the tears she knew she couldn't shed in front of him. "It's not right, Nick. Just two people can't save the world."

"They can if it's us. We will do this, Griet of the Irish Sea," he murmured against her skin. "We will accomplish what should have been done seventy years ago. And then," his mouth brushed against her ear, "then, we'll head for the land of long nights, find ourselves a cozy out-of-the-way inn and a very large bed. No fleas this time. I promise." He returned to her face and gave her a kiss that left her breathless before he released her and turned in the seat, securing the seatbelt across his chest and lap.

Jazz sniffed softly. "Okay, but if you get killed I will find whatever shadowy realm you end up in and come in and drag you out of there," she muttered, switching on the engine. "No one's going to kill you but me."

Nick's mouth curved in a smile. That was the Jazz he knew and loved. "Deal."

Jazz mentally switched Irma back on.

What happened? Did you two have sex? No, you couldn't have. It hasn't been long enough and I don't feel all that satisfied. What did you do? What did he do?

"Irma." There was no mistaking her warning.

Nick glanced at her.

"She's coming along for the ride," Jazz explained. "I just switched her back on." She pulled out of the parking lot and headed for her next stop. "If Tyge looks in the front seat, all he will see is a laptop computer. He won't think anything about it since he knows I watch DVDs or play computer games while waiting for him. But it's best if you don't speak. Any movement or sound you make will break the illusion." Her hands trembled on the steering wheel. She drew a deep breath to center herself. She looked at the moonstone ring gleaming on her finger. For a brief moment, the stone glowed with a milky blue ethereal light stronger than usual. The same light echoed in her moonstone pendant.

She suddenly felt stronger, more assured that whatever happened in the next few hours they would find a way to come out alive.

Seventeen

$\mathcal{F}$orty minutes later, Jazz parked the limo in front of Tyge Foulshadow's earthen dwelling. She waited with bated breath as the creature left his home and made his way toward her. Luckily Tyge was so preoccupied with his own thoughts that he said few words to her as he climbed into the back of the limousine. In the deepest recesses of her mind, she knew she should have been suspicious of his distracted behavior, but instead she was only grateful for his unusual lack of disgustingly salacious byplay while her own thoughts were diverted elsewhere.

"You know where the estate is?" he asked her before she closed the door once he was settled on the seat amidst a cloud of noxious dark-blue gas.

"Yes," she replied.

That's what you drive? Oh! He smells terrible! How can you stand it? Irma wailed in her head.

Jazz willed the ghost to be quiet and kept a faint smile pasted on her lips.

"Hand this to the gatekeeper. This will allow you to enter the grounds. He will not let you in without it." He passed over a card with his name written in fancy calligraphy on the heavy cream-colored vellum before settling back in the seat.

Jazz didn't glance at the passenger seat as she took her place behind the wheel. She felt Nick's comforting presence, and for now, that was enough.

As she took the freeway heading for Hollywood and its hills, she noticed that silence reigned in the back of the limo. For once Tyge didn't play his favorite music or make use of his cell phone. As one who didn't like seeing changes in behavior, this was something she didn't want to think about. Instead, she kept her focus on the freeway signs until she saw the off ramp she needed.

She later guided the vehicle up the winding, unlit road that she knew dead-ended at their destination. She looked up ahead and saw lights blazing from a three-story house that seemed to rule the hills themselves. Her stomach twisted so tightly she only needed some salt to turn it into a pretzel.

Is that where he lives? She heard Irma whisper. *It looks like something out of one of his horror movies.*

"Home of the devil," Jazz murmured to herself, stopping at the iron gates decorated with a large bat on each gate. She was positive the tall bald-headed man who approached her could easily bench press the limousine and not even break a sweat. "Master Tyge Foulshadow," she stated, handing him the card.

Instead of reading the card, he ran his fingers over the lettering and then stepped back. It wasn't until then that Jazz realized the man was blind and mute. He returned to his post and a moment later, the gates slowly swung outward.

"Here we go," she whispered, rolling through.

The moment the vehicle passed the gates, Jazz felt as if a hand squeezed the air out of her lungs. Instead of the usual white twinkle lights blanketing the shrubs lining the drive to give the grounds a fairytale appearance, tiny red lights gave it the ominous appearance she knew the host was looking for. She had a good idea the majority of his guests enjoyed the Goth ambiance. She studied the grounds, seeing them crowded with vampires and other creatures dressed in couture wear strolling around, unaware that something else flitted in and out around them. It was the latter that shook her to her toes. It was easy to see that the guests had no idea there were shadowy wraiths moving among them. Some of the wraiths looked resigned to their eternal fate, others held expressions of frustration as they followed the guests and tried to communicate with those who hadn't crossed into that shadowy realm. Their arms were outstretched in entreaty; mouths open, speaking words that obviously no one heard. It was heartbreaking to watch.

What are those?

"This is not good," Jazz whispered, automatically following the line of cars and limousines as each stopped in front of the mansion and released its passengers. She felt Nick's curiosity, but she couldn't acknowledge him in any way just yet.

She wasn't surprised to see that the Gothic styled mansion hadn't changed over the years, only looking even more forbidding with elaborate gargoyles guarding the huge wooden double doors. While gargoyles were known to protect the inhabitants from evil, she knew these were meant to keep all forms of good out and evil in.

"I'll return for you at two a.m.," she told Tyge as he slid out of the back seat. So she lied since she didn't intend to leave the grounds. She preferred he think she wasn't there in case all hell broke loose.

He smiled. If what his facial muscles did had anything to do with a smile. "Drivers are to remain on the grounds until the party is over, lovely Jazz. Perhaps you would rather wait inside the house than stay out here in the cold air. I am sure the host would not mind. We could have a glass of wine together."

"No thanks. I have enough here with me to keep me occupied." For a moment, she was startled to sense an unwanted intrusion inside her head. She instantly switched off Irma and did her best to repel the mental interloper. When Tyge slid backwards she knew she was successful. Her fingers itched to pull up a fireball. "Do not ever do that again." For one brief moment she was sorely tempted to slay him now and take the consequences later.

The slit doubling as Tyge's mouth curved downward in appropriate apology. Not that she believed him.

"I deeply apologize, my beauty." He inclined his head. He turned away and moved toward the stairs leading to the front door.

Jazz wasted no time getting back inside the limo and driving slowly to the rear of the mansion. It took all of her concentration to remain on the driveway and not turn around and haul ass out of there.

Nick coughed. "I don't know how you can stand driving that creature. Long dead animals don't smell as bad as he does."

"He is about as bad as you can get, but Dwcczil likes the gold bars he pays his bill with," she said, as she stared at the shadows on the grounds.

What are those shadows I see out there? Irma asked.

"So you see them too?" she asked.

"See what?" Nick asked. "What in Hades are you talking about?"

"This is so wrong." She moved away from the other cars, parking at the furthest end. She shut off the engine and stared through the windshield.

Nick looked from right to left in an effort to see what Jazz did. "What do you see out there?"

Jazz stared at the dimly-lit walkway that led down to the swimming pool she knew resembled a Roman bath complete with erotic statuary that many deemed pornographic. It had even been rumored that some of them somehow survived the destruction of Pompeii and centuries later ended up here. Clive had hosted many an orgy by the pool. She had considered herself lucky to have only heard about them and not actually been there. Of course, if she had, perhaps she wouldn't have become one of his victims later on because she sure wouldn't have come back. But what captured her gaze now were the shadowy forms that moved among the living and non-breathing without any notice, ignored by all.

"Shades," she whispered. "Lots of shades." She stared at three that crossed in front of the limo. One

paused and looked into the vehicle. She almost cried
at the look of despair on the indistinct face that
looked milky-white in the darkness. "This isn't my
gift, but ..." she closed her eyes, centered herself
and allowed herself to roam free. She ignored the
partylike emotions that suffused the majority of the
participants and focused on the others. *Sorrow. Fear.
Anger. Feelings of abandonment.* She opened her
eyes. "They're all his victims. Whatever he did to
them wouldn't allow them to have the peace to cross
over." She blindly reached over and gripped Nick's
hand. "They may as well be held prisoner here,
because there's no way for them to leave. They're
literally trapped on the grounds."

Empathy wasn't one of Jazz's gifts, but after all
the pain and anguish she felt from the shades it was
even easier to feel the waves of fury roll off Nick. He
sat perfectly still, his features looking as if they'd
been etched in stone.

"Then the only way they will be free to move on
is for him to die." He released her hand and climbed
out of the limo. "Let's do this."

Jazz got out and walked around the hood until she
stood in front of Nick. His anger had him shaking
from head to foot. When he looked down into her
face, she saw the fires of hell blazing in his eyes, a
fury she'd never seen before and never wanted
directed at herself. Nikolai the Destroyer stood in
front of her.

She placed her hands on his shoulders. "What
they see is not what we be. What they hear will be
unclear. Our truth will be a lie. Last until we say to

them good-bye." Her eyes glittered bright green in the darkness. "Because I say so, damn it!"

A chilly wind blew around them, twisting around them in a cloud of darkness. When it drifted away, Jazz looked at Nick, now blond with an obvious spray tan highlighting finely honed features; a movie star handsome man in a well-tailored tuxedo with a black silk shirt and tie while she now had golden-brown hair flowing in spiral waves down to her waist and wore a black-sequined strapless gown sporting a slit up to there. Her black high-heeled slides were nothing more than two narrow straps accenting scarlet tipped toes. Even her eyes had changed to a deep navy-blue color with a circle of red in the iris. Both of them had the appearance of extremely wealthy vampires whose focus was entirely self-involved.

She looked down at her breasts that had also increased two sizes. "The girls never looked better. But don't get any ideas." She grinned at Nick revealing a hint of fang. Even with her new disguise she looked like the Jazz he knew and loved. "Lock and load, Fang Boy."

"Fang boy? You better check out a mirror, sweetheart, because you now have a set of your own," he pointed out.

She tentatively ran her tongue across her top teeth and winced. "I don't know how you can put up with these things." She slipped her arm through his, conjured up two glasses of champagne and handed him one. "Shall we mingle, Rodrigo?" she purred with a toss of her head.

"Rodrigo?" He sipped the champagne. "Fine, Adelina."

But even crossing the grounds to the mansion proved to be difficult for Jazz as they passed the many shades all garbed in pale gray robes, some a darker shade of gray than others. And some so pale they resembled nothing more than a wisp of smoke. Jazz guessed the lighter ones were shades that had been there for far more years than the others. She saw the grounds crowded with faint vampire shadows and lost count of how many there were. The sight made her heartsick.

"You see us, don't you?" One shadowy feminine form asked. Her face was a pale blur in the darkness. Jazz doubted her face would be any clearer under bright light. She had been there too long. She wondered what would happen to the shade when she became so pale no one would be able to sense her. "I know you do. Please, tell me you see us. You are a witch, yes?"

What is she? Is she like me even if I don't wear something like that? Irma whispered inside Jazz's head. *I guess I should be grateful Harold chose that ugly dress or I could have been stuck in a robe like that for eternity.*

"Yes, I am. Please understand it would be dangerous for me to acknowledge you," Jazz said softly, keeping her gaze on the brightly lit house before them, acting as if a shadowy form wasn't walking with them. "We are here to help you if you can help us when the time comes. Do you know how many bodyguards he keeps inside?"

The shadowy form stayed with them, the woman telling her what she knew of the house when she was last inside, which she said was 1930.

"He placed wards around the house so we are unable to enter," she said, before they reached the French doors opening into a ballroom. "There is an underground dungeon where he plays with his victims. We hear them screaming for help, but we cannot go there. Please, be careful. He is a very evil man."

'Yes, I know," Jazz said grimly while keeping a vacuous smile on her lips.

She violently pushed down the multitude of dragons inhabiting her stomach as she and Nick stepped through the doors.

"We can do this," Nick whispered, sensing her unease. He moved closer. "Keep on smiling. We're being watched."

She obliged, looking like the sexy vampire she wasn't and acting as if she didn't have a care in the world other than having a good time that night. She scanned the room, easily picking out the staff from the guests. She noticed all the female servers wore pale-red silk gowns that bared one breast; a collar encircled each neck but did nothing to hide the bite marks that marred their necks and shoulders and, for all she knew, elsewhere. It was as if the revealing gowns were meant to display that the women were available for a quick snack. The male members of the staff were equally young, good-looking and wore only tight leather pants meant to augment their own charms. She was positive the smiles on their lips were more drug-enhanced than genuine. Once she saw the glassy eyes of more than one server, she knew she was right. The only way they were kept there was under the power of drugs and, she was certain, powerful magick.

She looked around and was relieved to find nothing familiar about the room. One of her biggest fears in returning here was that by stepping into the past all her nightmares would return. Instead, the furniture was more modern, even more lavish than back in 1932. Film stars back then lived excessive lives and Clive Reeves had gone beyond many with his wild lifestyle. He continued that more than seventy years later. Even so, memories were more powerful than the reality before her. It was too easy for her memory to overlay the room with the Roman-style couches and low tables that had dominated the rooms back then. Writhing figures sought a fulfillment that would be fleeting at best and only leave them empty and dissatisfied. The hunger would never end. Another room was candlelit, only one couch in there, a waterfall spilling down one wall, pornographic artwork adorning the other three. The presence of incense was so powerful it was a narcotic to the senses. Her screams were so loud, so strong, her throat burned, yet no one heard her. Or if they did, they ignored her. She swallowed the nausea that crawled up her throat.

Her impulse to turn around and run as far as she could in the other direction grabbed her and held on tight.

"Good evening."

Now there was a voice she would never forget. With Nick's reassuring presence by her side she was able to turn around and smile. "Our host, I believe." Her throaty Italian accent sounded nothing like her usual voice.

Even dressed formally in black slacks and a silk cream-colored shirt instead of the casual clothing she had seen in the parking garage, he was still a monster. All she had to do was look into eyes that held no soul, no humanity, to know she had to destroy him before he obliterated any more. Only Nick's slight hold on her arm kept her from drawing down whatever it took to burn the man into the ground.

Oh, that's him! He feels so evil! Jazz ignored Irma's distress that bounced around inside her head.

He smiled and sketched a shallow bow. "Clive Reeves. I don't believe we've met before." He looked from one to the other.

She held out her hand. Her razor-sharp nails matched the scarlet on her toes. When he lifted her hand she didn't expect him to turn it over and press a kiss into her palm. She resisted the urge to wipe her hand on her dress.

"Adelina," she said.

His face lit up. "How appropriate. Your name means noble."

"Rodrigo," Nick's normally deep voice was more baritone and Spanish in flavor.

"Charmed." Clive sketched another bow. "We enjoy new faces here." He glanced at their champagne flutes.

Luckily, Jazz had thought quickly enough to have the liquid resemble champagne mixed with blood before they entered the house. But there was still something in the man's gaze that unsettled her, especially when he took his time studying her face. She knew her illusion spell was still holding or he would have called her out here and now.

"We have been told by ones such as Master Foulshadow that you•have the power to return our true lives to us," she said softly. She knew even if Tyge was questioned, he wouldn't want to admit he didn't know anyone as beautiful as she. His nature wouldn't allow it. The slime.

He frowned. "How long have you walked only at night?"

Nick moved slightly in front of Jazz. "A little over three hundred years for Adelina. Four hundred for myself." He smiled and ran the back of his fingers down her cheek. "The first time I saw her I knew she was meant to spend eternity with me. But now we wish to return to our mortal lives." His expression was the ultimate bored vampire. "After all, it isn't as if we can't find someone to change us back if we so wish." He chuckled.

Clive studied their clothing, judging cut and cost. Jazz deliberately lifted her flute, displaying a ring bearing a diamond the size of Texas. She knew he didn't need, nor want, money, but she had to play the part. "What I offer is not cheap."

"Nothing of value is." Jazz chose to speak up. "Whatever you wish, we will pay it. We are weary of only seeing the sunset and wish to see a sunrise."

He smiled again. "Beauty is always welcome here. And anything you wish is yours. You only have to ask. We will speak more of your personal desires later." He bowed again and moved on, greeting more guests.

One of the female slaves walked past, offering them both a tentative smile. Nick gave a short shake of the head. She ducked her head and moved swiftly on. Within seconds, a vampire with glowing red eyes grasped her arm with a bruising pinch of his fingers and led her toward a curtained alcove. Judging by the way he hungrily latched his gaze on the young woman's revealed breast, Jazz feared the creamy skin would soon end up in shreds at best and she would be dead at worst. But then, by the time he finished with her, she might welcome death.

"Nothing is real here," Jazz whispered, taking in the champagne flutes filled with a combination of blood and champagne, the richly dressed guests and the lavishness of the mansion itself. "It's like something out of a surreal movie where the guests invited for dinner have no idea they could *be* dinner."

"We should circulate." Nick dropped his hand to hers and laced his fingers through hers.

"This is nothing new to you, is it?" While she had attended her share of preternatural parties over the centuries, she hadn't liked most of them. Most vampires cared for little other than themselves and instant gratification. Other preternatural creatures were the same.

The first time she had entered this house, it was filled with mortals and she felt as if she was truly part of the human world. By the end of the evening, she had been convinced she had faced the worst monster of all. For the next five years she slept with the lights on and Fluff and Puff huddled by her side.

"Admittedly, my kind have one-track minds when it comes to excess," Nick said in a low voice. "And for a time, I thought the same as they did. I was lucky to learn excess meant nothing."

"Good thing. You can make sure I don't make any mistakes, like throwing a few fireballs around here." She averted her gaze from a lovely female vampire falling to her knees before one of the male servers and unzipping his pants. Jazz really hoped Madame fanged-and-lovely wasn't about to literally gobble him up.

Is she doing what I think she's doing? Jazz guessed Irma would have a full education before the evening was over.

"A well crafted staircase," Nick commented, guiding her to the front of the house before her distaste was revealed to others. *Keep your cover* he deliberately murmured inside her head. *We've come too far now.* "This is the style I wish for our home, darling."

"Yes, it would work well, wouldn't it?" she replied, keeping to her persona. She noted the silk cushioned couches and chairs, highly polished tables, and elegant chandeliers. "Lovely." She paused to admire one of the chandeliers brilliant with candlelight.

"I purchased the chandelier from a seventeenth-century castle in England." Clive walked up to them. The contents of his champagne flute were a darker, richer color than many of the other glasses around. "The duke who owned it didn't want to give it up, but I made him an offer he couldn't refuse," he said, with a smile that was positively chilling.

Jazz didn't want to think what the exact contents of his flute were or what kind of offer he made the duke.

"You have excellent taste." Jazz forced a smile as she raised her flute to her lips. She was glad it tasted like cherry Kool-Aid instead of the alternative. "It reminds me of our own estate just outside of Paris."

He stared at her, visually stripping her gown from her body and finding her to be everything he would want in a woman. The need for a long hot shower with lots and lots of soap came to mind. "Still, I wonder why you are here. Ones as young as the two of you generally prefer keeping your lifestyle."

"We told you why," she said bluntly, ignoring Nick's tension. "Plus we were told you welcome vampires. Is that not true?"

"Yes, but as I said admittance is by invitation only. And the one you arrived with doesn't remember you." His smile turned deadly.

Jazz and Nick looked over his shoulder to see Tyge standing by a small mahogany table. Gold coins were scattered across the highly polished surface.

"The bas—" Jazz's words froze in her throat as Clive whipped a hand up, a large polished crystal nestled in his palm. The power glimmered across the surface.

Jazz and Nick stared at the crystal, seeing their true selves dressed in their black clothing instead of the formal wear Jazz had conjured up.

"Did you not think I wouldn't take precautions against unwanted guests?" Clive asked, a cruel smile tipping his lips. "Although, I must say I do prefer the lovely gown you're wearing, Jazz. It shows you at your best." His gaze fastened on her breasts.

"Your precautions are traitors who value gold over morals. How charming," she drawled.

"Nikolai." Clive turned to Nick. "It is nice to see you again. A friend of yours was here not long ago. We had an interesting chat before ..." his voice trailed off meaningfully.

Nick was professional enough not to react. "I have many friends."

"Yes, I'm sure you have, but how many of those friends served the great Roman Empire?" Clive asked.

Jazz felt Nick's hand tighten on hers until she feared the bones would be ground to dust.

She felt chilled to the bone as she stared at her enemy's face. He was enjoying their battles to mask their emotions. If it hadn't been for Nick standing next to her, she knew she would have unleashed the mother of all spells.

"Don't be so sure about that, Jazz," Clive said, reading her thoughts and intentions easily. "I have dealt with beings you cannot even imagine. With a word I could strip that lovely flesh from your hide before you could blink an eye. You would still be alive but feel pain you could never imagine. You would beg for death and I would only refuse to give you that release. I could also have you on your knees before me doing what I'm sure you do best. Don't even think about it, vampire." His icy stare whipped to Nick who took a step forward. "Because then I would be forced to get even more creative to the point where you would watch your lovely witch die a very slow and extremely painful death."

"You won't kill her, Reeves," Nick said, his tone and manner just as cold and deadly as Clive's, if not more, "because she's your card to my cooperation, and the only way you have any hope of remaining in one piece."

"Oh, you will cooperate, vampire." Clive nodded to the men who had silently surrounded the couple.

Jazz felt the buzz of power begin at her feet and move upward. She turned to Nick and saw by his expression he also felt the magickal bonds tighten around him.

What is going on? Irma shrieked inside her head.

Before Jazz could mouth Nick's name, her world turned black and she was lost in a void of nothingness.

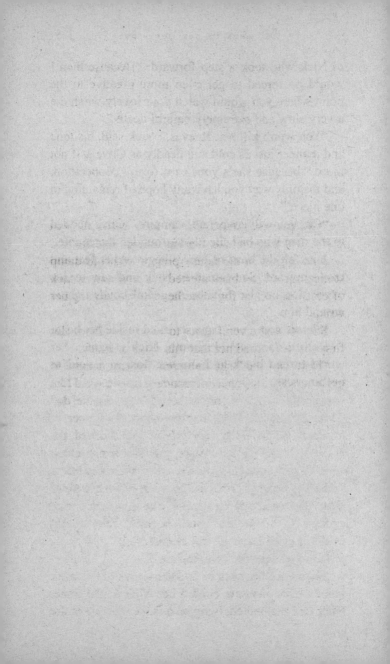

Eighteen

A pounding headache let Jazz know she was still alive. The chill in the air told her she was no longer in the house proper and cold damp stones against her back alerted her to a serious lack of clothing except for some heavy iron circling her wrists.

She blinked several times to clear her vision. Her first glance warned her that this was not good.

"Don't tell me," she muttered, looking around to get a better view of her surroundings that looked like something out of a movie set. "What did he do? Channel Vincent Price and transport the Tower of London to the Hollywood Hills?" She tested the manacles circling her wrists, but the heavy chain secured to the wall high above her head forced her to remain up on her tiptoes. She tried to wiggle away from the wall, but the heavy chains weren't long enough to allow her much room. "The bastard couldn't even leave me my clothes."

"Do you hear me complaining?"

She craned her neck to find the source of the weak voice. What she saw chilled her clear to the bone. Nick was also naked, lying on a stone altar set in the center of the room. Heavy chains had been criss-crossed across his body to prevent any movement. Even if there were no burns apparent on his skin, she feared there was enough silver embedded in the metal to weaken him beyond the point of any resistance. An obsidian bowl and matching goblet sat on a table next to the altar. She wasn't sure exactly what would happen once Clive arrived, but she had an idea it wouldn't be good. The rack dominating one end of the chamber looked much too authentic to merely be part of the décor and she was positive the rust-colored stains on the wood were blood. The same stains were visible on whips and various implements of torture that hung on a nearby wall. Her gaze swept the chamber, mentally cataloguing everything she saw. She wasn't sure what upset her more, the evidence the implements were well used or the huge embroidered tapestry hanging on one wall that detailed writhing and screaming victims tortured in unimaginable ways. She could feel power emanating from the tapestry as if what had happened in this dungeon was transferred into the tapestry as a permanent reminder. Her stomach plummeted at the thought she and Nick could end up as new portraits. Seventy-five years ago, she had learned just what a sick bastard Clive Reeves was. She saw that the man had only turned even more evil over the years. She dug deep, working to summon her power, but felt nothing.

"Damn it!" she swore, fighting the imprisoning chains.

"What's wrong?" Nick asked.

"There's something in here that won't allow me to tap into my power. He must have magick-dampening shields buried in the walls or something." She mentally searched for any hint of Irma inside her head but found only silence. "I can't even contact Irma. The one time I want to talk to that woman and I can't reach her!" If she hadn't been standing on her toes she would have stamped her foot in indignation.

The sound of a heavy wooden door creaking open sounded from above.

"We have company," Nick murmured.

Jazz looked around at the torture implements and bloodstained stone floor. "It better be the maid, because this place needs serious cleaning up."

"Good, you're both awake." Clive descended the stone steps wearing a black silk ankle-length robe and carrying a crystal wineglass in one hand.

Jazz noticed the symbols embroidered on the hem of the robe echoed those on the bowl and goblet. Only a few were familiar to her and those had to do with baneful magick.

Nope, not good at all.

"Your illusion spell was very clever, my dear, but I much prefer your true beauty." Clive approached her and reached out to stroke the line of her jaw. She snapped her head back before he could touch her and refused to wince when the back of her head connected with the wall. He smiled as if he expected her rejection, but she didn't miss the fury simmering in his dark eyes. Fury mixed with lust was not a good thing. "I believe you have grown even more beautiful than the last time I saw you," he said.

"Gee, Clive, you'd think we were upstairs partying away instead of our being buried deep within the bowels of your house in a dungeon straight out of one of your totally grade-B movies," Jazz said sarcastically, silently patting herself on the back for the less-than-subtle slur about Clive's movies. Judging by the tightening of his cheekbones, he got it. She'd mention she won the point for zingers, but she had a good idea he wouldn't take that well either. Plus, she wasn't exactly in a good place here.

While her skin crawled in reaction to the way he stared at her naked body as if she was a Thanksgiving feast on a silver platter, she didn't allow her thoughts to surface. She felt the dark power rolling off his body as it snaked around her like an icy cold wrap that penetrated her to the bone. She bit back her snarl when she noticed he was staring at her breasts, the nipples now rosy pebbles from the cold.

He and Tyge make a perfect pair.

"You know, I thought you were repugnant in 1932. I see my loathing back then was an understatement."

His features tightened to a mask that cracked just enough to reveal even more layers of the soulless insanity that resided inside. "Exactly how old are you, my dear?"

She stared deep into his eyes, looking at evil and madness in the black depths. Sickness and malevolence had overtaken an already forbidding soul, where years ago she had seen a faint hint of humanity. Now there was nothing left but a shell of the real man.

She wanted to crush that shell until there was nothing left.

"I am old enough to grind your bones to dust," she said levelly, digging deep within her very self for whatever hint of power might linger within her. She refused to believe there was nothing she could draw upon.

Clive chuckled as if she was a small child saying something clever. "Amusing, but we aren't talking about a child's fairy tale. I sense your power, witch, but what I have inside of me is more potent than anything you can imagine. With just a thought I can squash you like a bug," he bragged. "You thought you killed me once, but you didn't succeed. And now it comes to this." His eyes lingered on the chains.

She refused to give in to her terror over what he was obviously thinking. She would not. *Could* not. "This time I will make sure you are so dead you won't even be able to come back as a goldfish," Jazz said softly, with a menace that equaled his.

He half-turned and studied the resolve in her features, the ferocious fire that flared to life in her eyes as she stared back with no hint of the fear.

Just as swiftly his hand lashed out and she felt the sting across her face turn into a burn where he'd struck her. She refused to take her eyes from him as she spat blood from her mouth. She couldn't look at Nick as she heard his roar of fury.

"I believe you would, Jazz." Clive chuckled. "That is why I decided I would rather keep you alive as my pet. You have no idea of the untapped power within you. Power I can use. And perhaps, if you had some time to think about it, you would decide it would be more beneficial to be with me. There's no reason why we couldn't come to an arrangement suitable for the two of us."

"At the moment, I can't think of a totally witty response to such a disgusting proposition, but I can come up with something fitting. Eat shit and die." She added a smile to boost the insult even as moving her mouth hurt like hell. She was positive her lips were going to be puffier than any collagen injection could provide.

But Jazz wasn't through. She fought through the pain in her face and continued to mentally dig down deep, looking for any hint of magick that could help her and Nick out of this situation. A mental push to search for Irma only managed to push painfully back at her. Somehow Clive had managed not only to dampen all magick down here but he had also found a way to punish anyone who tried to use their power. So now she had a headache along with the burning pain on her face.

She glanced past him at Nick and saw that the silver she suspected was in the chains was a fact. Faint burn marks now traveled up his body. She could see his strength was rapidly draining. His jaw was tight as he fought the pain taking over his body.

Plan A was no longer an option, and Plan B had to also be tossed, so she'd have to move to Plan C.

There was only one problem. They hadn't thought to come up with a Plan C.

"Don't be sad, Jazz," Clive murmured, opening a secret cabinet below the altar and reaching inside.

"Once I have drunk your vampire lover's life force, I will have all that is his and you as my lovely pet. A man couldn't ask for anything more." He brought out a tube and IV needle. With a motion of long practice, he inserted the needle into Nick's wrist and blood dripped slowly down the tube and into the ceremonial bowl.

"Except you do not kill us, you bastard! You turn our kind into shades doomed to walk the earth and never have any peace." Nick flashed his fangs as he fought against the chains, but his strength was greatly diminished between the embedded silver and the blood exiting his vein. "No wonder you never leave the mansion. If you walked out the door you would have to face all of those who wander your grounds for eternity. That's why you learned astral projection. It was the only way you could leave here without encountering your victims."

If Jazz's gaze hadn't been centered on Clive she would have missed the flicker of fear cross his face and the way his hands hesitated in his tasks. She was pleased to know Nick had touched a nerve. Clive quickly regained his composure and turned to her. His expression wasn't so pleasant now.

"I have no reason to leave my beautiful house. Everything I require is here and I have staff to bring me whatever I need. Such as you." He walked over and roughly gripped Jazz's face and brought it around to him. She knew if she struggled he would snap her neck just because he could. For the time being, she vowed not to fight him, even if she knew it was a short-lived promise.

Except what Clive had in mind turned out to be more unpleasant than breaking her neck. His mouth savaged hers; he started biting and licking her lips and face like a ravenous dog. At the same time, he grabbed a breast and squeezed hard enough to leave bruises on her delicate skin. She held back a scream of pain and fury when he lowered his head and bit down on her nipple. She pulled on her manacles, but they were drawn up too short for her to slam the heavy chains down on his head.

"I will kill you for that!" Nick shouted, rearing up then falling back.

"Gross!" she spat out, while wishing for a large bottle of disinfectant to destroy the taste in her mouth when the monster finally pulled away.

Clive smiled cruelly. "That is only the first, my pet. And I do mean *pet*," he stated. "Because I intend to keep you naked and on a leash and you will do what I wish, when I wish, and for as long as I wish, and *if* you comply with my wishes, I just might decide to keep your vampire alive … for awhile." He walked over and pinched the tube closed. The blood stopped dripping into the bowl. He watched Jazz's face as he released the tube. The blood began dripping steadily into the bowl again. "It is your choice. Plus, I do admit the idea of keeping him on eternal tap is a lovely idea."

"She won't agree to it because I won't allow it," Nick shouted. "There is no reason for you to think you can achieve your goal by using my blood when you've drained so many and not succeeded. We are not food, human." His face had become that of a stone-cold soulless predator.

"I am no longer human, vampire. And I will be successful. Not long ago you and the witch not only fucked, but your shared power managed to create something new." He smiled at the shock on Jazz's face. "Oh yes, I have seen the two of you together and it was stimulating." He briefly touched himself, idly stroking his cock. "The shared power means that what she has is within you and vice versa. So by ingesting the essence of you both, mingling blood and sex, so to speak," his smiled widened, "I have the best of both worlds. By keeping you alive, vampire, I can have my elixir any time I wish. And by keeping Jazz around, I ensure your compliance—just as she will obey me to keep you alive. The two of you may claim you will only think of yourselves, but I know better."

So someone had been watching them make love that night. Jazz felt sick inside. She thought of the slaves he laughingly called staff who worked upstairs. She knew they were all slaves to his every whim. What they endured because of this creature and how he allowed the guests to have their way with them, biting, shredding of skin, and worse. A hickey from Clive would be minor compared to what his guests did to the poor unfortunates upstairs. She knew she would kill him before he would touch her again. She met Nick's gaze and saw the pain and sorrow in his eyes. She feared before too long he would be too weak to resist whatever ghoulish procedures Clive might think up next.

Do what it takes, love.

For once she wasn't going to complain about his entering her head.

He's going to die for good this time, Nick.

I never doubted it.

Nick's confidence in her was just what she needed right now. Along with a way to get Clive's attention no matter how much it hurt her. She looked around the chamber, looking for anything that what would startle him. When her gaze reached the tapestry she took a deep breath and closed her eyes. She finally found a tiny speck of power buried deep within her. She nurtured it the way she'd nurse a weak flame. The moment she felt the flicker grow, she opened her eyes and focused on the tapestry. It was a chance she had to take, no matter what.

Just do it, Jazz.

"Images I see. Images that hide," she shouted at the top of her lungs even as she felt the suffocating pressure build up inside her brain. "Images reveal to us what is beyond! Reveal because, damn it, I say so!" At that second, she pushed every ounce of that fledgling power toward the heavy fabric. Her vision momentarily clouded as whatever dampened her magick tried to punish her with waves of pain that screamed along her nerve endings, but she fought back just as hard. A heavy blast of cold air raced through the chamber, chilling Jazz to the bone before it struck the tapestry, the heavy fabric flapping in the wind as if it were nothing but paper. A moment later, the sound of the aged material tearing down the center echoed throughout the dungeon. Screams from within the cloth bounced around the room, sending more waves of chilled air as spirits escaped their textile prison. Just as Jazz thought, victims had been held captive there also.

Clive spun around. "*No!*" he screamed, starting toward the destroyed tapestry with his hands thrust out as if to stop what had already been done. Before he could take a step, he froze. A gurgling sound traveled up his throat.

Jazz tried to focus on the floor-to-ceiling window now revealed by the destroyed tapestry. At first, she thought the window had been covered with some sort of patterned paper. Now she realized the pattern was moving. The shades that populated the grounds now looked through the window, watching the imminent destruction of another one of their own.

"Flavius," she whispered, seeing the familiar features of Nick's sire in the forefront—confirmation that Nick's sire had been brought here and now would never walk and talk with Nick again.

"Look upon them!" She unconsciously pulled on her manacles until she chafed her skin raw and bleeding. The pain brought her back to her surroundings. "You are a beast who has lost all of your humanity!" she screamed loud enough to shatter glass. She only wished it had because then the shades on the outside would be in here confronting the one who imprisoned them on a shadowy plain with no chance of escape. "Look upon what you have hidden from all these decades! What you see are the products of your creation. Creatures you destroyed for a sinister power you can't even hold onto. No more, Clive, because before I'm done here they will be free and you will have *nothing!*"

"You bitch!" Clive screamed back, shrinking from the faces visible through the heavy glass. Mouths opened and closed in silent screams of anguish as they stared at the one who tormented them.

Jazz looked at Nick, noting the pain on his face, and knew whatever happened next could finish them both. Death wasn't her first option, but if she succeeded in freeing the shades and killing Clive in the process she knew their deaths would be worth it.

The flicker of power she'd diligently nursed to destroy the tapestry roared to an inferno. Clive's agitation caused a shift in the power in the dungeon that Jazz immediately felt. She wasted no time searching for any power trapped in the walls and started to tap into it, but she quickly realized his dark magick might override her own and in the end defeat her. It was a chance she'd have to take. She'd been lucky with the tapestry, but this next time around she'd have to pull out all the stops.

Do it, love. Nick's comforting voice inside her head offered her the grounding she needed.

"I call on the Goddess of Judgment! I plead that you do to this creature of the dark arts what he deserves for twisting power for his own personal gain and not respecting the existence of others," she called out, searching for all she could tap into even as the pain inside her head increased to the point where she feared her head would explode. As she drew in a deep breath, she knew exactly what to say for maximum effect. "Show no mercy for this one who has shown no compassion for the children of the night. Show no mercy for this one who steals that which gives them their existence. Let those victims who walk between the two worlds judge him as he should be judged." A rumble rolled through the chamber, causing Clive to stumble. He reached out to grab the edge of the altar to keep his balance. The air grew thick with power making it difficult to breathe while the flames from the torches flickered wildly under the wave. For a moment Jazz feared they'd start a fire they'd have no chance of escaping. Her hair lifted up and waved around her head with the crackle of magick while her skin seemed coated with multi-colored sparkles. Her moonstone ring glowed a white hot blue that burned her skin, but she was beyond feeling either the burn or the pain pressing inside her head. She was a witch on a mission to destroy the bad guy.

Clive was wild-eyed as he felt her power envelop his with a strength he hadn't expected. "*What are you doing?*"

Her gaze could have sliced him to ribbons. "Making things right." She closed her eyes again, took a deep breath of the thick air and embraced what rushed through her. "I ask that he not be allowed to create anything more that walks between the worlds!" Jazz nudged her control up that extra notch. For a moment, as it moved through her, she felt as if her head would fly off but she managed to hold on by her fingertips. "I beg that things be made right." She lifted her face, her smile wide with the sense that right now she could pretty much do anything. It was suddenly very clear what was needed.

A thunderclap slammed through the night sky as if the magick she brought up would split the atmosphere in two. Jazz didn't flinch when a lightning bolt struck the stone floor leaving the burnt scent of sulfur behind and splitting the floor in half. Fire licked up from beneath the stones.

"I ask that the one who can finish this be brought here. Grant her the chance to face the one who harmed her, so that she may make things right!"

The air fairly sizzled with the nostril-burning smell of electricity as her power again rolled around her.

"You fucking bitch! You won't ruin this for me! I'll see you dead first," Clive roared, starting towards her with his hands outstretched.

Jazz knew if she didn't finish it now he would surely tear her limb from limb, and in his fury he wouldn't spare Nick no matter how much he wanted Nick's blood. As she looked at his enraged features she realized that by drawing what power she could from the house she'd effectively barred Clive from using it. She spared a quick glance at Nick. Guessing her intent he managed a brief smile.

"Allow the one who can finish what I have begun to leave her protected surroundings and join me. Because I say so, damn it!" Her lungs burned, but she wasn't about to shut up now. "Irma! You can do it! Leave your refuge to pass judgment on the one who has harmed so many! *Because I say so, damn it!*"

Nineteen

orget my screwing you to death and then handing you over to the others to feast on. I *will* kill you now!" Clive almost reached her when the entire room shook as if a monster earthquake rolled around them.

Jazz lost her balance, falling forward with only the manacles around her wrists keeping her upright. Clive fell to the floor in an undignified sprawl. He rose onto his hands and knees, his features distorting even more. His earlier arrogance had been wiped clean and he now looked more like a terrified animal than a man who was confident he was invincible.

The air around them glistened and shifted until it appeared to tear in the center and part. A woman's shriek was abruptly cut off as a figure stumbled into the chamber.

"It worked! Jazz, honey, you did it! You got me out of the car! I told you you could do it," Irma squealed looking around. She exhibited shock at Jazz's state of undress and then paused to give Nick an admiring glance. "My land, child, what kind of shenanigans have you been up to in this horrible place? As she turned away she came face to face with Clive. "*You!*" She lifted her handbag as if ready to pummel him. "You're the bastard who put all that nasty oil on my car! You scared me half to death! Well, you know what I mean." As her anger intensified, her form shimmered in and out until it appeared solid. "You are an evil man and you need to be held accountable for your crimes."

"You can't be here. This isn't possible." He scrambled to his feet and backed away from her as she advanced on him. His anger had been replaced by stark fear that shook his limbs. His pale features turned an unearthly gray color. "No shades can pass the mansion's threshold! I set those wards myself years ago. Many shades have tried to breach them and they all failed."

"They failed because the shades you protected yourself from were ones you created. She's not your shade, asshole," Jazz snarled, ignoring her raw throat and the searing pain in her wrists and arms as she again pulled on her chains. "You have no control over her. No one does." With Clive losing more of his power, she felt the return of her own with a vengeance. She smiled as she watched Irma pause long enough to look around the chamber. Disgust crossed the ghost's face as she turned back to Clive who backpedaled to keep out of arm's reach. "And she's going to kick your ass," Jazz finished with relish and more than her share of witchy malice. She so loved watching the bad guy get what he deserved.

Irma turned back from the faces pressed against the glass. "What kind of wickedness have you been doing here, you son of a bitch? What you did to me that day was bad enough, but this …," she gestured toward the window, "is beyond words." She marched toward him, her handbag still upraised ready to inflict damage.

As Clive threw up his hands in self defense, Irma walked right though him. The horror his victims experienced at his hands was now transferred to him. A thin stream of blood trickled down his forehead then a second followed as his skin began to blacken and split. Trails of blood soon leaked from his mouth, nose, and ears.

"Go get 'em, Irma," Jazz whispered, before gearing up one more time. "I ask that the shades be released to exact their own judgment!" Her voice fractured on the last word, but it was enough. The sound of glass cracking was first, followed by window fragments falling to the floor and shattering. Chilly night air whooshed inside along with what Jazz sensed were thousands of shades. She knew she would have screamed like a girl if one of them had touched her, but all of their concentration was centered on Reeves. He fell to his knees, covering his head as the shades converged on him. His screams of terror echoed throughout the dungeon.

With the dampening spell completely gone, Jazz managed to release the manacles and sink to her knees. She stood up and ran over to the altar and gently pulled the needle from Nick's wrist. She winced at the blood trickling from his wound. Thankfully, before her eyes, the wound closed up and healed.

She turned her attention to the chains and tugged on the thick links then looked for the lock. She cursed under her breath when one couldn't be found.

"Release the one that doesn't deserve this. Because I say so, damn it!" she commanded, holding onto one of the links.

"I'm glad to see you haven't lost your touch," Nick whispered with a faint smile. "By destroying Clive, the mansion will be brought down too because his magick kept it going. You need to get out of here now."

"If you think I did all that only to abandon you, you've got another think coming, mister. I'm not leaving without you." Grim resolve gave her that extra strength as she zapped the links. She fell against the stone, feeling the sharp edge cut into her palms.

"I can survive the house coming down. You can't," he reminded her.

"We've survived the Black Plague, the *Titanic,* and Pearl Harbor just to name a few. Not to mention the Disco period. We leave here together." She wiped her bloody palms on her bare thighs and pushed the chains to one side until Nick could easily slide out from beneath them. He stood up and staggered a bit.

"I'd say he's very much dead this time. I heard his heart stop beating," he said, accepting the shoulder she offered him.

Like stop-motion photography, Reeves' salt and pepper hair lengthened, turning a yellowish white, while his blackened and split skin peeled away from his skull, leaving white bone behind. The same happened with his hands and legs, skin and muscle disappearing until only bones were left behind. Within moments, the robe flattened to the floor and all that remained was a grayish-white powder. Just as his body returned to what it should be, the torture equipment around the room slowly crumbled to dust, the iron now rusty from age and old blood. All the whispers she'd heard when they first entered the property were now silent.

"They judged him and were released from their final bond to earth." She looked past Nick at the scorch marks and hole in the floor. "Oh man, Mother Nature is going to get me for that one." She winced each time her bare feet found a splinter of glass.

"I did it, Jazz!" A beaming Irma appeared in front of them. "I left the car." She swung in a circle.

"Yes, you did." She smiled back.

Irma looked at what was left of Clive's body and her smile disappeared. "It was for an excellent reason." She turned back to Jazz. "Thank you." She suddenly looked startled and vanished in the blink of an eye.

"And now she's gone," Jazz said, feeling a tear leak from her eye. "Probably just as well." She felt the floor trembling under their feet. She struggled to keep a tight hold on him. "You're right. We need to get out of here."

Nick leaned on her heavily. "While we're getting the hell out of Dodge as they say, we might want to find some clothes. As much as I like seeing you naked, the authorities might not understand and they're going to show up here very soon. An exploding house doesn't escape notice easily."

"That's all you want? Piece of cake." She swept her hand over them. Nick wore the tuxedo from before while she again wore her gown. "No reason for us to attract any unwanted attention in case any of Reeves' goons are still around." She started for the stairs, but Nick tugged on her arm to halt her.

They turned toward Clive's remains. The faint shadowy substance that had once been Flavius stood there. He smiled and held up his right hand, palm forward.

Nick echoed the gesture. A second later, Flavius disappeared.

"Come on," Jazz whispered, keeping her arm around Nick and helping him up the stairs. Between the two of them they were able to lift the heavy wooden bar across the door and wrench it open.

They found the main floor of the house in chaos. Those Clive had enslaved were running through the house toward any exit they could find, while vampires, unaware they could have been the next victims in Clive's quest for dark power, were likewise swarming out. Bodies lay scattered in each room they passed. Flames licked at the walls, turning the silk window coverings into torches.

"If you need blood we can find someone," Jazz whispered, aware of his weakness.

He shook his head. "No, I won't use them the way he did."

Jazz considered his weak state and muttered a curse that brought a hint of magickal smoke to the air. She propped him up against a wall and ducked into a room. She came out holding a goblet. "Drink it. I'd say this is the pure stuff, but you're the real expert here." She waved it under his nose.

Nick's fangs appeared at the rich coppery scent. He grasped the goblet with both hands and downed it in one gulp. He had barely finished when she snatched it from his hands and gave him another.

He finished the second and cocked his head. "Police."

Jazz grimaced at the resonance of sirens that didn't sound all that far off. "Not my favorite people even if they adore you. Should have known they'd get up here fast. The higher-priced the neighborhood, the faster the response."

"Maybe if you were nice to them once in a while they wouldn't give you so much trouble." He grinned.

"Come on. If we're lucky we can get out of here in time." She almost lost her balance when the house shifted again.

As they crossed the threshold, the house began buckling, folding into itself. The earth shuddered so severely they were thrown to the ground.

This time, it was Nick who grabbed Jazz and pulled her to safety as the house sank into the ground and flames shot up into the air, igniting a few nearby trees. Nick flinched.

"Save the trees," Jazz said for want of anything else and because she was just too damn exhausted to come up with a better spell. The fire immediately died. She gave a sheepish shrug. "Considering everything, that's the best I could do. Do you feel it, Nick?" She looked at the destroyed house. The only vehicle remaining was her limo parked nearby.

Judging by the dents in the sides, some of the fleeing guests weren't careful in their retreat from the catastrophe. Neither of them were surprised that all the vampires had left the property immediately. After all, fire was their enemy. She looked around, pleased to see the absence of the sad-faced shades wandering the grounds. "They really are all gone. They were able to fully cross over and be free. We did it."

He looked sad as he scanned the expansive property, the three-story house now nothing more than a fiery pit. Even the swimming pool had collapsed.

"They didn't deserve to die the way they did," he murmured. "Flavius was denied the warrior's death he earned long ago."

Jazz wrapped her arms around him.

"Still, they're free, Nick," she whispered against his shoulder. Her smile and tears were luminous in the moonlight. "They're free." She reached up and kissed the side of his neck. She turned her head when his arm around her waist tightened. "Uh-oh." She stared at the unmarked sheriff's car moving up the long driveway behind the approaching fire trucks. "Uh, Nick, if there was ever a good time for you to play big bad cop who totally can bond with these guys, this is it."

The vehicle stopped nearby and a man wearing a rumpled suit climbed out. Jazz made sure their clothing appeared rumpled and torn, their faces smudged with smoke. The man sighed as he stared at them.

"How did I know you'd be here?" Detective Larkin tugged at his loosened tie, looked toward the destroyed house and back at Jazz and Nick. He stabbed a meaty finger at Jazz. "And don't give me that mom and apple pie shit, hear me?"

Jazz kept her snarl to herself. "I hadn't planned on it. I swear to you I had nothing to do with this, Detective Larkin," she said, for once telling the truth. In the strictest sense of the word, she had nothing to do with the fire, only what happened before that.

"And you two decided to stay here like good little citizens to make a statement, right?" He turned to Nick, clearly seeing him as the voice of reason. "Either of you need a paramedic?"

"We've suffered nothing more than cuts and bruises from the stampede out of the house. We were here for the party and next thing we knew someone yelled fire," Nick explained. "People started running for the doors and we were pushed outside with everyone else. Jazz and I were parted in the melee and by the time I was able to find her again, everyone else had left the grounds." He rubbed his head as if it was aching. "Look, Detective, I know you'll want a statement, but can it wait until morning? It's been a rough night."

Larkin glared at them both. "Wait here for now." He headed for the fire chief directing the operation.

"I don't think he believes us," Jazz murmured.

Nick smiled. "Oh, he believes me. It's you he doesn't trust." He looked upward at the sound of thunder rolling overhead. "Not a good idea right now." The thunder grew silent.

Larkin walked back to them. "They won't know what happened for sure until they can look through the rubble, but the firemen think it might have been an electrical short," he told them. "House is pretty old and who knows when the wiring was last looked at. We need statements from you two, so be at the station at nine."

Nick held tight onto Jazz's arm so she wouldn't say anything. "We will be there, Detective." He steered her toward the limo.

"So what are you going to tell Detective Larkin when you don't show up in the morning?" she asked. "Weather Channel said tomorrow will be a bright and sunny day."

"He only said nine. He didn't specify if he wanted us there in the morning or the evening."

Before Jazz rounded the hood to climb into the driver's seat, she took one last look at the destruction and then lifted her face to the sky as a drop of rain hit her face. In moments, the misting rain turned into a downpour. She stood there for a moment enjoying the cleansing power of the cold water on her skin. She noticed the fire soon died under the downpour.

"Thank you, Mother Nature," she whispered, climbing in.

Cocooned in the dark confines of the front seat, she turned to Nick.

"You did it, Jazz," he said softly. "You dug deep within your power and you brought forth the one who had the power to destroy Clive."

"I did, didn't I?" She grinned, proud of her accomplishment in bringing down the enemy. She released a weary sigh and rested her head against the headrest with her face turned toward him.

"You do good work, love." He leaned over and cradled her face with his hands, covering her mouth with his.

Jazz slipped her tongue inside, tangling it with his while she pulled at the lapels of his tuxedo jacket. She was tempted to just end the spell, but she liked the idea of stripping him. Nick pulled the front of her gown down, baring a breast. A muted growl left his lips as he gently touched the purple bruises marring her skin.

"One of Lilibet's poultices will take care of that," she whispered.

But Nick had a different idea. He trailed his lips along the rounded flesh, soothing the lingering pain.

"I wanted to tear his throat out when I saw him do that," he murmured against her skin. "Rip him to shreds when he slapped you."

"I wanted to tear his throat out when he started taking your blood." She cradled his head against her breast, stroking his hair. Needing more, she pulled his face up to hers.

With their adrenaline running high, kisses weren't enough.

"If we don't get out of here soon, Detective Larkin will decide to check on us," Nick muttered, circling her ear with his tongue. "I don't know about you, but I don't fancy the idea of spending the rest of the night in jail with a charge of indecent exposure hanging over my head."

She nodded. "Ditto." She cranked the engine.

Nick looked over his shoulder at the lowered privacy screen, detecting a lingering fetid odor. "What do you think happened to Foulshadow?"

"Who knows? But I intend to find a way to make sure he never betrays someone again." She guided the limo down the driveway.

"Is Krebs home?" Nick stroked the length of her thigh.

"Yes."

"My place, then."

Jazz smiled and pressed down on the accelerator.

With a little witchy magick it was easy to literally blow through red lights and make it to the boardwalk in record time. Jazz parked in the lot and followed Nick around to the rear of the building and downstairs to his lair.

He didn't bother turning on lights and she remained on his heels.

Once her eyes adjusted to the dark, she noted a neatly designed apartment with an open design. But she noticed the large bed the most. No coffin for this vampire.

"How—" anything else was cut off as Nick spun her around and kissed her deeply. She jumped up, wrapping her legs around his hips. She laughed as her labia brushed against his erection.

"I could have cancelled the illusion spell earlier, but it was more fun to wait," she said, rising up then lowering herself onto his cock.

Nick widened his stance and pressed his palms against her hips, giving her the lead.

Jazz's breath hitched in her chest as she stared at the shadows crossing his face.

"I don't want to hurt you," she whispered. "You lost so much blood back there."

He rocked his hips against her, driving up into her. "Do I feel weak now?"

Jazz threw her head back and laughed. "We survived!"

"Yes, we did." His mouth took hers as she took him.

∽

After a shower that continued what they had started the minute they arrived at his apartment, Jazz was ready to collapse into bed. She felt Nick's body curved against her back. She had barely closed her eyes when a dizzying sensation overtook her. She snapped her eyes open and found herself wearing her lilac robe and standing in a familiar stone-walled hall. Women of varied ages in robes of different colors sat behind the stone table. But it was the woman in emerald green who snared Jazz's attention.

Hope mingled with uncertainty filled her. A part of her wanted to point out she did it even without their help. But she didn't think this was the time to brag. Did her being brought here mean her banishment was to be lifted? And if that were the case, what would happen to her? She already knew she couldn't return to the life she had first been trained for. Too much had happened over the past seven hundred years. She wasn't the young witch she had been back then.

"I understand the Protectorate is very happy with your endeavors, young Griet," Eurydice spoke. "You righted many wrongs this night."

"I am sure the Protectorate is only happy that their kind is no longer in danger from Clive

Reeves," Jazz replied, ever cautious. Since the members of the Witches' High Council didn't look all that ecstatic or even invite her to sit, she had an idea that saving the vampires somehow managed to land her in trouble … again. She decided to test her theory with a positive spin. "I hope you are also pleased that Clive Reeves has finally received the judgment he deserves."

The elder witch's faint smile wasn't the least bit comforting. "I said the Protectorate was pleased. Not that *we* were."

"Excuse me?"

"Did you think we would end your banishment just because you claim to have destroyed Clive Reeves?" Eurydice asked.

"Uh, yeah. Yes," she quickly amended. "I realize a life was destroyed, but it was a life not worthy of continuation. He did not deserve to live considering what he had been doing for so many years. By taking his life, many others were released from their earthly bonds. And it's not like I killed an innocent. In fact, if you want to get technical, I had killed him more than seventy years ago even if he managed to find a way to transfer his life force into another body at the moment of his death. So I only corrected that mistake."

"Do not be smart-mouthed with us," Kabira, the powerful, who sat on Eurydice's left, snapped. "You are an arrogant witch who still has not learned her place. Did you honestly expect us to lift your banishment and welcome you back to our ranks just because you finally cleaned up your own mess?" Her smile was as tight and prissy as The Librarian's. "Besides, what proof do you have that you were successful? The house is nothing more than a memory, the property devoid of any evidence of what went on there. Not to mention Mother Nature was not the least bit happy that you brought down lightning. She plans to deal with you later on that matter."

"From what you said, the Protectorate seems to have no trouble believing it," Jazz argued, at this point past caring what happened to her. "The shades killed him and freed themselves. The house buckled under the loss of Clive Reeves' magick and I plan to go out there to cleanse the property of any of his power lingering there. Done deed!"

Eurydice looked at each of her companions, nodding several times as if their conversation was all done on a mental plain. She turned back to Jazz.

"If you remain out of trouble," she sounded doubtful about that, "we will review the situation again in one hundred years."

Jazz's jaw dropped. "One hundred years? Wait—" Just that fast she was back in bed with Nick.

She rolled over with the intention of waking him then realized there was no sense in it.

The sun had risen and after their tumultuous night and Nick losing blood, she knew he needed to rest in order to regain his full strength. For now, he was beyond rousing.

Instead, she slipped out of bed and watched his still figure while she rummaged through his clothing and pulled out a t-shirt and a pair of shorts she hoped wouldn't fall down before she got home.

Thanks to her being called before the Witches' High Council she wasn't in the best of moods. As it was, she still had collateral damage—aka the limo—to deal with. She had a pretty good idea Dweezil was going to be hopping mad once he saw it. But that would be minor once he learned he had lost Foulshadow as his prized client. One way or another, Jazz intended to find that putrid and treacherous creature and make him pay for what he'd done.

Including Irma.

∽

Krebs was carrying a mug of coffee out of the kitchen when Jazz crept in the back door after a quick trip to swap the limo for her T-Bird. But Irma wasn't in the car.

"Whoa, that fashion statement is definitely not you."

"No kidding." She plucked the mug out of his hand and drank deeply. "Thank you." She cradled the mug against her chest as she headed for the stairs.

"Any chance you're going to tell me what happened?" Krebs called after her.

"No," she called back, climbing the stairs.

"Would it have anything to do with a famous horror actor's mansion burning down last night?"

She stopped on the fifth step. "The only fire I like is the one on the stove or in a fireplace." She continued up the stairs where she took a long hot shower and then dressed in her own clothing. She picked up the t-shirt, pressing the soft fabric to her nose. She imagined she could smell Nick's scent on the cloth even though it was clean. She carefully folded the clothing and left it on her bed.

As she descended the stairs, she heard Billy Joel crooning from the second floor.

"Wonder who caught his attention now?" she murmured, dancing down the rest of the way and stopping in the kitchen long enough to refill her coffee mug before she went outside. The moment she stepped outside she heard a pounding beat coming from the carriage house. Queen singing *We Will Rock You* was accompanied by a reedy very off-key voice.

"Irma's alive … er, around?" she said with a sense of wonder and hastened her steps.

When she stepped inside the carriage house, she found Irma standing on the passenger seat swiveling her hips in a way that no woman her age should ever do.

"Now that's just nasty." Jazz stared in horrified fascination.

When the ghost turned around, Irma opened her eyes and smiled broadly.

"We did it, Jazz! You found a way for me to leave the car!" she squealed.

Hip-swinging with squealing was definitely not a good look for Irma. But Jazz would keep that piece of information to herself.

"You did great, Irma," she said, smiling back, lifting her coffee mug in a toast. "You were the only one who could have accomplished it."

"I still don't understand how that was possible," the ghost said.

"It's simple. Clive was afraid of the wraiths wandering his grounds because he knew how much they hated him. They were doomed to stay there until his death, but he'd ensured they couldn't cross the mansion's threshold to kill him. Because you weren't one of his victims, you could cross the threshold and be the means to destroy him. You were the last thing he expected and it was perfect."

Irma's grin mirrored Jazz's. "Then I'm glad I could be of help. Is Nicky all right?" she asked, floating back to her usual seated position. "He looked a little worse for the wear last night. Although, I must say he's a *fine* figure of a man."

"He's recovered," she said, remembering just how well recovered. "And a good day's rest will finish the job." She walked over to the chair Nick had sat in the night they watched *Arsenic and Old Lace* with Irma. "We really couldn't have done it without you." She knew it was taking a chance admitting that to the ghost, but she figured Irma deserved the kudos.

Irma beamed under her praise. "And I left the car too." Her smile faltered. "Those ghosts killed him, didn't they?"

"Yes, they did," Jazz said gently. While she was too familiar with death, she sensed Irma, even in death, was not familiar with it, especially not violent death. "He deserved it, Irma. He had taken what was left of their existences and he would have continued doing it to others if we hadn't stopped him."

"Oh, I don't feel guilty he's dead," Irma said. "I just wish I hadn't been sent back here. I think I was ready to move on." She made a face as she slapped the dashboard with her gloved palm. "So I guess you better get working on a spell to get me out of here permanently."

Jazz toyed with the idea of not telling her, but if Irma found out on her own, there would be hell to pay. "Actually, you're free of the car. You can go anywhere you want."

The look on Irma's face was a true Kodak moment. "Anywhere?"

Jazz nodded, watching her take in the news.

"Seriously?"

Again Jazz nodded.

"You're not fooling around like you usually do, are you?"

Jazz laughed. "No Irma, I'm not fooling around. You can cross over or run amok in Nebraska or whatever you want to do."

Irma scrunched her face in thought and then came to a decision.

"Well, since everyone I know is dead or close to it, I guess I should stay here." Irma looked around the carriage house. "But can we paint the interior a lovely shade of pink or maybe a soft green? And get some curtains? A lady needs her privacy. And a portable heater is very necessary now. Or perhaps we could fix up that small apartment overhead. You once said there's only junk stored up there anyway. It wouldn't be perfect living quarters, but better than what I've had for the past fifty years." She continued prattling on.

Jazz turned away muttering that some people just couldn't be content with what they had when she felt her foot sink down. She looked down to find a huge glob of ectoplasmic goo all over her shoe. "What in Fates—"

Irma froze. "Oh."

Jazz turned around. "Oh? What is this?" A faint whimpering sound drew her attention to a shadowy corner of the carriage house. "No. No, no, no, no, no …" She stared in horror as part of the shadow separated from the corner and made its way into the light. She reckoned the figure was the size of a small horse.

For the first time, Irma looked uncertain as she walked over to the ghostie mastiff and placed her hand on top of its head. "He followed me home after I was returned from the mansion," she said in a weak voice. "I can keep him, can't I?"

Jazz stared at the huge slobbering creature who offered her a lopsided doggy grin, complete with strings of ectoplasmic drool hanging from its muzzle. "Damn. I should have gotten you that canary," she sighed.

Epilogue

*J*azz didn't need to look at caller ID to know Nick was on the line. Sunset had occurred thirty seconds ago.

"Come on, Nick, we've saved the vampire race. What's next? Saving the world?" she asked, the minute she picked up the phone. "I even had it easy this time around. I only had to deal with the sheriff's department twice during all this, and I didn't have to see what one of the county cells looked like. Although Detective Larkin has already called three times today, so I think we're going to have to go down there and make a statement just to keep him on my side."

"I think we can wait on the saving the world bit for a day or so. Same thing with Detective Larkin." He chuckled. "No, I had something else in mind."

"Oh really?" She started thinking about a repeat of the previous night sans Clive Reeves, the dungeon, fire, and so on. Although, a naked Nick stretched out on an altar wouldn't be such a bad idea. Maybe with some silk scarves instead of the chains, central heat instead of cold dank air, and some warm scented massage oil to add to the experience. Yeah, that she could do. She was so lost in her lascivious thoughts that she almost missed his next words.

"Jazz Tremaine, would you do me the honor of having dinner with me tonight?"

Her jaw literally dropped. "Huh?"

His chuckle was warm in her ear. "You really need to do something about your communication skills. Yes, dinner. I will pick you up at your house, take you out to a nice restaurant, and I don't want to hear any arguments from you that I can't eat solid food while you can. Then perhaps we can go somewhere to hear some music or go dancing."

Jazz swallowed. "That, uh, that sounds like a date," she ventured, wanting to make sure she wasn't imagining his words.

"It does, doesn't it? And do you know that's something we've never done in all the time we've known each other? I would like to take you on a date, Jazz."

Witches and vampires didn't date. She and Nick, especially, did not go out on dates. They fought, they made love, and then fought some more. She threatened to behead or stake him. He called her crazy and vowed he'd go to the other end of the earth to stay away from her. Then they parted for ten or twenty years.

But the idea of going out on an actual date was appealing. To wear something sexy, go all girly-girl, and share a truly romantic evening with Nick was downright appealing.

She pretty much had her life back. As she predicted, Dweezil had screamed about the damaged limo, but she reminded him his insurance would cover the repairs. There were calls on her voice mail asking for her services as a curse eliminator. She wouldn't be dealing with the Witches' High Council for another hundred years as long as she stayed out of trouble. Yeah, like that was going to happen.

And Nick wanted to take her out on a date like they were two ordinary people. Except he was a night person on a liquid diet and she could turn people into frogs and no amount of kissing would turn them into any form of a prince.

But for one night they could pretend they were … well, real people.

"I would very much like to go out to dinner with you tonight, Nick Gregory," she said formally. Then she grinned as her true nature kicked in. "But you might want to be aware of one thing."

"What is that?"

"I don't put out on the first date."

Acknowledgments

The road to creating and ultimately finishing *Hex* has been wild and fun. And I couldn't have done it without the help and support of some fantastic people.

My husband, Bob, who understands that I "hear" voices in my head. My mom, Thelma Randall, who always told me I could do it.

My agent, Laurie McLean of the Larsen/Pomada Literary Agency, aka, Batgirl, who has totally gone way beyond the call of duty. I wanted to write outside of my comfort zone. She made sure I not only wrote outside my comfort zone, I pretty much demolished it. Thanks, Batgirl, I love ya for that.

My editor, Deb Werksman, who read Jazz and loved her as much as I do. If I ever find a pair of bunny slippers like Fluff and Puff, they are yours!

Thanks to my beta readers, awesome authors in their own right, Elaine Charton, Lisa Croll Di Dio (who gave me a great line about holy water), Lynda K. Scott, Lynne Michaels, and Terese Daly Ramin who kept me on track many a time.

To Lisa again and Yasmine Galenorn for making sure all my witchy stuff was right. And for Yasmine screaming at me in an email, "Take your finger off the delete key!"

The Witchy Chicks, Yasmine Galenorn, Terese Daly Ramin, Lisa Croll Di Dio, Madelyn Alt, Candace Havens, Kate Austin, and Annette Blair. Your support is much appreciated.

Jazz, Nick, Irma, Fluff and Puff, and I thank you from the bottom of our hearts—whether they beat or not.

About the Author

Linda Wisdom was born and raised in Huntington Beach, California. She majored in journalism in college and then switched to fashion merchandising when she was told there was no future for her in fiction writing. She held a variety of positions ranging from retail sales to executive secretary in advertising and office manager for a personnel agency.

Her writing career began when she sold her first two novels to Silhouette Romance on her wedding anniversary in 1979. Since then she has sold more than seventy novels and one novella to four different publishers. Her books have appeared on various romance and mass market bestseller lists and have been nominated for a number of *Romantic Times* awards as well as the Romance Writers of America Rita Award.

She lives with her husband, two dogs, two parrots, and a tortoise in Murrieta, California.

When Linda first moved to Murrieta there were three romance writers living in the town. At this time, there is just Linda. So far, the police have not suspected her of any wrongdoing.